Matt Gemmell is the author of the KESTREL techno-thrillers series, the continuing flash fiction anthology series Once Upon A Time, and *Raw Materials*, a collection of personal essays. He has also published several non-fiction books on writing.

He is a former consultant software engineer, and he lives in Edinburgh, Scotland with his wife Lauren, their son Calum, and their labradoodle named Whisky. He can be found on the web at mattgemmell.com.

For exclusive bonus stories and chapters, plus previews of new novels and more, sign up for his occasional newsletter: mattgemmell.com/news-subscribe

Middleshade Road

Matt Gemmell

For my brother, Martin.
We always knew each other.

Middleshade Road

"The life of the dead is placed in the memory of the living."

Marcus Tullius Cicero

Monday

Chapter 1

The week started badly.

The call came a little before 5AM on a November morning, abruptly pulling Dair Lewis from a dream he couldn't remember. He was disoriented, and it took several seconds for him to identify the source of the sound that had woken him, and then to pick up his phone and answer it.

"Hello?"

"Can I speak to Mr. Alisdair Lewis, please?" said the voice on the line. The man sounded stern, and his voice made no allowance for the hour, as if he'd already been awake for a while. Lewis woke up a little more.

"Uh… speaking. Who is this? Do you know what time it is?"

"I'm sorry about that, Mr. Lewis," the voice replied. *"This is Sergeant Howarth, Dunleven police."*

Lewis was suddenly completely alert, and he sat up and swung his legs out of bed without being consciously aware of it. The other man had stopped speaking, and in a flash of insight, Lewis knew that he was being given a moment to prepare himself.

Because when the police call from your home town in the middle of the night, there's usually something to prepare for.

"It's my mother," Lewis said. It wasn't a question, but he heard Howarth inhale deeply.

"*Yes, sir,*" Howarth said. "*I'm afraid I have some bad news.*"

"Meaning that she's dead," Lewis replied immediately, and he was surprised to hear the detached quality of his own voice. He could hear a buzzing, whining sound inside his head, growing in intensity.

There was a long moment of silence, and then Howarth sighed. "*Yes, sir, I'm sorry to say that she is. My condolences.*"

The world seemed to tilt sideways for a moment, and Lewis's free arm shot out, his hand pressing onto the mattress, fingers spread. His pulse pounded in his ears, and he had to deliberately take a breath. His bedroom had taken on an air of unreality.

"*Mr. Lewis?*" Howarth said on the phone, and Lewis nodded at first, only responding after a further couple of seconds.

"Yes. I'm here," he said. "What happened?"

Howarth sighed again, and Lewis could actually hear the man scratch at what must have been stubble on his chin.

Not the only one who was wakened early today, he thought, and to his alarm he found that his mother's face swam into his mind, as she'd been when he last saw her. It had been several years ago.

"*She was found at home about half an hour ago, sir,*" Howarth said, his tone all business now. "*A paperboy saw the front doors open. Mrs. Lewis was in the entrance hall. The lad called an ambulance, of course, but there was nothing to be done.*"

"The doors were open?" Lewis asked, not sure he'd heard the man correctly. *At four-thirty in the morning? She's in her sixties.*

The paperboy's visit was no surprise. His mother had always risen very early, and liked to have a news-paper waiting for her. Her position in the community made it possible. It had always been that way. Even be-fore Lewis left.

"*Oh, there was no sign of foul play, sir,*" Howarth said quickly. "*It seemed that Mrs. Lewis had been out in the gar-den for some reason. Tracked some soil back in. We're check-ing, of course, but at the moment it looks like she passed away naturally.*"

"Naturally," Lewis repeated. *After being outside in the garden, alone. In the middle of a winter's night.*

"*That's correct, sir,*" Howarth said impassively. "*She was still in her nightclothes, in fact. Bare feet. Sometimes, once people reach a certain age...*"

He tailed off, the rest of the thought being either unnecessary or indelicate, or perhaps both.

Lewis blinked. Again the world seemed to tilt side-ways, and then right itself again.

"I'll... I'll be there in a few hours," Lewis said.

"*Very well, sir. I understand you're familiar with the area. The place to head for is the community hospital; it's on —*"

"I know it," he said, a chill settling on the skin of his back. *I remember it quite well.*

Another tilt. Another sweeping feeling of unreality.

"*Alright then,*" Howarth replied. "*And my condolences again.*"

"Thank you," Lewis said, and he was about to hang up when something occurred to him. "Ah, Sergeant?"

"*Sir?*"

"There was no sign of anyone else there at all?"

"*None, sir. It rained last night. Plenty of footprints, but they seemed to all be hers. There was no-one else in the house. We've locked up, and you can collect the keys from the station when you arrive.*"

"I understand. I have my own. I… thank you. I'll be going now."

"*Of course, sir. Drive safely,*" Howarth replied, and then Lewis heard the call end.

For almost a minute, he just breathed.

She's gone, he thought, dropping the phone onto the bed and then slowly standing up in the darkness. He hadn't even switched on his bedside lamp.

And I'm going home.

After another moment, he lurched across the floor and into the en suite bathroom, fell to his knees in front of the toilet, and vomited.

Lewis thumbed the switch to lower the driver's side window a little further, letting more of the icy morning air into his VW Golf. It wasn't yet 6AM, and still fully dark, but even at this hour there was a reasonable amount of traffic. The cold waters of the Firth of Forth, far below the vast suspension bridge he urged the car over, looked like a black void.

He had wandered the handful of rooms of his own flat in darkness after Howarth's call, but only for a few minutes. There was a sense of inevitability about the morning; almost like deja vu, but he couldn't trust his own impressions at the moment. He briefly considered calling someone — a friend; just *somebody* — but it was still early, and what would he say? The only thing to do was pack a bag, and start the long journey north. He stepped out of his own front door barely twenty-five minutes after Howarth had hung up.

Dunleven was a mining town, or at least it had been in the past. Coal in its day, and then a steelworks, but both industries had long since fallen to ruin. His mother's family owned the mine and the factories, and at one time — his great-grandfather's lifetime — had employed the bulk of the town's menfolk. The population was higher then. Now, it had dwindled, and the place sat under a permanent pall of melancholy, and a sense of having lost the grander days of the past.

The drive would take three hours at least, not taking traffic into account. He would take the motorway as far as Perth, and then head off to skirt the Cairngorms, and go steadily north-east. The morning would be well underway by the time he arrived, and Lewis found himself thankful that at least it would be full daylight by then.

He would have to go to the house, of course.

His mind skittered away from the image of it, leaving only a blank space in his thoughts. There would be time enough for that later. He supposed he'd be there for at least several days, so there would be plenty of opportunity to reacquaint himself with his childhood home.

It's empty now, he thought. *Actually empty, after all these years.*

An image almost rose up in his memory — something from his dream last night — but it slipped away before he could fasten onto it.

A side-wind buffeted the car, sending a lance of frosty air in through the window, and Lewis hunched his shoulders and pressed the accelerator a little harder.

It was no warmer once he'd reached the other side of the bridge and was passing North Queensferry, but at least there was some shelter from the arctic breeze blowing in from the North Sea. Snow was forecast for much of the north this week, and dread sat heavily in his stomach, like something greasy and undigested.

A new-build housing estate slid by on the far side of the three-lane tarmac, and he saw a glimpse of someone's back garden, the grass unnaturally vivid in the harsh light of the moon. His fingers clenched around the wheel when, without warning, his mind served up an image of his mother barefoot and wearing an ankle-length nightdress, trailing damp earth back up the front steps of the sprawling residence that loomed over her. A tiny, frail woman, living alone by choice, on what was the final night of her life.

The breeze from the window caught him again, and he could feel the even colder tracks running down his cheeks. He didn't bother to wipe the moisture away.

There'll be more tears before all is said and done, his mind whispered, and he wasn't surprised to find that it spoke in his mother's voice.

The world awakened around Lewis as he drove. Windows lit up one by one, in the infrequent stretches of housing that were visible from the motorway. He switched the radio on briefly, but the cheerfulness and normality of it were intolerable.

The police sergeant's words — *What was his name, again? Howard?* — were running on a loop in his mind. *Once people reach a certain age...* and then the man had tactfully omitted the rest of the sentence. *They lose their marbles*, Lewis thought. That's what the sergeant meant. Something like that.

She was a lot of things, but she wasn't senile. She didn't have dementia, no matter what the local police might think.

He'd spoken to her several weeks earlier, but he pushed away the memory of the phone conversation. It was too much right now. There were too many emotions and regrets attached. But he could picture her exactly as she would have been.

On the morning she died — on *this* morning, by god — his mother was sixty-three years old. Margaret Ellen Lewis (née Lambert) stood less than five feet and four inches tall, her skin was pale, and her hair was silver, bearing no remaining trace of the auburn of her youth. Her nails were immaculately manicured, pragmatically short, and constantly drummed upon whatever surface was ready to hand, in a nervous habit that had accompanied her for her entire life.

Lewis's stomach clenched at the innocuous phrase that had taken on a new and bitterly poignant meaning in these hallucinatory, pre-dawn hours of a day that was certain to be one of the longest he'd ever experienced. *Her entire life*. It had now been quantified. Fixed as a number of years and months and days that would never again increase.

Margaret's mind was sharp, just the same as both her wit and her tongue. She didn't suffer anyone gladly, and fools not at all. Her isolated existence was by choice; living amongst the last vestiges of a very different time.

The Lambert family had been at the centre of life in Dunleven for more than a century, and their influence was considerable. When Margaret, the great-granddaughter of the man who started it all, married an employee of the Lambert Mining Company in 1976 at the tender age of twenty-three, the warning signs of a waning industry were already visible. A further ten years had removed any doubt, and Dunleven was now a changed place. Faded, reduced, and more and more boarded-up. Left in disrepair, and ultimately abandoned by its youngest residents, who sought a better life and newer types of work in the cities to the south.

Dair's father, Ross Lewis, had driven trucks for the company, worked his way up into shipping administration, and had befriended the owner's daughter when she also took a strongly-encouraged interest in the family business. It was an unconventional romance, especially as he was three years older than her, but to their credit her parents hadn't stood in the way. Their primary desire was for their daughter to be happy, and a suitor already involved in the business allowed them a certain measure of influence. The wedding was the talk of the town for weeks.

Alisdair Gordon Lewis was born the following year, on a stormy Tuesday night a little before 9:30 PM, and the marriage lasted twelve more years before Ross Lewis packed a bag and left — on a Friday at a similar time, in much the same weather conditions.

The divorce was quick and efficient, with Ross neither asking for nor receiving very much, and Margaret had nevertheless kept the surname ever since, for reasons only known to herself. She'd been only thirty-six when once again unattached, and she had never remarried.

But there were some close calls, Lewis thought, as he grimaced and switched on the Golf's wipers to clear a flurry of light snowfall. He felt a twinge in his back, and he shifted in his seat, refusing to acknowledge the sick feeling in his stomach that accompanied the pain.

His father had mostly disappeared for a while after the divorce, returning to a solitary life of long-distance delivery driving across the UK and Europe. He was gone for weeks at a time, and his phone calls to his son were intermittent at best. He saw the boy a handful of times each year, with the inevitable estrangement that the separation brought, though their relationship had steadily improved once the young Lewis reached his twenties and was living far south of Dunleven in the city of Glasgow. Ross Lewis had never been truly comfortable with the shift in fortunes that brought him into a large and wealthy family and its surroundings, and perhaps that had been part of the problem in the closing years of his marriage.

He certainly seemed much more content to once again be earning a living behind the wheel of a truck, eating up miles by the hundreds each day, and beholden to no-one and nothing except his schedule. When he got home for an infrequent and brief stay, it was to a rented, two-bedroom first-floor flat in a satellite town less than half an hour outside of Glasgow. The second bedroom had no bed, the double glazing misted up in the mornings, and the green and leafy outlook was mostly onto an immaculately-maintained cemetery. As far as Lewis knew, his father had never been happier.

The earlier flurry of snow had vanished as quickly as it arrived, and it wouldn't be long before he reached the Perth bypass, and left the motorway for the A9 towards Pitlochry and eventually Inverness and beyond.

I'll have to remember to call Alan later, he thought. Alan Butler was the technology editor at *The Sentinel*, a prominent broadsheet newspaper in the UK, and the source of Lewis's current writing commission which had a deadline later in the week.

Lewis had been a freelance technology journalist for a number of years, drifting into the job as something to occupy his time after an abortive attempt to pursue a career in the legal field. He'd inherited a substantial trust fund in his name upon graduating from university, and he lived fairly modestly, so paying the bills hadn't been a concern. His mother had never pushed him to make more of himself, and his father certainly had no advice to offer one way or the other. From time to time, Lewis toyed with the idea of writing something other than opinion-pieces on the vagaries of the technology industry, perhaps even an honest-to-god crime novel, but both the motivation and the ideas always eluded him.

He was drifting, and he knew it. Always waiting for something, but he didn't know what. He'd been in a holding pattern for his entire adult life so far, without any sense of what could break it.

Where has the time gone?

But there was no answer to that. Thirty-eight years old, still mostly intact and serviceable, but with only a broken string of short-term relationships in his past. The longest had lasted fourteen months, all told, and that had been several years ago.

Lewis thought that the sky might be beginning to lighten in the distance, and the thought only brought tears to his eyes again. His mother was gone. Their relationship had been turbulent, with long periods of little to no contact, but she was still his mother. She had done the lion's share of raising him, and whatever else had happened, he'd never wanted for anything.

He swiped at his cheeks with one hand, glad of the icy air blowing in, and asked himself how he honestly felt at this moment.

I always thought we'd have time, later. Sometime. To rebuild.

A reconciliation — a real one, not just lip service and politeness — that he'd never made the effort to initiate. There had been plenty of time, really. But it had run out on this cold winter's morning, in the very last place he wanted to see. He was going there right now, getting closer as each mile rolled under the car's tyres.

And how do I feel, really? he wondered. The answer was complicated, and not entirely palatable. *Shocked. Bereaved. Relieved. Like the other shoe finally dropped.*

The road stretched ahead, as the scenery began to change once more. Hills rose up as dark curves on the horizon, blocking out starlight but offering nothing in its place, and he knew that before long he'd be on winding stretches of tarmac between peak after peak, with dense forest on slopes ending far from the blacktop. Miles of gorse and heather, and perhaps the occasional solitary stag, a majestic monarch of the glen, watching dolefully from afar. The trees would be pine and oak and rowan, many trimmed with snow, and it would all have a desolate beauty to it, like a land somehow paused since time immemorial, and puzzled at impudent human intrusion.

Eventually, he would pass Inverness and venture farther north, into the Highlands. And in time, he would reach Dunleven at last, as the day brightened under a cautious and watchful sunrise. He would drive along the old lanes and streets and avenues, and he would make one last turn (to the left, when coming into town from the south), and then it was a road curving gently uphill for longer than it seems at first.

Through the gates, always open. Up the approach road. Onto the gravel turning-circle. And then he would be there again.

Pale House.

Another twinge of pain from his back. Another feeling of nausea. And a flash from his dream, just briefly — a dark place, vast and labyrinthine, stretching out around him. There was something he had to do, but there was no time left — and then it was gone.

He braked as the road veered sharply to the right, smoothly shifting gears before accelerating again. His gaze flicked momentarily towards the horizon, and he thought that the brightening sky must just have been his imagination.

Chapter 2

Lewis made the journey with only a single break for coffee and a cursory breakfast in Inverness. The rush-hour traffic was clogging the roads by then, and it was better to sit in a cafe than in the car.

He set out again after forty-five minutes, and by the time 10 AM arrived, he had passed the welcome sign for Dunleven, followed the well-known route towards his childhood home. He made the final left turn, glancing at the blue metal street sign on the corner, attached to two short poles.

Middleshade Road, it said.

He felt a bolt of unease chase through him, and he frowned as he manoeuvred the car up the gradually increasing incline.

The road wound up a gentle hill, ending at the stone gateposts that gave entrance to an enormous plot of land that the Lambert family had owned for more than a century. There were a handful of smaller houses clustered around the very bottom of the road, where Lewis had turned from the main thoroughfare, but most of the uphill stretch was simply walled private land belonging to the estate further up.

It took only a few minutes to reach the gates of the property, and he allowed the car to come to a halt, holding it on the footbrake.

Home, he thought. *After… how long has it been? At least a couple of years.*

He usually visited briefly every second Christmas or so, and his mother had accepted it on account of their tentative relationship and the distance involved. He hadn't visited last year at all. He knew that she'd have preferred to see him more often, and he also knew that there was a small part of him — rarely allowed to intrude upon his consciousness — that would have preferred that too. But the time for it had now passed.

And nobody's there, he thought, peering through the gateposts and further up the approach road, until it curved out of sight amidst pine trees. For the first time in living memory, his family's ancestral home had no occupant. Lewis himself certainly wouldn't be living there, beyond the next few days at least. It was a sobering thought. The mansion had been inhabited continuously since its main extent was completed in the mid-1800s. But the Lambert line had dwindled with the town's fortunes, and now he supposed that he was the heir to it all.

I'm alone here. The realisation provoked a visceral dread, and he felt his pulse spike in his chest. The strangest part was that there was a strong sense of familiarity about it, as if he'd been expecting to feel this way ever since he left his apartment long before dawn that morning. But there was nothing to fear in this place. Bad memories, yes, but also plenty of good ones.

It's just the situation, Lewis told himself. *Completely understandable.*

He wound the windows back up nonetheless, and then urged the car forward. It rolled through the gateposts and onto Lambert land, and if he'd been expecting some ominous darkening of the day, none came.

It took only half a minute to travel up the approach road which curved back and forth through the trees, before he finally turned onto the final stretch with a clear view up towards the house.

And there it is, he thought.

Pale House stood gaunt and rambling against the sky. Its name came from the unusual light-grey stone used in its construction, brought in from quarries much farther north and at great expense, but it had darkened with the grime and the weather of more than a century, rendering it only marginally brighter than the landscape around it. Its estate was prodigious, but mostly hidden in thick forest, with some large but isolated areas of clearing.

The main and original part of the building was four tall storeys high, in a square arrangement that stood imposingly beyond the expanse of gravel at the head of the access road. Two asymmetrical wings had been constructed almost immediately after completion of the primary house, both five stories tall, stretching further back and almost giving the impression of a grand museum. Much of the interior space was given over to expansive rooms that, in Lewis's lifetime at least, had seen only occasional use. A ballroom, a music room, an elaborate dining room, a reception room too large to be practical, several lounge and sitting rooms, a smoking room that had ceased to fulfil its intended purpose decades ago, and more besides. Hallways and stairways and galleries. Archways, doorways, and corners. Shadows and stealthy sounds.

Lewis drove fully around the turning circle, facing the car away from the house and back towards the access road, then he reluctantly switched off the engine and got out.

The ground was wet from last night's rain, just as the police sergeant had said, but the weather was currently dry and cloudy. A part of Lewis's mind had been expecting to see crime scene tape, or a constable standing on guard down at the gates, or just some kind of evidence of the momentous event that had taken place here just a few hours earlier, but there was none of that. There wouldn't be any gawkers. There wouldn't be any trespassers. It wasn't really that kind of town, and it certainly wasn't that kind of building.

Pale House was many things, and chief amongst them was that it was left alone by those who didn't belong there.

He looked up at the house, which sat in its own shadow like a window into a different time, and the house looked silently back at him.

Always feels like it's watching, he thought, but he knew it was just the emotional strain of the day, and his own tiredness that was talking.

It was so easy to imagine walking up to the front door and pressing the bell — he always rang when he arrived, even though he had his own keys; a mark of politeness which doubled as a means of maintaining a certain distance from his own background here — and then at length his mother would answer the door, welcoming him home. He could picture it vividly. By contrast, it was impossible to believe that this place was now devoid of life. That his mother was gone; from here, from the world, from his future.

He heard the caw of a raven from somewhere in the trees nearby, and it was a scolding sound — perhaps at his presence, or perhaps for his absence until now, when he was too late.

I've dreamed of here recently, his mind whispered, and he pulled his coat more tightly closed in response to the jolt of unease that twisted through him.

He could feel three sets of keys sitting heavily in his pocket, but the set he withdrew was for the car. With one last glance up at the brooding roofline of the place, he turned and got back into the still-warm vehicle, closed the door, and started the engine. He felt an instant of panic when the starter motor was slow to fire, but it did, and the engine was suddenly very loud in the silence.

He manoeuvred the car across the gravel and started back down the access road, peripherally aware of the house receding in the rear-view mirror. He didn't look back, and when he passed the first turn, he was glad.

The community hospital was modest but functional, and exactly as he remembered it.

A series of long, low buildings, all made of institutional concrete, with paint peeling from the metal handrails that led up short ramps or handfuls of steps to enter each department ￼ directly from the outside. The main entrance to reception was a double set of automatic doors at the top of a flight of five steps, and an elderly man was standing to one side of them, smoking in silence. Lewis walked towards the doorway, hands shoved deep into his coat pockets.

The last time I was here, I went in the other door, he thought.

He glanced off to his right, a couple of hundred feet along the edge of the car park which bordered one half of the hospital, and saw the Accident & Emergency entrance farther down. An ambulance was parked there, and he wondered if it was the same one that had collected his mother in the early hours of the morning.

Probably, he thought. Dunleven wasn't a large town, and this was the only medical facility in the area.

He took a deep breath of the still-icy air, and walked up the steps to the main doors, nodding at the old man as he passed by. The nod was returned with a cough that sounded ominous, and Lewis thought that the man would probably be inside the hospital for a too-brief stay before many more years went by.

The reception area was well lit, and quiet at this hour. There was a nurse behind the counter, typing away on a PC that had seen better days, and Lewis was about to approach her when he heard a voice from nearby.

"You're… Margaret Lewis's son, aren't you?"

He turned to see another nurse, short and with brown hair, standing about fifteen feet away at an open doorway. She was holding a clipboard and looking at him with undisguised curiosity, but there was also sympathy in her eyes.

Better get used to this now, he told himself. *There's going to be a lot of it over the next few days.*

"That's right," he replied, taking his hands out of his pockets but keeping his arms at his side. The nurse nodded, then she took a half-step back into whatever room lay beyond the door behind her, set the clipboard down on a table, and stepped back out into the reception area, closing the door behind her. She approached him slowly, and Lewis supposed that she'd probably been trained to avoid upsetting people who were facing difficult situations.

He expected her to offer her condolences, but instead she simply said "Come with me." Now it was

Lewis's turn to nod, and he fell into step alongside her as she led the way down an adjacent corridor.

They walked in silence for almost a minute, going beyond the primary part of the hospital and through a connecting covered courtyard towards the rear. Lewis couldn't help but glance at the signs they passed by, showing the various departments, each colour-coded and with an arrow of the same colour pointing in its direction. After the courtyard, there was another sign and an arrow, with only a solid rectangle beside it. It was black.

Lewis came to a halt so abruptly that he almost tipped forward and fell, and the nurse was immediately at his side. Instead of a question, there was only understanding on her face.

"I know," she said. "It's difficult. We're all very sorry for your loss."

My loss, he thought. *Because up ahead is the mortuary. And my mother's body is there.*

When he didn't respond, a frown creased the nurse's brow. "Did you… I mean, if you don't want to see her now, that's fine," she said. "Lots of people wait. I can get you the paperwork and everything you need, if you'd like?"

He shook his head immediately, and he was surprised at himself. "No," he replied. "I just… I hadn't really prepared myself. That's all. Which is strange, because I just drove hundreds of miles after getting a call from the police here, and I've had hours to…"

He just trailed off, and again the nurse nodded, with the same look of understanding on her face. Lewis had a momentary flash of insight into the emotional cost of the job that this thirty-something woman had, going through the same mundane tragedy again and again with strangers of every age and background. He felt a surge of compassion for her, and then he felt tears prick the corners of his eyes once more.

Steady, Dair, he thought. *Let's just get through this without a public breakdown.*

He inhaled deeply, and tried to give the woman a small smile. "I'm alright. I'm ready to see her now. Sorry."

"Nothing to be sorry about," the nurse said, eyeing him for a long moment as if making an assessment. Finally, she nodded again. "It's this way."

She walked at his side now, instead of leading him. The corridor was completely quiet except for a mechanical hum that hadn't been present in the main building, and Lewis realised after a moment that it was refrigeration machinery. In his mind's eye, he imagined an American TV-style morgue ahead; all stainless steel tables and fluorescent strip lighting, with a medical examiner in blue scrubs standing respectfully nearby. There would be a spotlight on an adjustable mechanical arm, and a telephone on the wall, and there would be clipboards stacked on a writing surface along the edge of the room. Boxes of disposable latex gloves. The strong smell of antiseptic.

The image was completely out of place here, in a small community hospital and health centre in the Highlands of Scotland, but it was difficult to dismiss. He was actually surprised when the nurse gestured towards a windowed door just a few feet away, which already stood ajar. The room beyond was more like a patient's private room on a ward, and it was naturally lit by the grey daylight. His pulse quickened.

"She's just in here," the nurse said, and he looked around at her almost incredulously. His mind chose this moment to notice the name-tag she wore — it said *Kerry*, without a surname — and he opened his mouth to say something, but no words came out.

She's in here, he thought. *Like she'll be sitting up in bed, maybe reading a magazine. Waiting for me to get here. Or to call her.*

He felt his stomach twist, but he just nodded to Nurse Kerry, and she gestured again, letting him walk ahead of her into the room.

There was a bed, and at first he looked at it only obliquely, careful not to let his gaze travel up towards the pillow. There was certainly someone lying in it; a woman, covered by a sheet that was folded down at the chest. Across her legs, there was a bright yellow blanket. A clock ticked on the wall. There was a vase of lilies on a small table, alongside a chair in the opposite corner of the room. Beside the vase, there was a blue plastic folder.

There were no magazines.

And suddenly Lewis felt vacant. Like he'd already walked into this room, and seen his mother's body, and wept and grieved, and got himself back under control, and maybe said a few words to her lifeless form, and taken her cold hand and kissed it before laying it gently back down again, and now he was ready to leave. He felt like all of his emotion was already spent. A distant part of his mind registered curiosity at his response, and he wondered if this, too, was normal.

He inhaled deeply, and then he finally looked.

Margaret Lewis, or at least her mortal body, lay there. She was perfectly still. Her eyes were closed, and her hair had recently been brushed, but not in the way she usually wore it. Her skin was grey.

"Christ," Lewis said, his voice choked, and the nurse's hand was immediately there against his arm. Somehow he was already crying, without any transition that he was aware of.

The reality of it struck him like a hammer-blow, and without any conscious thought he moved forward, lurching, and laid his hands on the bed just inches from his mother's body. The sheet was cool and crisp, and a little starchy. Nurse Kerry was at his side again, watching in silence. He sensed her, rather than saw her.

After a moment, he reached out and placed his right hand over his mother's. Her skin was like ice, and the bones beneath were steel pins. Her hand was unusually rigid. It didn't feel real. But then he inhaled reflexively, and there was the lingering scent of yesterday's perfume — always the same one. A wave of nausea passed over him, and he took a gasping breath, wiping the wet track from his cheek with his free hand.

"I'm so sorry," Nurse Kerry said gently, but Lewis was barely listening.

"How… how did she die?" he asked, and a crease briefly appeared on the nurse's brow.

"The police didn't say?" she asked, and he had to wrack his memory for the sergeant's exact words on the phone that morning.

No sign of foul play.

"They said it was natural causes," Lewis replied. "But she didn't… I mean, she was in good health. She was only sixty-three."

The nurse gave a sympathetic smile, then crossed the room to pick up the plastic folder. She opened it and looked at the contents for a moment, then met his gaze again.

"It's just as they said; she passed away naturally," she said, in a kindly tone that seemed to imply that this news should be of some comfort. The nurse kept eye contact for another moment, then quickly leafed through the several sheets of paper in the folder before closing it again.

"Everything you need is here. There's a note that says you can pick up the keys to her house at the police station." She came back over to where Lewis still stood beside the bed, and handed the folder to him.

"Thank you," he said, and she nodded.

"Is there anything I can do?" she asked, and Lewis shook his head. He appreciated her thoughtfulness, but he was quickly realising that what he most needed was to be alone.

"You've been very kind," he said simply. "I'd like to stay for a few minutes, if that would be alright."

"Of course," she replied. "Take as long as you need. And again, I'm very sorry."

She gave him one last compassionate smile, then left without another word. He took a deep breath, and turned back to look at his mother.

It was only a couple of weeks ago that I spoke to her, he thought.

The memory came easily, and it was uncharacteristically vivid.

Lewis had been crossing the street in Edinburgh, going uphill towards the centre of town. It wasn't his usual route, but the weather was bright and clear, and he'd wanted to get some fresh air. There was a red phone box on the corner, and only the very last of the leaves still clinging to almost-bare trees.

His phone suddenly vibrated in his pocket, and he frowned as he fished the device out and looked at the screen, just as he reached the safety of the kerbside. The frown deepened as he read his mother's name, then he sighed and tapped the green icon to answer the call.

"Hello," he said, consciously brightening his tone. Making an effort.

"*Hello Alisdair,*" his mother replied. "*Am I catching you at a bad time? It sounds like you're outside.*"

"Just out for walk," he said. "Is everything alright?"

A pause, for a fraction of a second too long. Then: *"Everything's fine. Just puttering around. I thought I'd see how you were. How are you?"*

"Oh, ticking along," he replied, pushing away the helpless irritation that began to rise up. *She's your mother. You can spare a few minutes to talk to her.*

"Keeping busy?"

Lewis closed his eyes for a moment, and considered stopping and ducking into a doorway to have the call, but it was too cold for that. He kept walking instead, opening his eyes again in time to see a black Labrador puppy being dragged away from a lamp post by its presumed owner, a girl of no more than fifteen.

"Of course. I have a few different pieces due in the next week or two. The usual."

"Mm," she replied, clearly distracted, and again the irritation rose up. She had called *him*, after all.

Another pause. He pressed the phone closer to his ear as a bus rumbled by, but there was no voice on the line.

"Still there?" he asked, and he could have sworn he heard her inhale.

"Yes, sorry, I'm here," she said. *"I'm just going through some things."*

Lewis suppressed a sudden yawn. "Some things?"

"Just some papers. Having a tidy-out. Organising. You know how I am."

"But everything's alright," he said. It wasn't really a question. He heard her sigh.

"As I said. Why do you keep asking?"

He swallowed the remark that threatened to bubble up from his throat — something like *I hardly think that twice qualifies as 'keeping asking', mother* — and just pressed his lips together for a moment.

"Just checking," he replied. "Making sure. How's the old place?"

"The House is still here," she said immediately. It was her long-accustomed response to this question; the asking and answering was something of a ritual for them. He asked because he knew the question annoyed her; a reminder that he visited only very rarely. And she answered in that way because she knew it annoyed him in return. Always the implicit capital *H* in *House*. Because in Dunleven, there was only one building truly worthy of the name.

Lewis nodded, even though she couldn't see him. "And how's Moira?"

"She's her usual self," she replied. *"Nosy. But she means well."*

Moira Rankin was his mother's neighbour and friend — if Margaret Lewis could be said to have friends. Moira had began as a sort of housekeeper, helping out around Pale House. She was five years older than Margaret, and was for all the world like an elder sister, though Margaret kept her at arm's length. Moira's home was at the foot of Middleshade Road, before the winding path up towards the Lambert estate. She was one of only a couple of other people with an address on the street. Like Margaret, she now lived alone. Her husband had died years before, and her daughter had some kind of administrative job in Brussels, and visited only a handful of times each year.

It took Moira twenty minutes to walk from her own modest dwelling up the long hill and then along the approach road to Pale House. In winter, it could be treacherous — but she always came. She was a daily fixture in Margaret Lewis's house, however much the latter claimed to be annoyed by the fact.

"You're lucky to have her, mother," Lewis said. It was another well-worn response, and a part of their ritual.

"Have you settled on your plans for Christmas?" she asked, and Lewis felt an unpleasant twinge of guilt at the suppressed hope in her voice.

"I'm pretty busy right now," he replied, "so I'm not sure yet."

"Oh. Of course."

"But I'll try to come up," he added, without knowing he was going to say the words.

"Well, I'd like that very much, if you can manage," she said.

Lewis could tell that she was trying not to get her hopes up, and again he felt guilt twisting through him.

"I'll let you know as soon as I work out my schedule for December."

There was another pause, this time for several seconds. "Is there something on your mind, mother?"

Lewis asked, and it took several more seconds for his mother to respond.

"Oh, nothing really," she said. *"It's just been a while since we had a chance for a talk. If you do make it up, we should catch up properly."*

Lewis frowned. It wasn't the sort of thing she said. She tended not to push, knowing that he'd react poorly to it, and make an excuse to change the subject, or end the conversation. The very last thing she'd usually do was try to arrange a heart-to-heart in advance, since he in turn would take that as his cue to avoid travelling north to visit her in the first place.

There's something on her mind. Something important.

"Uh… of course. We should," he said simply. He also knew very well that his mother would talk when she was good and ready, and that trying to draw her out beforehand was futile, and would only provoke an argument.

"Well, I'm sure you're busy. I should let you go."

This particular gambit tended to mean that *she* was finished with the conversation, and ordinarily he could feel the tension in his shoulders loosen as soon as he heard it. This time, though, he still felt uneasy — but there was nothing for it.

"Alright," he replied. "It was good to hear from you. I'll let you know about Christmas. And say hello to Moira for me."

"I'll be sure to. Take care of yourself, Alisdair."

"And you."

He heard the clack of the landline handset being placed into its cradle, and then the call cut off.

Lewis came to a stop in front of a furniture shop, and a mother pushing a pram had to swerve around him, raising her eyebrow impatiently. He mouthed a distracted apology in her direction, but she was already gone.

He was still holding his phone, and he looked down at the now-dark screen as if expecting answers to be written there.

First time for everything, he thought.

He sighed, glancing across the street at nothing in particular, then he pocketed the phone and started walking again.

Maybe he'd call her in a few days, just to check in. He could do it just before lunch, so that they both had a reason to keep it brief, but he'd still have a chance to gently press her for at least a clue. He nodded to himself, and increased his pace.

Overhead, the sky was still clear, but he could feel the temperature beginning to drop.

He had never got around to calling her. Not within the next few days, and not during the following week either. He'd vaguely planned to do it sometime *this* week — maybe even at lunchtime today — but of course that chance was now gone.

Should have made the time. Should have called her more often. Should have visited her even once this year. Jesus.

He had to silence the voice in his mind, because the picture it painted was stark and unforgiving. As a part of him had always known, he'd been failing as a son for a long time now. And though there were reasons for their estrangement, the fact was that he was the one who could have bridged the gap between them — or at least tried to. He knew that she was willing, with only her pride, and a fear of losing him entirely, standing in the way.

He could have reached out. He could have come halfway. And he *planned* to; it was always on the to-do list, somewhere. He knew, each year, that there was one fewer year ahead; he knew that the window of opportunity was closing. He knew that, in a way, he was letting her down — even if she'd let him down first.

And now *failing* had become *failed*. The indeterminate future was now settled. The part of his own story that overlapped with his mother's life had ended, just a few hours ago, while he was asleep and unaware hundreds of miles away. A stranger had to call and wake him to let him know.

She'd been alone, and he knew that when she'd thought about it — and it was certainly *when*, not *if* — she didn't really expect him to visit her this Christmas at all.

Lewis reached for his mother's grey hand, and it was still cold, and rigid, and strange, but it was hers. He had no more strength, and in that moment, he utterly hated himself.

He bowed his head until his nose was only inches from her hand, close enough to fill his nostrils with the faded scent of yesterday's perfume, and he wept.

44

Chapter 3

Lewis didn't see the nurse again as he left the hospital, but he wasn't paying much attention to his surroundings. He found himself standing in the car park without clearly recalling how he got there. The wet tracks on his cheeks caught the breeze, and he shuffled forward towards his car, swiping at his face with his gloves.

It was less than a ten-minute drive to the town centre, and at first he missed the turning for the public car park. He felt depleted and entirely unlike himself. The day had a dreamlike quality, and he had no idea what time it was. Once he'd parked, he sat in silence for a couple of minutes, just breathing. Eventually, he got out and walked towards a low sandstone building that housed the local funeral director. Squaring his shoulders, he went inside.

He didn't have an appointment, but he was seen immediately, and the arrangements were surprisingly easy. He was in and out in less than half an hour. It seemed anticlimactic, somehow — as if such a moment-ous event as the death of a parent ought to warrant more complexity and ceremony. The funeral would take place three days from now, on Thursday, in the late morning. Lewis was given a business card by the man he met with, and also a leaflet for a local family pub and restaurant that specialised in catering to large parties on such occasions. Once he'd left the funeral director's of-fice, he could no longer even remember what the man had looked like.

He called the restaurant, whose owner immedi-ately recognised the family name and assured Lewis he'd cater for however many people attended, no prob-lem at all, and gave his sincerest condolences. Lewis thanked him and hung up, and the feeling of unreality returned in earnest.

His next stop was the police station, and as he walked into the reception area, he knew with an almost precognitive certainty that the man with the bushy moustache and tired, doleful eyes standing behind the duty desk was the same Sergeant who had called him that morning. When Lewis approached the desk and read the black-on-silver name badge, sure enough, it said *HOWARTH*.

"How can I help you, sir?" Howarth asked, and Lewis was momentarily surprised that the man hadn't recognised him in return, before realising how bizarre the thought was.

"We spoke on the phone at five o'clock this morning, Sergeant," Lewis replied. "I'm Alisdair Lewis."

If Howarth was taken aback at his directness, he didn't show it. "Of course, sir. You made it here safely, then. I'm sorry for your loss."

Lewis only nodded, unsure which statement he was responding to. "You said I could collect my mother's set of house keys here."

"Indeed you can, sir," Howarth replied. "I have everything here waiting for you. There's the report too, if you'd like a copy. I'll just need a signature and some identification, if it wouldn't be too much trouble."

Lewis took his wallet from his jacket pocket, extracted his driving license, and sat it on the scarred wooden surface that separated him from Howarth. The counter was waist-height, and smelled strongly of institutional disinfectant. The varnish was long since gone, and some of the gouges must have been a centimetre deep.

Howarth examined the driving license carefully for a few moments, then sat it back down with a cursory smile, and placed a pink form beside it. He produced a black biro, and indicated the two boxes where a signature was needed. Lewis obliged, wordlessly, and when he returned the pen and the form, Howarth handed him a keyring he'd seen hundreds of times in his life. His mother's house keys. The sound they made was too loud, and Lewis swallowed as he slid them into his trouser pocket beside his own set.

Finally, Howarth produced two green sheets of paper bearing a multitude of checkboxes, ruled lines for text, and indecipherable abbreviations. Most of their surface was unmarked, but Lewis recognised the date, name, and address at the top of the first sheet. There were also three dense paragraphs of handwriting in block capitals further down, and the second sheet bore three different signatures.

The incident report, he thought. *The incident of my mother's death, alone, after going outside in the middle of the night in her bedclothes.*

"Thank you," he said, picking up his license and the copy of the report, and Howarth nodded solemnly.

"Anything else I can help you with, sir?" he asked, and Lewis looked up at him for a moment as if the question was in a foreign language.

"I… no. I appreciate your help," he said at last.

"You're welcome, sir," the sergeant said. "And again, my condolences."

Lewis gave a final nod, and then turned and walked towards the entrance. He was nearly at the doors when he heard Howarth's voice behind him.

"Forgive her."

He came to a stop, feeling gooseflesh break out on his forearms. Slowly, he turned and looked at the sergeant. Howarth's brow creased, and he adjusted his stance.

"I'm sorry, but what did you say?" Lewis asked, his voice carefully even. Howarth's shoulders visibly relaxed.

"I said we'll miss her, sir — your mother. She was an important part of this community. It's a sad loss for Dunleven, if you'll pardon my saying so."

Lewis's arms were still prickling, but he just nodded slowly. "Oh. I see. Well, … thank you again, sergeant."

"Of course, sir," Howarth replied.

After another moment, Lewis turned and left.

The cafe was vaguely familiar, but he assumed it had changed its decor and probably even its ownership many times in the intervening years. Lewis was almost certain he'd sat at a small, round table near the window years ago, looking out on nearly the same street scene, with his mother across from him. But memory was a fickle thing, and he could barely trust his senses today.

He wondered if his mother had ever come here on her own, or perhaps with Moira, to get out of the house for a while and enjoy a change of scenery besides her twice-daily walks around the Lambert estate that stretched out around Pale House. Just a lunch out, like ordinary people — but he knew the answer immediately. Of course she hadn't. She didn't do that sort of thing. Because Pale House was her home, in every sense. She lived in the safety of its surroundings, where time flowed much more slowly than it did beyond its walls. In a way, it was every inch the museum that it resembled from the outside — of a family's past, and better days, and a mournful echo of what might still have been.

The waitress brought his food, giving him a smile but barely another glance. She was young and she was rushed off her feet, and a part of him was irrationally relieved that she had no idea who he was. He could pretend for half an hour or so that he was simply a stranger, passing through on his way even farther north, and that today held no special sharpness or regret.

Just a Monday, like the Monday of everyone else in the cafe. Not a dark and indelible milestone of his life, unexpected and sudden, already filling his consciousness, and to be remembered on every subsequent day.

He caught movement outside from the corner of his eye, and turned to see a man walk past the cafe with a large Alsatian; black with bands of tan fur along its sides. He tracked the dog's progress as it sauntered past the window and out of sight.

I'd forgotten about that, he thought. The dog — not the one outside, but a similar animal, from years before. Their own family pet, for the brief few years between its rescue and its untimely death from a heart condition. There had been other dogs at other times, but this was one he hadn't thought of in a long while.

He lifted his coffee cup and took a mouthful of the bitter liquid, trying to remember what age he must have been. Young, certainly; a boy. Barely a teenager, at the end of the animal's life. The dog's name had been Angus, according to a name-disc attached to his collar when Lewis's father had brought the dog home one afternoon, after a trip to the regional animal shelter some twenty-five miles distant.

Angus was quiet, attentive, undemanding, and obedient. Lewis's father had called him *civilised*. It wasn't until Lewis was in his early twenties that he realised it was actually a euphemism — deliberate or otherwise — for *mistreated*.

The dog was loved, and immediately became a part of the family. Angus would roam the house and its grounds, sometimes staying out overnight for one or even two days in a row, before being found sitting nonchalantly on the front steps when the storm doors were opened in the morning. He would glance up as if to say good morning, and then dart inside to find a secluded spot for a nap. Inscrutable and stoic. His past was a mystery, and always remained so.

They would walk the dog along the coastal cliffs a couple of miles from Pale House. At first, there were three of them: his father, his mother, and himself. The dog tended to range ahead, but not too far, keeping an eye on the humans who accompanied him. He wasn't a ball-fetching sort of beast, but he did love to explore the landscape, as if he was perpetually looking for something he'd long ago lost. Or maybe he just liked the sense of freedom.

Those memories were hazy, and had the soft lines and bright colours of childhood half-recollections, probably constructed as much from subconscious editorialising as actual events. They'd become a part of Lewis's mental furniture; always present, but unexamined, and blurred by time.

Later, as he reached the cusp of adolescence, it was just himself and his mother. Angus wouldn't range quite so far anymore, knowing that their circle had a break in it now, and instinctively staying nearer to try to close it. Some animals had a way of knowing things — important things — and Angus was certainly among them.

The conversations were fewer then. Margaret didn't seem to have anything to say, and Lewis lacked the words to help. Years later, he'd wondered if the growing silences between them had been mutually mis-interpreted — if his mother had thought he blamed her for the divorce, perhaps; and if he, in turn, had been wrong about some of her resentment towards him for his similarity to his father. He'd decided that there was probably some truth to both assumptions, but they'd never discussed it.

Angus had died, peacefully in a drug-induced and very brief sleep, one morning after Lewis had gone to high school. Just before he left, his mother gave him a piece of sausage-meat to feed to the dog, which was un-precedented. He'd done so, and petted the animal, and then washed his hands before leaving to catch the bus. He knew that the vet was coming later that morning to check how Angus was doing after a period of failing health, but nothing more had been said. He refused to think about the implications of it, steadfastly not putting two and two together. When he arrived back home in the evening, Angus was gone, and so was his bedding from the warmest corner of the kitchen. His collar, with the now-faded metal name disc attached, sat on a countertop. Lewis wasn't surprised, and when he cried, he did so privately.

In the years following, there was another dog, but the ritual had been broken. Clifftop walks were for Lewis alone, and at irregular hours of the early morning or late evening. He thought only of his wish to leave Dunleven and go as far away as he could.

I was as civilised as the dog was, he thought, still staring out the window of the cafe at the passing people and vehicles.

For not having given any thought to the animal in so many years, he could now picture Angus clearly. Brown, watchful eyes, seeing and clearly understanding. Like a counterbalance, for as long as he was able.

You got out first, Lewis thought, and he wasn't sure whether he was talking about the dog, or his mother.

Chapter 4

Moira Rankin's house was the sort you'd find on the cover of local tourism magazines. A whitewashed bungalow surrounded by a low stone wall, a forest-green wooden gate that always looked freshly painted, window boxes, and ceramic plant pots lining the short path leading up to the front door.

There was a driveway but no car, and even from outside the garden gate Lewis could hear the whistle of an old-fashioned kettle that boiled on the hob. He wasn't looking forward to this visit, but he knew that the police would already have informed the old woman about his mother's death. Moira had been Margaret Lewis's companion and friend for years, and almost everyone in town recognised her when she was out and about on her endless errands.

Lewis opened the gate and stepped onto the front path, closing the gate behind him before reluctantly approaching the door. Finding no doorbell, he knocked twice on the painted wooden surface, and after half a minute or so, he heard a latch being opened within. A moment later, the door swung inwards to reveal Moira.

Her eyes lit up when she saw him, first in recognition and then in sorrow, and Lewis barely had the chance to realise with shame that this woman had taken his mother's death worse than he had, before he was embraced by her slender and fragile arms. She smelled of rose water, and fabric softener, and somehow also of that vague and unsettling sense of borrowed time that lingers around the elderly.

"I'm so terribly sorry, son," she said. Lewis could hear the sincerity of it, and the intensity of the woman's own bereavement, all through her surprisingly strong voice. "Come in, come in," Moira said, releasing him and gesturing to the simply furnished but welcoming space within.

"Thank you," Lewis said, stepping past her with a nod, already feeling bound to this person he'd spoken to on only a handful of occasions before. He took a few steps into the wooden-floored hallway and stopped, respectfully waiting for Moira as she closed and locked her front door, and when she turned to face him she shooed him into the room to the left.

"Don't be silly," she said. "Go on in and sit down. I've just boiled the kettle."

Her accent was of the area, bending the vowels into lyrical things of more than one sound, and despite all of the events of the day so far, it was only now that Lewis was struck by a deep sense of nostalgia, and then a moment later by the same loss he'd felt in that chilled room in the hospital.

Moira had evidently returned from her kitchen to ask him something — what he'd like to drink, probably — and as their eyes met, a look of understanding passed over her face.

Makes her look younger, he thought. He could imagine the young woman that she'd been, and for the first time he wondered what her life had been like. *Another question I should have asked years ago.*

Moira moved towards him, placing one of her small hands on his elbow.

"I loved her too," she said. "And she wasn't an easy person to love. I told her that myself. I know you two had your problems, but I think she understood why you moved away. Don't fret. She was my family, and so are you. Now let's get you some tea."

She turned without another word and went through another door, leaving Lewis swallowing past the lump in his throat and pressing his fingernails painfully into his palms in an effort to regain control of his emotions. He heard the clink of cups and saucers, and he sat down in an overstuffed chair near the room's modest fireplace.

It was so simple. The clarity that had evaded him for years — decades, really — had arrived with devastating swiftness, and all it had taken was the irreversible loss of his mother. He realised now just how much he'd wanted a reconciliation, and how his careful preservation of distance had been self-sabotaging. He'd often told himself that it was merely self protection, logical and fair, but he'd always known that he was lying to himself. Sitting here in the home of this old woman who had been his mother's friend and companion during these many lost years, he caught just a glimpse of the inevitability of it all, given his own temperament, his need to blame others for the circumstances of his life, and even how he in some ways had been using the unresolved estrangement from his mother as an excuse to keep his own life endlessly paused. The truth was devastating, and he raised his hands to his face, pressing on the ridge of bone above his eyes as if he could force the realisation back into his subconscious.

Moira chose that moment to come back into the room, and Lewis heard her step falter briefly before resuming course towards where he sat. With his eyes still closed, he heard a tray being placed down with the telltale rattle of china, and he took a deep and ragged breath before letting his hands fall away. He looked up at her, and was horrified to see wet tracks on her own cheeks. The guilt rose up within him again.

I'm mourning my own shortsightedness and stubbornness, and she thinks I'm mourning my mother.

Lewis looked away immediately. The tears of the old were particularly painful to witness. So many more lines and creases to run through, leaking from eyes that have surely seen more than enough of life's arbitrary cruelties. It was much worse when they offered pity that was undeserved. He cleared his throat.

"Moira, thank you for everything you did for my mother," he said. "There's no way for me to repay you for that."

"Nor would you ever need to, son," she said, with gentle chastisement in her tone. "It wasn't just a one-way street, though I know you like to think otherwise."

Lewis looked at her for a moment, but she had busied herself with pouring tea. The cups were of fine china with bright floral patterns, the colours still strong, and he somehow knew that this was a tea set she very rarely used. He wondered if his mother had ever taken tea here like this, but he doubted it. She had always preferred the safety of her home environment, drawn around her like a mantle of faded authority.

Moira handed him a steaming cup of breakfast tea, strong and golden-brown, after he declined the offer of milk. He glanced at the silver tray, seeing that it held a serving plate of assorted biscuits, but it was the sugar bowl that caught his eye. It was mint green, in contrast to the rest of the set, stirring a hazy memory of something. He blinked, and now all he saw was the same off-white china, emblazoned with purple and yellow and blue flowers.

My mother had the green tea set, he suddenly remembered. It had become an ornament of sorts, sitting in the centre of a round table in the blue drawing room which she favoured for its views out towards the rear aspect of the house. It hadn't actually been used in Lewis's memory, and he'd never known why she kept it there to gather dust. And now he'd seen that sugar bowl here, just for a moment, in place of Moira's own.

Forgive her, his mind whispered in Sergeant Howarth's voice, and he licked his lips before taking a gulp of the tea that was still too hot.

"Have you been to the hospital?" Moira asked, in a tone that she might have used if she were asking about the supermarket instead, and Lewis just nodded.

"And the funeral director," he replied after a moment. "It'll be Thursday morning. There's a lunch afterwards."

"I'll make sure everyone knows. You didn't have to arrange all of that on your own," Moira said, with the same gentle chastisement as before, and Lewis wasn't entirely surprised to feel a great surge of affection for this woman who seemed determined to step in and assume a kind of parental role for him.

But we don't really know each other, he thought. *Even if she knew my mother better than I did.*

He shrugged. "I picked up the keys too. Her keys, I mean. From the police station."

Moira had been reaching to pick up her teacup again, but changed her mind and clasped her hands in her lap. She looked at him strangely.

"Have you been to the house yet?"

Lewis nodded. "I drove up as soon as I arrived. I didn't go in. I just… felt that I wanted to see it."

"Because it's hard to believe," she said. "I felt the same way when my husband passed on."

"I think I wanted to check she wasn't still there. Like it was just some kind of mistake. It's ridiculous." Lewis made a small laughing sound that wasn't entirely steady, but Moira only looked at him with pity and understanding. The understanding was worse.

He shook his head, then took another sip of tea. After a moment, he asked the question that had been on his mind ever since he was woken that morning by Howarth's call.

"How had she been recently?"

A look of guilt passed across the woman's face, and Lewis quickly spoke again before she could reply. "You've taken wonderful care of her. I'm really glad that she had you. I don't know what she would have done otherwise, honestly. The police just said she'd been out in the garden in the middle of the night, barefoot. Like she'd got out of bed and went straight outside."

"And they're wondering if she'd been losing her marbles," Moira replied evenly. "She was only sixty-three, Alasdair. There was nothing wrong with her mind. Don't let anyone tell you otherwise."

"That's what I thought. So what do you make of it then?" he asked, hiding his curiosity behind the rim of his cup, but he knew that she could see right through him. Moira sighed, setting her own cup down on its saucer.

"She'd been... troubled lately," she said. "Had things on her mind. She wouldn't talk about it much, of course, but she had been agitated."

Lewis frowned. "Did she mention anything at all about what was bothering her? She didn't say anything to me."

Moira shook her head. "All I know is that she was looking for something in the house. I'd find her going through drawers and cupboards upstairs, and she'd say she was thinking of having a clear out, or redecorating."

"Redecorating?" It was difficult to believe. His mother's taste in interior design had ossified decades ago, and while she did get people in to refresh the place once every eight or ten years, it was always kept the same.

"I didn't believe it either," Moira replied. "She was spending time in a particular room, but there's nothing in there that I know of. I asked if she wanted me to clean it, and she said no. She kept it locked."

"Which room was that?" Lewis asked, leaning forward now. There were dozens of chambers in Pale House, some vast and some modest, all connected by stairways and hallways and landings. Even as a boy, there had been parts of the house that rarely saw human inhabitants except for cleaning, but lately his mother had used only a handful of rooms, leaving the rest to fade.

"On the second floor, along the eastern wing. Where the gallery runs past that room with the piano. There's a room on the garden side. There's a—"

"Clock outside it, yes, I remember it," Lewis said. The room had served a few functions during his time at the house, including an ancillary guest bedroom, and —

if memory served — as an ironing room when his mother had deigned to perform the task herself instead of relying on household staff. He had only the vaguest notion of what it looked like now; he couldn't even quite recall its layout. He must have walked past it well over a thousand times, but he almost never had cause to go in.

"I might have hidden in there once when we were all playing hide and seek," he said, and Moira gave a small smile that was wistful, even though she hadn't been present at that time in his life. After a moment, Lewis realised that she was probably remembering something similar from earlier in her own life, perhaps with her daughter.

Moira's smile faded, and she pressed her lips together. They were a greyish pink, and paper thin, surrounded by lines that spoke of a lifetime of laughter. But there was no amusement upon them now.

"There have always been secrets in that house, son," she said, looking down at her teacup as if she were a scryer about to foretell his destiny. "And lately I've felt that... well, you'll just think I'm a daft old woman."

"No chance of that," he replied. "I'd like to hear what you think, no matter what that might be."

She looked at him appraisingly, weighing up something in her mind. Then she sighed. "The truth is that I felt she wanted to lay some old ghosts to rest. She was going through her past, and yours I suppose. Going through that house, searching for whatever she was after, but finding other things instead."

"Other things?"

Moira gestured as if waving away the question, but then she answered it anyway. "I'd find things sitting out that hadn't been there before, after she'd been going through a room. Sometimes it was ornaments, or pictures, or even toys that I assumed were yours. I had no idea she kept so much, or where she had it hidden."

"Me either," Lewis said, frowning now. His mother hadn't been an overly sentimental woman, and had always preferred tasteful decor to keepsakes and nostalgia. He certainly couldn't recall seeing any of his childhood things for twenty years at least. He wondered what could have prompted all this.

"But the old things were never out for long. Between one day and the next, she'd put them away again. I tried asking her about that too, once, and she gave me the most peculiar look."

"But you're sure that she was... alright," he said. "It sounds like she was under a lot of emotional pressure, and you said she was agitated."

"She wasn't going senile, son," Moira replied insistently and with a note of defiance now. "I spoke to her every single day. I'd have been the first to notice."

Lewis nodded thoughtfully. He believed her, and it only confirmed his own impression. Whatever had been going on with his mother, she had remained *compos mentis* to the end. Which was perhaps worse, in a way, because it meant there were questions with no convenient answers.

"You should have a look for yourself," Moira said, interrupting his thoughts. "You might even have a better idea of what she was trying to find, I suppose. Oh, and I almost forgot: you'll want to look in her filing cabinet for the legal documents you'll need. I have her solicitor's phone number here for you. You should call him as soon as you can."

She got up and crossed to the small circular dining table that would barely seat three people in comfort, and which had very clearly not seated more than one in years. Her leather handbag sat upon it, somewhat faded and creased but having lost no more of its comportment and essential elegance than its owner had. Moira retrieved a spiral-bound notebook from it, flipped through the pages for a moment, and tore out one of the sheets.

"Moira, where's my mother's filing cabinet?" Lewis asked. "I don't remember her having an office in the house at all."

She gave a sad smile, and nodded. "She'd been using the old staff kitchen, facing out to the back lawn. She liked the view, and she liked walking through the east wing to get to it. The filing cabinet is under her desk in there; you'll see."

He nodded. He'd always liked the old kitchen too, despite it getting almost no use since the much more modern one had been installed nearer the front of the house.

Lewis took the piece of notepaper, and typed the number into his phone. "I should probably just call him now. Mind if I step outside for a minute?"

"Oh, of course," she replied. "I'll be here."

There was a hint of sunlight behind the clouds as Lewis went out into Moira's front garden, but it only added a yellow hue to the grey, making it feel almost like twilight. He looked to his right, up the long road leading towards the Lambert estate. Pale House was up there, but it was hidden behind a curve in the road and hundreds of pine trees beyond.

The solicitor, whose name was Laird, was temporarily out of the office for lunch according to his secretary, but she was happy to create an appointment for the following day in mid-morning. She had asked if Lewis wanted to come in that same afternoon, but he declined, saying he had some things to take care of. It was only after he'd hung up that he wondered just how many residents of the little town had yet to hear about his mother's death.

Moira was busy in her kitchen when he went back inside, and he stood awkwardly in the doorway until she noticed him.

"I have a meeting in the morning," he said. "So I ought to go and find those documents, I suppose. Thanks for the tea, Moira… and for everything else."

She stepped forward and embraced him for the second time, and told him not to be silly. She made him promise that he'd call if there was anything she could do to help, and he said he would.

Moira stood at her front door and waved as he drove off up the hill, and Lewis had the thought that after keeping his distance from his own mother for so long, on the day of her death he found himself all too willing to accept a surrogate. The realisation troubled him, but it flitted away as he once again set eyes on the gateposts that led to the expanse of land beyond.

No excuses this time, he thought, as he eased the car over the threshold and into the avenue of trees whose branches seemed to drain what little dull light was left in the day.

Chapter 5

The house stretched overhead, and the atrium was unusually cold.

Because the doors were left open for half the night, Lewis remembered, his eyes searching for the spot where his mother had been found. But there was no police tape, no markers, no chalk outline — because that's not what real life was like when no foul play was suspected.

Her footprints were visible, though.

Small tracks, almost like a child's, but heavy on the balls of the feet. Some of the prints were still virtually complete, showing just how much dirt and mud she must have brought back in from the grounds. An image flashed through his mind, of his mother's feet still coated in mud beneath the white bedsheet and the bright yellow blanket that lay over her legs in the hospital. He blinked it away, again troubled at the trajectory of his thoughts.

"It's been a difficult day," he said to himself, flinching at the sound of the words spoken aloud amidst the silence. The house offered no response, and Lewis was unsettled to realise that a small part of him had perhaps been expecting one.

Then the absurdity of the situation struck him. He was standing in the entrance hall of his family's home, in the very chamber in which his mother had been found dead less than twelve hours earlier, with his favourite carry-on backpack slung over his left shoulder and stuffed haphazardly with clothing and toiletries plus his laptop and its charger. A black suit that had never fitted him well — hanging from his frame, always making him look like an appropriately sickly vulture at the occasional funerals that were its only outings — was in its own bag in the boot of his car outside. And what was he expected to do next, exactly?

Put the kettle on in the still-new kitchen where his mother probably made tea each morning, now knowing she would never again stand upon those cold tiles, looking out the window as the steam rose from her cup?

Sort the handful of bills and junk mail that sat askew on the thick mat beneath the letter box, and begin to make a list of companies who would have to be informed that she no longer resided here?

Would the funeral director need a dress for her to wear? Probably. Where did she even keep her clothes? Shouldn't Moira be the one to choose her final attire? And what about jewellery? Does it just go with her into the —

Lewis took an unsteady breath, pushing the clamouring thoughts away. A part of him knew that it was unwise to be alone right now, but there was no other realistic option at this point. He couldn't ask Moira to come up the hill or even go and collect her; that was unfair, and was just delaying the inevitable.

He didn't feel like eating or drinking. He didn't feel like doing anything at all, but he especially didn't feel like doing nothing. So he dropped his jacket and bag right there in the atrium, retrieved the blue plastic folder he'd been given at the hospital, which he'd stuffed into the backpack's laptop compartment, and began to walk deeper into the house.

The downstairs reception hall creaked and clanked as the central heating made its usual brave but hopeless attempt to evenly heat the chamber. Lewis had a flash of memory: playing with toy cars on the floor here, because it was hard and uncarpeted so the wheels ran much better than in his own bedroom. He had sat on the varnished planks in one corner, right in front of a large radiator, and whenever he moved away from the wall to collect one of his vehicles, he could feel the temperature drop by several degrees.

He looked at the staircase now, and tried unsuccessfully to picture his mother's small frame descending it each day. He knew intellectually that she had lived here the whole time — *until this morning* — but his own separation from the place had given it the quality of a house that had been well-known years ago, but had since transferred into other ownership and gradually lost the hundreds of little elements of familiarity that a home possessed. The house was two places: the one from his memories, and this shell that soldiered on, fading, as time ticked onwards beyond its walls with little concern for whether it survived or not.

Most of the doors were closed. Though it was impossible to really know — Moira might have fastidiously closed doors to keep the place warm, for example — Lewis suspected that many of them had probably been closed for a very long time. Weeks, months, and perhaps even years in some cases. The house was too large for any kind of consistent occupancy throughout most of its extent, and he already knew that his mother stuck to a handful of rooms during her daily routine. The remainder were left alone, to remember whatever it was that rooms remembered, and lament the passing of their usefulness.

Morbid thoughts again. He found he was irritated at himself, and he unconsciously quickened his pace.

There was evidence of an isolated and highly habitual existence. Lewis swore he could see the faint trace of a path worn into the thick strip of carpeting that ran along the centre of each passageway radiating from the hall. He followed the rightmost branch, reasoning that he might as well locate the folder of legal documents that his mother's solicitor would want to see the following morning. The afternoon was darkening rapidly despite the sun now peeking intermittently through the clouds, and the light coming through the occasional high window or infrequent open doorway was the feverish yellow of an approaching winter twilight.

For years now he'd dreaded being in Pale House when darkness fell, but only because it would mean the awkwardness and tension of an evening and then a morning with his mother, both making polite conversation but so very aware of the gulf that had yawned between them for years. The things unsaid, and questions unanswered; a detente after a period of genuine non-communication, that was in some ways worse because the silences now punctuated every conversation instead of being concentrated.

Now, though, the house just felt empty. It was still vast, still looming, and still pregnant with the past and a history that felt like someone else's life. But no longer a threatening place. It was just… melancholy.

Already holding its own funeral service for its last remaining occupant, he thought, and he abruptly realised that he very much wanted a drink.

The Old Kitchen — he heard the initial capitals of its title clearly in his mind — was almost shockingly bright and airy compared to the passage that led to it. It had been exclusively for servants in previous decades, but it had changed a lot since Lewis had last seen it. The countertops spanning two of its four walls were still there, as was the large central island, but the shelves above the counters were empty. The pot hooks and assorted racks had been removed, the stovetop was concealed by a metal cover, and the island was now clearly a makeshift desk of almost ridiculous magnitude, with a stool pulled up to it on the side opposite the large window that looked out towards the expanse of grass beyond.

On one of the side counters there was an electric kettle plugged into a socket that probably dated from when the house was first wired for electricity, and there was a teapot and a solitary mug standing nearby, along with a ceramic jar which Lewis presumed contained tea bags. The objects were almost brutally conspicuous there on the surface which must have spanned a full twelve feet along the wall.

The more he looked at the scene, the more disproportional it became, and his mind whispered that it was a sort of microcosm of how she had lived in the house itself; pockets of occupation and utility, amidst an expanse of orphaned places with no further hope of use.

Of course she'd have an extra kettle and things here, he thought. *It's a fair walk to the actual kitchen.*

The teapot had an air of expectation about it, or perhaps confusion and impatience at the unprecedented tardiness of its usual user, coupled with the unanticipated appearance of the virtual stranger who now stood in front of it. Lewis's mind summoned an unasked-for image of the magically-animated kitchenware of some cartoon he dimly remembered from childhood, and he imagined that the crockery was silently watching him, waiting for him to leave so it could continue its dance.

"Christ," he muttered to himself, turning away and dropping the blue folder onto the island before placing his hands on the surface. He let his gaze bounce off the few neat little stacks of papers, a pen pot and accompanying block of notepaper, and then finally an object that abruptly brought the grief surging back up into his chest.

His mother's diary sat upon the sun-faded and heavily scarred wood.

Lewis instinctively reached out towards it, but then he drew his hand away without touching the black leather cover. It was a diary in the sense of a schedule and appointment book, not a personal journal, but no collection of intimate thoughts could ever hope to so perfectly encapsulate its author as this book did.

She had always kept a diary, for as long as he could remember. It was a constant fixture in the house, written in and amended multiple times per day, both governing and chronicling not just a life, but also an approach to living.

Every task for the day was listed, no matter how minor — indeed, the more trivial the better, since the end of the day would bring a bigger list of checked-off items. It was her means of control over her own existence, and Lewis knew very well that he'd inherited both the propensity and the habit.

He reached for the book again, and this time he flipped it open at the page marked by its slender fabric bookmark. He frowned. The page's date was three days ago, and his life-long experience was that almost nothing would stop his mother from attending to her diary each day. The list of tasks there was completely checked off, and was mostly miscellaneous household or administrative matters, with the exception of one item which simply said *Keep looking*.

Moira said that his mother was looking for something in the house, and this seemed to confirm it. Lewis closed the diary again, feeling a surge of childlike guilt for opening it in the first place, but he knew that it probably belonged to him now. Its previous owner certainly wouldn't be asking for it.

He took a step back from the central island that had served as his mother's desk, and looked underneath it. Sure enough, at the corner nearest the large windows, there was a metal filing cabinet pushed in, out of the way. There were two drawers; a small upper one and a much larger lower one. Lewis chose the latter, pulling it open to find a series of hanging files, each labelled in block capitals on its tab. Everything was there, including details of his mother's bank accounts, her will, insurance policies, tax documents, utility supplier details, and so on.

Always organised, he thought.

He had a similar filing system of his own, back down in Edinburgh. He wondered if he should start using a paper diary too. Dismissing the thought, he took a series of documents from the cabinet and tucked them into the blue folder along with the handful of forms the hospital had supplied. It would have to do.

Lewis retreated from the overly bright room back into the comparative darkness of the rear hallway, taking the folder with him. He still found himself expecting to see his mother around every corner. For a brief moment, he considered getting out of the house and finding a pub so he could drown his sorrows, but he knew it was a spectacularly bad idea. It was much more sensible to try and eat something, then get whatever rest he could.

He moved through the house, partly retracing his steps, but he took a small detour on a whim, towards an area that he'd rarely found himself in even when he had last lived there. As well as the grand staircase in the reception hall, there were several other stairways spread through Pale House. Some were elegant and carpeted, clearly meant for the family or their guests, and some were narrow and hidden away behind doors, reserved for the household staff. One such narrow stairway led directly from a part of the south wing, up two levels to finally come out in the corridor leading to the master bedroom that his mother had surely continued to use. He had no idea what the room looked like these days, and he had no desire to find out today.

Lewis passed by the open doorway that revealed the stairway going up, purposely not glancing towards it. He continued instead towards the front of the house, and was about to emerge into the reception hall again when a flash of colour registered in his peripheral vision.

There was a sideboard along the left of the corridor, just before it opened out into the large and gloomy space. Sitting on it, and staring back at him with large, dark-stitched eyes, was a blue rabbit.

"My god," he said, coming to a halt immediately.

The toy was smaller than the creature it playfully recreated, but not by much. It was made of cloth, faded to a pale eggshell blue by the work of sunlight and years, and its stuffing was lumpy and compressed now, giving it a crumpled sort of look. Its pose was upright even if its posture could no longer quite claim to be, and its nose and whiskers were stitched entirely flush to the fabric. Its mouth was a closed line, and Lewis had always thought the thing looked disapproving.

Is this what she was looking for? he wondered, but then he immediately dismissed the possibility. The rabbit — or *Blue Rabbit,* to use its proper name — had been in his mother's bedroom for as long as Lewis himself had been alive, and even if it had migrated to this sideboard for some reason, it would readily have been visible as his mother went about her daily business. The question of just why it was sitting here was one that would have to wait.

He approached the stuffed toy with caution. It was immaculate despite its faded colour; not dirty in the slightest. The sideboard itself had a fine covering of household dust, but Blue Rabbit itself had none.

Of cOurSe I DoN'T, Blue Rabbit said in his mind. *RaBBiTs rUn Too fASt To GeT DusTY!*

The voice was high-pitched and clownish, with an exaggerated accent. It was really his mother's voice, disguised so as to puppeteer the toy, as she'd done when Lewis was a small boy. Blue Rabbit had never been his, exactly — it had always remained hers — but it had been on loan for a while, to help him get off to sleep in the large, dark, and never entirely quiet house. He hadn't thought about it in years, and with good reason.

The night before she went away, he thought.

It had been when he was at high school, during his early teenage years. His mother was suffering from stress, but Lewis hadn't known quite how severe her condition was until that particular evening. Months had gone by where she became increasingly withdrawn, clearly having trouble sleeping properly, and steadfastly refusing to answer any questions as to why. Lewis himself had settled into a quiet, watchful, anxious sort of sullenness.

The day was a Tuesday; Lewis had always remembered that. He had barely seen his mother all day, and by the time he'd finished a late and solitary dinner, he assumed she'd just gone to bed early. He was walking through the house when he saw a light on in the kitchen. She was sitting on the same stool as always; in the same position, even. Already in her robe, and make-up removed. The newspaper was on the table, as usual — but closed. He asked how she was. She didn't answer.

He asked again, more loudly, but she still didn't respond, so he moved into her line of sight. Lewis felt the first stirring of unease. He tried to get her attention several more times, even approaching and reaching out towards her, but she only flinched away, remaining in silence. He gradually realised that there was something genuinely wrong.

Upstairs in her bedroom, she had a rocking chair. It had always been there, to the best of his recollection. It held various plush toys and animals, at least some presumably having been her own from childhood. He had never asked. In all those years, he had never once asked. One of the animals was Blue Rabbit. Its presence there with her in the kitchen was the final bizarre detail that pushed everything off-balance.

The small voice in his mind that wondered — desperately, by that point — if this was a prank of some kind had grown silent. She wasn't given to that sort of thing, and the other explanation was all too plausible. Whatever pressure and stress she'd been under had evidently been slowly crushing her. It was just the suddenness that was so shocking, as if it had all taken place in the space of an hour.

He decided to call for help. There were still household staff at that time, and even though the hour was late, he would be able to rouse someone via the additional button on each of the phone handsets in the house. An obscure instinct told him that he should call from another room, rather than using the phone that sat in front of her in the kitchen. He withdrew from the room, letting the door close, and went in the direction of the front of the house. Finding a handset, he realised that she had already taken the kitchen phone off the hook, and would depress the switch when he tried to dial.

His concern changed into frustration, and he returned to the kitchen to find her again. She stood strangely by her stool, holding the keys to the main entrance and also a small keyring which opened the door leading directly from the kitchen to the side grounds. He knew that she had locked him in with her. In her other hand, she clutched Blue Rabbit.

Lewis briefly tried to reason with her, and was met with only blankness — but there was a light in her eyes; intellect and insight still shining there. He assessed the situation, as much as his panicked mind would allow. She was strong, certainly, but she was also only marginally over five feet tall, and with a slim figure. He was by no means powerfully built, but he was a teenaged boy, and he was taller and heavier. He could take the keys from her, if it came to that. For her own good.

As if sensing his conclusion, she put the keys into the pocket of her robe. Then she took out the knife.

These things don't really happen, he thought to himself at the time. He had a clear and vivid recollection of that phrase in his mind. That was all he consciously thought about for some time.

Even now, Lewis could remember the taste of adrenaline in his mouth, and the hyper-awareness. He remembered the characteristic looseness then immediate pre-tensing of muscles; the slight and automatic stoop in his own posture; the utter, exquisite *detail* of every object and surface and sound. If she had lunged at him, he could have caught her wrist; he knew it. Lewis the *person* was entirely vacant during that long two or three seconds. There was only primal threat-assessment and observation.

She turned away, back towards the rear of the kitchen. He immediately went the other way, along interlinked hallways and to the front of the house, then up both main staircases in sequence. He went from the bottom to the top instantly. He made no sound. He required no breath. He was a shadow, flitting up the wall like a wraith.

He stood at the top balcony, looking over the railing and downwards, but no-one was in sight. He considered going up to the attic, out one of the skylights, and over the roof in the dark. Then it would be a scramble down the tiles to two lower levels of roof, somehow, and then a long, sheer drop which would break his legs at the very least. Pale House was not designed to be scaled or descended-from outside its walls. Pale House was also not designed to be escaped from.

Lewis had hid in one of the guest bedrooms, under the head of the bed, with his back pressed against the skirting board amidst the dust. It had tickled his nose maddeningly, but he had not sneezed. He could hear his heart pounding in his ears, and every creak of the house seemed to be a slipper-clad footstep, bringing death in the guise of a worse betrayal than he had ever contemplated.

He didn't know what happened in the house later that night. Even now, he couldn't recall any of it. He couldn't remember falling asleep there on the floor, hidden away. He couldn't remember waking up the next morning. He couldn't remember any part of it at all. All he knew was that he had survived unscathed.

The following day, his mother went away for a while, to rest. The word was always *rest*, and Lewis supposed there was more truth than euphemism in it. No other terms were used. Everything continued.

Blue Rabbit was already back on the rocking chair when he dared to venture into his mother's now-vacant room the next evening. The household staff took exceptionally good care of him, and his late aunt who lived elsewhere in town spent several nights at Pale House in the aftermath of it all.

When his mother returned a couple of weeks later, she was paler than he remembered, but her eyes were clear, and they were haunted in odd moments with a hint of something he didn't understand at the time. Years later, he came to realise that it had been misplaced embarrassment, and perhaps slightly less-misplaced guilt.

They never spoke of that night again, and if Lewis had ever wanted to, the opportunity had now been lost permanently.

"Fuck," he said, but Blue Rabbit made no more response this time than before. Lewis decided to leave the damned thing where it was. Maybe it was fitting that it turned up today of all days.

At least it wasn't in the old kitchen, he thought. A small voice in his mind remarked that it was unusual he hadn't remembered the incident when he was in the room where it happened, but he knew that memory didn't work that way. People were good at selectively forgetting things. It was a survival mechanism.

He decided that tea might be a wise choice at this point, not trusting his stomach with food just yet. He also decided to forego the solitary kettle in the room that had become his mother's office, instead seeking the incongruously new staff kitchen area elsewhere on the ground floor. He had a cup of jasmine tea in his hands within minutes, and decided to take it outside.

The steam from the hot liquid curled up into the fading light of the sky like a funerary offering, and Lewis could see a few stars beginning to appear. The only sound was the incessant rustle of the wind through a thousand trees, and the occasional distant cry of a woodland bird. There was no traffic sound at all, and the centre of Dunleven might as well have been a hundred miles away.

It's like another world up here, he thought, and it had the distant ring of familiarity to it, as if it was something he'd stood here and thought at another time.

Lewis walked a short distance from the main entrance, noticing that the gardens running off alongside the east wing were still being kept in good order. He was lost in thought for a while, then he turned around abruptly when the electric lanterns framing the open storm doors came on. For a moment he wondered if he might not be alone after all, before he remembered the timers his mother had insisted on having installed.

Even so, he tilted his head upwards, eyes flicking back and forth between the many unlit windows stretching in all directions on the main facade. He blew on his tea, making more steam curl into the now visibly darkening evening.

He looked at Pale House, and Pale House looked back at him.

Lewis wasn't sure how long he stood out there, but when he tried to take another sip from his cup and found it already empty, he also became aware of the chill that the wind had brought, and his jacket was still inside the house. He sighed, and patted his pocket to confirm that he still had the keys he'd obtained from Sergeant Howarth. They jangled, and he had another flash of sensory memory — they'd jangled in the pocket of her robe too, on that same night — and he had to suppress the urge to bend over and vomit for the second time that day.

The feeling passed with a few steady breaths of evening air, and then he sighed. There was nothing for it. For better or worse, he would be spending his first night in Pale House for years, and he would be alone. He went back inside, locking the doors behind him.

Lewis picked up his belongings from the reception hall and decided that he would see if any of the guest bedrooms were still made up for visitors; he knew that his own room had been cleared and repurposed years ago. Perhaps he would even just have a very early night, then see what tomorrow would bring. He certainly felt exhausted enough.

He trudged across the reception hall towards the main staircase, passing the mouth of the corridor that

he'd arrived from earlier. He was too preoccupied to notice that the top of the sideboard was now entirely bare.

Tuesday

Chapter 6

His sleep had been dreamless, as far as he could remember, but Lewis woke with the strong sensation of having just forgotten something of great importance.

The room around him was unfamiliar and disorienting for a few moments, and then everything fell into place. A weight dropped onto his chest, and in the emotionally unguarded moments of awakening consciousness, he felt a burst of acute anxiety at being back in Pale House again.

It was still dark outside, but he could sense that most of the night had already passed. He reached for his phone on the ornate and dusty bedside table, and when its screen illuminated he saw that it was past his usual breakfast time. Hunger immediately took hold of him. He hadn't eaten much the day before; probably not enough. He briefly wondered if there would be any food in the house, and then the compressed timescale of it all struck him once again.

Of course there will. The supermarket delivery arrives here every Sunday morning, and that was only two days ago.

He sat up in bed, not bothering to switch on the lamp he'd had to plug into the wall the previous night. The unremarkable room was dimly visible around him, frozen in time. The house made all the noises that houses do as they're roused from their own slumber, by light and heat and the intrusion of people who form only the current chapter of their narrative. Lewis pushed back the covers, swung his feet onto the cold floor, and ran one hand roughly over his face.

The sudden shrill ringing of his phone badly startled him.

For a moment, it was as if he'd been thrown back in time and the previous day had never happened. The phone screen was illuminated again now, but the glare made him instinctively close his eyes. He was certain it would be Sergeant Howarth, and—

Can I speak to Mr. Alisdair Lewis, please?

—he would be told of his mother's death all over again. Then the long drive north, and the hospital, and the police station, and—

"Get a hold of yourself," Lewis said aloud, tapping the large green button to answer the call. He held the phone to his ear, listening over the accelerated thump of his own heart.

"*Hello, son,*" said the familiar voice on the line.

"Dad," he replied. "Where are you today?"

His reply was ingrained from long habit. Lewis could hear the rumble of a truck engine over the line, and the road beneath its big wheels, and he knew that his father was driving. It wasn't unusual for Ross Lewis's infrequent calls to come from the cab of his vehicle. Lewis assumed that it was the monotony of the unfolding road that led the man's mind to drift to other connections. It had become customary to ask for his location as the first question.

"Just about... uh... still a little north of Luton," came the reply. *"Going for the tunnel again."*

Lewis knew it meant that his father would be in London before long, and his destination was continental Europe via the tunnel underlying the English Channel. He thought it was a route his father drove often, but he wasn't really sure. They didn't dwell on those matters when they spoke. Or on any matters at all, really.

"And how are you getting on?" his father asked, not waiting for Lewis to respond. *"Still writing?"*

It had long ago ceased to bother him that his father would even need to ask, rather than keeping tabs on Lewis's work for himself. Ross Lewis wasn't that kind of man, and there was no inconsideration or callousness in it; it was just how he had been made. But their usual duel of performatively familial pleasantries couldn't be less relevant today.

"I'm at the house, dad," Lewis said. "I drove up yesterday. Mum's... she passed away."

Later, Lewis would wonder if he had been too blunt in sharing the news, but the silence that now filled the line was short lived.

"I'm very sorry to hear that, son," his father replied, and Lewis could hear that the sentiment was genuine. *"What happened?"*

That's the question, he thought.

"They said it was natural causes," he replied. "They found her here at the house. I got the call yesterday morning, early."

"Do you need me to come up there? It would be next week, but I can do it."

"No, no," Lewis replied quickly. "I'm handling it. And there's Moira. I already talked to her."

"That's your mother's friend from down the road?"

Lewis nodded. "Yes."

"Alright," Ross Lewis replied after a moment. *"Well, if there's anything I can do, you let me know. Are you sure you're alright?"*

"I'm sure." It was a lie, of course, but it was the expected and usual one. It was impossible to be alright in a situation like this. It would probably remain impossible for quite a while, and the future definition of *alright* would be different than before, changed irrevocably. Lewis knew all of those things. But certain relationships had their own parameters, and he would not be crying on his father's shoulder today or ever, metaphorically or otherwise.

"OK. Let me know how the funeral goes. I'll have my phone with me. Maybe we can catch up in Edinburgh when you're back home."

"That would be good. Drive safely, dad," Lewis replied. Again it was a scripted statement; his portion of their dance.

"*You too,*" his father replied, "*and call me whenever you need to.*" Then the line went dead.

Lewis sighed and finally switched on the bedside lamp, trying to remember the last time his mother and father had spoken to one another. There had been a few occasions since their paths through life diverged, and they had been cordial enough, but he found that he couldn't remember any within the last five years or more. His mother did periodically ask how her ex-husband was doing, and always sent her best wishes via Lewis, but that was as far as it had gone. He wondered what his father was thinking now, but he knew he'd never ask.

Breakfast was a sombre affair, sitting in the new kitchen and watching the sun climbing into the sky, filtered by the trees all around. His task for the day was clear enough, but the problem was that it would be over too soon. Once he'd seen the solicitor, there would entirely too many hours left to account for.

Lewis stood up and took his meagre dishes to the sink, gave them a cursory rinse, and set them on the drying rack. The day looked to be brighter than the one before, and as he looked out at the lengthening shadows of morning, he decided that there were exactly two pressing matters besides the funeral and related arrangements.

One: Why did a healthy woman in her early sixties suddenly die?

Again, Howarth's early-morning call swam back into his mind. It seemed like it was either five minutes or five months ago. He pushed it away again.

Two: What was she looking for here, and why did it take her out into the garden in the small hours of the morning?

Perhaps he'd even visit the Sergeant again and press him to investigate further, Lewis thought, but then he immediately dismissed the idea. His mother had still been a respected figure in Dunleven, and her passing was surely the talk of the town already. The last thing he wanted was to taint that memory with idle speculation and gossip. He wasn't naive enough to believe that any enquiry he placed with the local police would remain private for more than a few hours, despite the best of intentions. It was too small a place. So he would pursue answers to those questions on his own for now.

Satisfied for the moment, he cast one more glance around the quiet room and decided to just head into town early, on foot. If he was going to spend the afternoon and evening rattling around in Pale House, he could at least have a few hours out beyond its doors first.

Raymond James Agnew was thinking about the future.

His father had finally dropped dead at the age of seventy-three, and if Agnew had been a better-educated man, he would have mused that the expression was true both literally and figuratively. The elderly James Maurice Agnew's sudden stroke had come while he was sitting on the toilet in resignation, and he fell forward and cracked his skull open on the chipped floor tiles. The carer who visited once a day had found him bare- and filthy-arsed, soaked in his own blood and piss, and dead as a doornail. Agnew the younger had laughed at the image every day since.

The stroke's mercy was given not just to the old man himself but also to the world for taking him away from it, and Agnew had since expressed that sentiment — though less eloquently, to be sure — to each of his very few friends.

The funeral was busy, and at least half of those attending had just wanted to make sure the man was truly dead. Agnew counted himself among that group, a paranoid part of him always wondering if maybe it was all an elaborate trick, and his father would sit up in the coffin and give him yet another clout around the skull with the calloused heel of his hand. But that didn't happen, and when the coffin slid silently downwards into the podium at the crematorium, Agnew wished that the flames would come right up to claim it.

He resented even the meagre money spent on the cremation and service, but it helped that it didn't come from his own wallet. Agnew ran the rural bus company that his father had started as a young man, and as he edged past the age of thirty-nine years, he had started to wonder if perhaps his great destiny had got lost somewhere on the winding roads north to Dunleven.

He spent most of his time in the garage, leaving the business administration to the secretaries and the office manager. While everyone was technically his employee, he had very little interest in interacting with any of them except the mechanics he'd known since high school. He was very happy, however, to spend the company's money when it suited him, but Raymond Agnew derived little pleasure from material things. He drove an ordinary car, and he didn't care. He lived in a modest and faded house that had once been his mother's, inheriting it after her death fifteen years earlier. He didn't care about that either.

It was difficult to care about anything when you were angry all the time.

He had days that were good, and days that were bad, but he never had a day when he didn't want to destroy something, or punch someone, or maybe to take the utility knife he kept in his pocket and run its blade between somebody's ribs. The feeling was always with him, even if there were times when it was quieter than usual. Those times didn't last very long, because there was always a new reason to be upset.

Upset. It was what his father had called it, deliberately to annoy Agnew further. The tactic worked well. His father had mostly loved with his fists instead of his heart, but there were worse things in the world. At least he was paying attention. At least, during those many, many moments when Agnew had felt the pain that passed for fatherly affection, he knew that the old man was focused solely on him. In his own way, he had loved his father back for that, because he understood it so well.

So, yes; Agnew got upset a lot. And he took it out on anyone who was within reach, which was a big part of why his modest and faded house had not felt a woman's touch since his mother's death, and hadn't even felt a woman's presence for more than an hour or two, here and there. He didn't care about that very much either.

Just the drumbeat of anger that endlessly churned and slithered in his belly, and in his chest, and would sometimes reach up into his head and take control. Just the anger, which was the shape and essence of his entire life. Everyone in town knew it, and most people avoided him for it, and honestly that just made Agnew even more angry. The way they looked in the other direction, and pretended not to see, and not to hear. The way that a path cleared for him when he was in the pub, or especially when he was on the way out afterwards. He knew they were aware of him, but sometimes it really seemed like they weren't paying enough attention.

That kind of treatment, day in and day out, had a way of making a man feel like he was outside of himself; like he was someone else entirely. And so Raymond James Agnew was thinking about the future, and how to deal with this creeping anger that gnawed at his skull every minute of the day and the night. About how to show people that they ought to respect him, not just give him a wide berth. Because the one thing Agnew could tell you for sure was that he was meant for bigger things.

The hell with the people in this shitty, broken-down little town. The hell with what they thought, or didn't think. The hell with James Maurice Agnew, whose corpse would go up in flames before morning. And the hell, too, with James Maurice Agnew's only son, because when Agnew the younger looked in the mirror, he didn't think of the dark-eyed, hunted-looking thing he saw there as a person at all.

That was his biggest secret: deep down, he saw himself just as everyone else did. He revelled in it, in fact. If you asked anyone in town who he was, they might use his given name, but that's not how they spoke of him privately. It wasn't how they thought of him, even. And rightly so.

Most people knew him as Rage.

Chapter 7

Lewis wandered the streets, allowing the muscle memory of his childhood to guide him.

A lot more of the town centre was pedestrianised than he remembered, but otherwise it was every bit the place he'd visited so often while growing up. Many of the shops had the same names, though he was sure that a couple of them had switched premises during the intervening years. There were also plenty of boarded-up retail units, and what had been the job centre now seemed to be a holistic health shop. There was probably a joke to be found in that fact, but Lewis knew it wouldn't really be funny; not down where the truth of it lay.

Dunleven had seen better days; that much was clear. It might see better ones again in the future, because you never really knew what direction fate would take you in next, but for now it gave the impression of something that was clinging to life, or which perhaps had already just slipped over the edge towards oblivion, and had yet to accept that it was in free-fall into darkness.

There were plenty of people around, though. Going about their lives as usual, and no-one gave him any special scrutiny. Lewis was glad of that, and his thoughts were mostly consumed by Pale House and what would become of it. Should he keep it? Would there be enough money to allow for taking care of it? Would Moira want to retain that responsibility, or would she now prefer to distance herself from a place that would surely be a source of mixed emotions for her?

Lewis's brow was furrowed and he wasn't paying much attention to where he was going, and so it was inevitable that he bumped into the woman who came out of a small cafe with her gaze fixed upon her phone.

"I'm sorry," Lewis said, instinctively reaching his hand out towards her elbow, but not actually touching her. The woman had almost dropped her phone, but when she looked up from behind her curtain of dark brown hair there was an embarrassed smile on her face.

"It was my fault," she said, and then something shifted in her gaze. An instant later her eyes widened, and then she abruptly threw her arms around his neck. It took Lewis's brain a moment to catch up.

"Anne?"

She released him just as quickly as she had embraced him, and Lewis looked upon her large, dark and almost liquid eyes for the first time in at least fifteen years.

Anne Sutherland had been a childhood friend, and while Lewis had moved away from Dunleven a couple of years before he would have finished high school, evidently Anne had either found herself back there again, or had never left. The two had almost been something more than just friends, and Lewis had always sensed it was what she wanted, but for whatever reason it had never happened. His move south so long ago had been abrupt, and to his knowledge she'd never been given an explanation for it. They had never spoken again until this moment.

"I'm so sorry about your mother, Dair," Anne said, and he nodded gratefully. "We all heard about it. Everyone was talking about it at school."

"At school?" he asked, and she gave a small smile that he immediately recognised, and had perhaps even missed.

"I'm a teacher now," she replied. "Ages six to nine. Down at St. Margaret's, too."

Lewis thought it was strangely appropriate that she would be teaching at the school they had both attended as children, and he said so. He started to ask how she'd been, but Anne's phone buzzed and she gave him a regretful look. "I'm sorry, but I don't have very long. I should really be back already."

"Of course," he replied. "It was really nice to see you. It's good to see a friendly face."

She looked at him for a moment, and he could see that she was considering something. Then she glanced around before pressing her lips together.

"Listen, I know you must be busy with… everything you have to deal with right now, but if you don't have anything on tonight, do you want to catch up a bit? Or if you're heading home again—"

"No, I'll be here for a few days," Lewis said. He realised that he was going to accept her invitation, and he smiled gratefully. "That would actually be great. Otherwise I'll just be rattling around up at the house."

"The *Hat* is still open, if you can believe it," she said, and Lewis laughed. *The Admiral's Hat* was a pub in town that had a zero-tolerance policy regarding both underaged drinking — or at least it had when Lewis was the laughably underaged and squeaky-voiced potential drinker in question — and any kind of entertainment, so it had always been renowned for being quiet and respectable on most nights of the week. He had been in a few times for a meal with his father and sometimes his mother too when he had been younger. It would be an ideal place for a conversation.

"What time?"

"Eight?" she replied almost immediately, and Lewis remembered that this, too, had been part of how Anne had been with him when they were children. Attentive to the point of eagerness. How much else had he missed when he was focused only on himself?

"I'll be there," he said, and she nodded.

"I really am sorry about your mother," she said again, then with one last look at him she hurried off and was lost in the crowd.

Anne Sutherland, he thought. Her appearance had caught him off guard, and again he was struck by the strangeness of it. Anne had been a significant figure in his childhood, and for a time she had often been at Pale House. Looking back, Lewis remembered how his mother was polite and even friendly towards the girl that Anne had been, making her feel at ease as much as she could. But there had always been a lingering question. Lewis supposed that the two women had understood it instinctively, but he himself had been blind. Anne had been a friend; that was all.

You knew how she felt, though, a voice in his mind said, and he couldn't place whose voice it was. A tawdry little feeling of shame chased through him as he was forced to admit that the voice was right. He hadn't strung Anne along, but nor had he allowed anything to happen one way or the other. It must have hurt her when he suddenly disappeared from her life and moved away without any word.

I had other things to think about, he thought, and while it was true, it also wasn't really an excuse. Now he suddenly felt a note of nervousness about the idea of meeting her tonight, but so many years had passed, and she'd seemed only friendly and concerned.

She was probably married, too. Primary school teachers were always married, weren't they? At least the ones that hadn't been born at the age of fifty, preconfigured for spinsterhood.

He shook his head at the inanity of his own uncharitable thought, then looked at his watch. He thought he should probably get some coffee or even something to eat, but he wasn't sure he had much of an appetite.

Lewis chose a direction at random and started walking, deciding to forego refreshment until later; perhaps after meeting the solicitor. He didn't particularly relish the idea of being indoors anywhere just at the moment.

Lost in his own thoughts, he didn't notice the pair of dark eyes watching him with interest from further up the street.

The solicitor's waiting area was strangely spartan, and Lewis didn't know whether that was what passed for professional now, or there was just little need for adornment. He was the only client there, and the sole receptionist on the modest front desk kept shooting him glances of guileless curiosity.

He was just beginning to think the reason the appointment was for mid-morning was that the man he was meeting with didn't come to work before then, when the receptionist told him he could go in now. She indicated a conspicuously wood-panelled door at the end of a short hallway — all the others were simply painted white — and he nodded in thanks.

Lewis knocked once and then opened the door, and the man behind the large desk inside stood up with a moderated smile on his face that had already conveyed his condolences before he spoke a single word.

"Good morning, Mr. Lewis. I'm Cameron Laird. I'm very sorry indeed for your loss," he said nevertheless.

Only the great and the good get an "indeed" in that sentence, Lewis was immediately certain.

"Thank you," he replied. "I appreciate you seeing me so promptly."

"Not at all," Laird countered. "Please have a seat. Can I get you a coffee, or tea? Something stronger?"

Lewis mentally raised an eyebrow, but he supposed it wasn't so extreme a suggestion when the appointment was about a last will and testament. He politely refused the offer, and produced the folder he'd brought from the house. Laird took a few minutes to look through it.

"That should be all we need," he said at length, then he closed the folder and clasped his hands on top of it. After a few moments, he met Lewis's eyes.

"As you may know, Mr. Lewis, I've been your mother's solicitor for quite a number of years," he said. "There hasn't been so much call for my services since some of your family's businesses were wound up, but she's continued to be kind to this town in a variety of ways. She spoke of you on several occasions. This has come as a shock to a great many of us here in Dunleven."

Lewis chose to just nod, unsure what the other man was getting at.

"It's none of my business, of course," Laird continued, "but if you wouldn't mind my saying so—"

You've been a terrible son, Lewis's mind whispered in Laird's voice.

You have a lot of nerve coming back here now.

She deserved so much better than this.

Forgive her.

Lewis blinked, alarmed again at the direction his thoughts were taking. He acknowledged that he felt guilt about his mother, but apparently he'd drastically suppressed the scale of it.

"—you should know that she cared about you a great deal. Her primary stipulation in her will, even with the recent modification, was to ensure that you were the majority beneficiary."

Laird took a document from one of the drawers of his desk and set it in front of him. Even upside down, Lewis could see that it was his mother's will. The strangeness of it being here instead of in the house struck him, and he reflected on how death wasn't so much a matter of removing a person from your life, but rather of distributing the many pieces of their existence between places they almost never had cause to visit while alive. A private person instead becomes, in the course of only a few days, a sort of temporarily public property, where their anecdotes and experiences and documents and often even their home are opened to acquaintances and strangers alike. There was a scavenger-like element to it, and he couldn't think of anything his mother would have wanted less.

"The recent modification?" he asked instead, and Laird nodded.

"It was about six weeks ago that she arranged an appointment with me — at the house — and we talked about some changes she wanted to make. It was three things, in all. First, a sum is to be given to one… Moira Rankin. I understand that you know her."

"I spent part of yesterday afternoon with her," Lewis replied. "She was very important to my mother. I'm not sure what my mother's last few years would have been like without her. It's good she'll be taken care of; I'd have done the same myself."

Laird nodded again. "I believe your mother said as much. The second stipulation added to her will was that a sum be given to the local Maxwell Church."

Lewis frowned. His mother had never been particularly religious, beyond what was obligatory for reasons of decorum in a smaller community. She'd never given the impression of being someone who believed in a higher power or an afterlife.

Just a final gift to the town? And a way to keep the family reputation in good order for a while longer?

He had no problem with it; he was just a little surprised. But it was her own money, and if the act had given her comfort, he was grateful for it.

"She was always very fond of this community," Lewis said. It sounded a little flat to his own ears, but Laird only smiled before taking an envelope from between the sheets of the will itself. It bore Lewis's own name, in his mother's handwriting.

"This is the final addition she made: you're to have this," Laird said. "She requested that you read it in private, whenever you feel is best. She asked me to tell you that it has no bearing on the will or her estate."

Lewis nodded slowly before reaching out to take the envelope from the other man. He looked at it, front and back, and then slid it inside his coat. Something for another time and place.

"Everything else — the vast majority of the estate — has been left to you, of course," Laird continued. "The house itself and its contents and grounds, the surrounding land, your mother's liquid assets, and also the buildings and lands of both the mine and the processing plant, including all related rights. Properly managed or sold, I daresay you'll be able to live very comfortably for the foreseeable future."

Lewis blinked at him. He hadn't really thought about the specifics of his inheritance, because he didn't see it as *his*. Nevertheless, this new reality he was confronted with would make profound changes to his lifestyle whether he wanted it to or not.

"Well, thank you for handling these matters on my mother's behalf," he said, feeling a little detached. "May I ask what exactly you need from me at this point? I'm really not familiar with the process at all."

Laird smiled sympathetically. "Of course. Almost no-one is, and it's actually fairly straightforward. You just have some papers to sign, to accept the various transfers of ownership, and I can handle most of the rest of it for you. You're most welcome to give me instructions regarding your wishes for any of your new properties, or we can defer that conversation until a later time, as most people do."

"I hadn't thought about it at all, to be honest," Lewis said, and Laird nodded once more.

"I'll give you my card and we can follow up whenever you wish, whether you're here or elsewhere. In the meantime, we'll handle the paperwork now — if that suits you, of course — and you'll receive all the relevant deeds and information at your nominated address in due course."

It sounded fine, and almost routine. Which it was, of course, for Laird and anyone in his line of work — but it could never be routine for the person on Lewis's side of the desk. It would always be anything but.

It took less than twenty further minutes to sign a host of documents, many of them identical-looking, and mostly in triplicate. When it was all done with, Lewis felt a strong need to get out of the suddenly too-warm office and get some fresh air, and Laird seemed to understand instinctively.

The two men stood and shook hands, and Lewis offered his thanks once again. Laird assured him that it was no trouble, and repeated his earlier condolences. With that, the meeting seemed to be over, and Lewis stepped out into the reception area without a glance at the woman behind the front desk, and then went gratefully out into the cool air.

Chapter 8

This belongs to me now, Lewis thought as he stood in one of the many corridors within Pale House.

It was a bizarre concept. The place that had been his home but always his mother's family's house, was now his property. Lewis was almost certain it would never really feel that way, no matter how long it might be in his possession. Even if he chose to live here — a thought he could barely stand, even now — he would always see himself as merely an inhabitant, haunting rooms and hallways that belonged to another person and another time.

He had eaten a quick lunch in town after his meeting with the solicitor, and then walked home via an indirect route, wanting to see if he could dredge up any sense of comfort at being back in the place where he spent his childhood, and which featured in so many memories. But youth and innocence, apparently, were more of a perspective than the product of any particular place and time. He could only see Dunleven through the eyes of an adult, with its brighter past incarnation forever hidden to him. It looked like just what it was: a place that had seen better days, and whose better days were perhaps even an illusion born of a child's limited experience and limitless hope.

"Cheerful as always, Dair," he muttered aloud.

It was still hours until he would go back into town to meet Anne, and every time he thought about it he felt anxious, so he was doing his best to keep it out of his mind for now. Lewis was on the second floor of the house, wandering without any particular destination in mind, opening doors and allowing himself to remember inconsequential events that had taken place in those chambers.

Hide and seek, in bedrooms that only saw occupancy at Christmas. A model railway within a countryside diorama, overtaking what had once been a billiards room. The impossibly alluring and dangerous aromas of tobacco and alcohol, choking the air in the library when his father's own friends had visited to play cards every few weeks — before his mother had put a stop to it.

Lewis opened another door with some trepidation, expecting a pang of loss, but instead he stopped short in the doorway. The practice room was still there, incredibly, and it looked like it hadn't changed at all.

Why would she keep this in such good order? he wondered. While she'd been a lover of music, his mother hadn't played a single instrument, and his father's interest didn't extend beyond live cover bands in crowded pubs. The practice room had been inherited from Lewis's own grandfather who played the piano with great enthusiasm and somewhat less-great technique, and Lewis had taken lessons from the ages of six to fourteen.

The grand was still there, covered and slightly off to one side. The upright was against the wall too, just where he remembered it being. On impulse, he strode over and pulled the cover away, lifted the lid, and without sitting down he struck several notes, and then a series of chords. The sound was shockingly loud after the near-silence.

Perfectly in tune.

His mother could no more tune a piano than play one, so she must have kept paying someone to come by and maintain the beautiful instrument. From the sound and feel, it couldn't have been more than a few months since it had last been serviced — particularly since Pale House was an old building, and subject to the usual huge variations in temperature, which tended to hasten the deterioration of instruments.

He considered the possibility that the lovingly maintained piano was a gesture of some kind towards him, but then he dismissed the idea immediately. He hadn't really played in years, for one thing, and it had never been a particular special part of their relationship. It was just something she had wanted him to be able to do, and he had dutifully studied the instrument for as long as could reasonably be expected of a young man.

Lewis re-covered the upright piano then left the practice room and continued along the wide hallway, then he stopped when he reached the landing that connected this floor to those below and above. He looked upwards, where he could just see the railings that looked down from the third floor.

For a moment, there was a boy there, dressed in red and blue.

Lewis's pulse stuttered in his chest and he instinctively took a half-step back, but the child was no longer visible. After a moment of indecision, he ran up the stairs, reaching the next floor in only a few seconds. There was no-one to be found. He looked left and right down the corridor, and then approached the nearest door, which led to his own childhood bedroom. It was slightly ajar.

He pushed the door and it swung silently inwards, without even the slightest creak. Lewis had a flash of memory from years earlier, when he'd lubricated the hinges to ensure there was no sound when he entered and left his room. He shook his head, banishing the irrelevant thought.

The room was empty.

Not a stick of furniture, and only a carpet to cover the bare boards. It had been fully redecorated after he'd left Dunleven for good, and he had no idea what purpose it might have briefly served before it was stripped down again and left as a vacuum behind a noiseless door. There was certainly no small boy hiding in it.

Lewis took one last glance around and then went back out into the hallway, closing the door behind him.

From this vantage point, the railings looked taller somehow. There was still no sign of the boy, but an uneasy feeling of familiarity was bubbling up from Lewis's subconscious, and he found himself crouching down to look through the gaps between the elegantly shaped iron rods below the bannister.

I listened to them fight from here, he thought.

It had been close to the end of his parents' marriage, but he hadn't known that at the time. He was only a boy at the time, and preoccupied with everything but his own family life. High school brought a glimpse of the world that awaited him in later years, and girls were becoming the subject of increasing interest. He had been paying so little attention to his mother and father that he barely noticed they weren't spending any time together anymore, or that his father was more often than not absent from the dinner table.

On one particular night he'd been wakened by noise from downstairs; he thought it might have been a glass object breaking, but he'd never found any evidence of it when he took a detour to search on his way to breakfast the next morning. Lewis had been sound asleep, and so he was slow to rise in the darkness, make his way to his room door, and creep out to crouch behind the railings. His parents' voices carried easily through the large house, bouncing off cold stone and polished wood.

He was ashamed even now, years later, that he hadn't managed to put the pieces together at the time. It had been the first of several occasions when he'd eavesdropped on his mother and father's arguments, long after his bedtime. He could only make out the occasional remark, and they all tended to follow the same theme.

I've got to get out of this fucking place, his father had said on that first night. It couldn't have been more obvious, particularly in the context of how their relationship had been clearly deteriorating, but Lewis was in complete denial. It had been an interesting and vaguely exciting peek into heated adult discourse, and nothing more. He remembered feeling like he was a super spy.

It became a weekly event, and then twice weekly, and then eventually he just stopped listening. A part of him knew, deep down, that he had been straining to overhear the death knell of his parents' marriage, but he buried the realisation so deep that he had still been shocked when the inevitable finally happened, on a Friday evening only a few weeks after he'd last listened in to their late-night confrontations.

His mind shied away from that particular recollection, and instead produced an image of his most beloved pyjamas of that time of his life: they'd been soft cotton, fashioned into a likeness of the costume worn by the then-cartoon iteration of Spider-Man. Red primarily, with flashes of blue down the arms and torso, and mostly blue trousers with red cuffs. Just as the boy had been wearing.

Because that must have been all he'd seen; a memory of himself. Lewis was immediately certain of it, his mind latching onto the idea with a panicky gratitude, and it even made a perverse and melancholy sort of sense. But it had been so real, no different from the people he'd seen while he was in town earlier.

That's how these things tend to be, though, he thought. Hallucinations brought on by emotional trauma, pressure, exhaustion and so on seemed completely real at the time. He had past experience of the phenomenon, after all.

"It's just the stress of all this," he muttered to himself. "That's all it is."

Lewis stood up again, letting his hands rest on the bannister. He was struck by how silent the house was — enough to hear the breeze in the trees outside, even from here — but he supposed this had been its usual state for years now. Just his mother, and often Moira, rattling around somewhere or other, leaving most of its expanse empty. Pale House was a lonely place, and it had always been so. Too large for its occupants, and never entirely comfortable with itself.

For a moment, it seemed like lunacy to be here on his own, and Lewis briefly considered just getting ready now and then spending the day in town, waiting for the evening when he would meet Anne. But that would be an admission that something was wrong, and he wouldn't allow himself that.

"This is my house," he said aloud, and his voice was steady and calm, even if he didn't actually believe the sentiment at all.

He made his way back to the old kitchen, and he saw that the few objects on the central island had been rearranged and tidied, so he assumed that Moira must have been here in his absence. Lewis found the thought comforting more than anything, but he knew he'd have to talk to her at some point about access to the house, and who else might have keys. Perhaps he could even see if she'd be interested in helping with its upkeep on an ongoing basis.

Or perhaps he should just sell the place and be done with it.

Lewis considered the idea. Not ever being able to come back to Pale House; drawing a line under the part of his life which intersected with it. How would it feel, he wondered, to know that its doors were forever closed to him? Or to see it demolished to make way for a stack of two-bedroom apartments, more likely.

He wasn't ready to make that sort of decision yet. Whatever else it was, Pale House was a repository of childhood memories and experiences, and it had played a key role as the stage for the formative part of his life. It was also the place where his mother had lived, and where she'd maintained a single point of connection between him and his family. Until yesterday.

He wouldn't talk to Anne about the house unless she asked, he decided. She had memories here too, after all, and they would raise an uncomfortable topic. He'd focus on her own life instead, and what had happened during those absent years. Lewis found that he was actually looking forward to it now, and to thinking about something other than what had brought him back to Dunleven.

He told himself that it would be an enjoyable night, even though he knew the conversation probably wouldn't stray too far from this place and from his own past within it. Not for long, at least.

Virtually every memory she has of me took place within this house.

The thought troubled him, but he couldn't quite articulate why.

Agnew tore the top flaps off the cardboard box, even though they weren't sealed. It was time to get this stupid task done.

The woman at the care home had been gentle and kind when she gave him the box of his dead father's few remaining possessions, and she said that she was sorry for his loss. Agnew had told her it wasn't a loss to anyone, particularly him, and that she could go and fuck herself. The woman's face had changed then, but he didn't care.

He was back at the garage now after getting lunch in town. The office seemed like the right place to open this particular package, since the room had once been his father's too.

Agnew leaned over a little to peer into the box, and his nose wrinkled in disgust. Even the box smelled of the damned care home. Like disinfectant, and piss, and old people waiting to die. The thought of it made him angry. The thought of most things made him angry. He had to restrain the urge to dump the contents on the floor, smash them to pieces with the heels of his boots, then rip the box to shreds.

Plenty of time for that, he thought.

Most of it was just paper. There were documents like the old man's birth certificate and bank book, his pension card, and that kind of thing. There was half a pack of cigarettes, their smell faded now, so he knew they'd been left sitting for months or even years. At the end, his father could just about breathe well enough to get to the toilet and back. No wonder he never finished smoking them.

There was an address book made of black leather, and Agnew flipped through it with a vague grin on his face. Most of these people were dead. Even the doctor listed in it was dead, which was very funny when you thought about it. Then he found his own phone number, listed only under *Raymond,* and he wondered if he was the only entry in the book that was still alive and kicking. He closed it and threw it into the bin beside his desk.

There was a bundle of letters, still in their envelopes and held together with an elastic band that was starting to break down. He recognised his mother's handwriting, faded almost to nothing, and immediately he was furious again.

He knew that these must have been from the old man's time in the army, when he was stationed overseas. Agnew didn't fully understand why he resented these tokens of connection and affection between his parents, but he instantly wanted to burn every single one to spite his father. He picked up the bundle and began to squeeze, feeling a rush of satisfaction as the paper began to crinkle, but then he loosened his grip again. Maybe he'd even read them later. Maybe that would have annoyed his father even more.

Setting them down, he fished around in the box for anything else of interest, not finding very much. He had almost given up, deciding to just dump the box in the industrial bins outside, when his hand closed upon something small and cold. He saw an image in his mind even before he drew his hand back out of the box, already knowing exactly what he was holding.

His mother's locket. After she died, his father had worn it every day, never taking it off. There had been a time about ten years ago, right before the old man started to get ill, when someone in the pub noticed it and made a joke about men who liked wearing women's jewellery. Agnew's father had broken the guy's jaw, and fractured his own hand in the process. Agnew had grudgingly respected him for it.

He opened the locket, fumbling to work the catch, and found just what he expected. The photo of his parents was in surprisingly good condition, but it had been hidden away from the light for all these years. They were younger, and happier. Agnew found that he was furious about that, too.

Impulsively, he drew back his arm and prepared to throw the thing as hard as possible against the bare brick wall, then he froze.

You useless little bastard, his father's voice said.

Agnew spun around, pulse stuttering in his chest as his eyes sought the office door, but it was still closed. There was no-one there. He felt a sharp pain in his hand and realised he'd clamped his fist shut around the locket. The anger rose up again, and once more he decided to smash the thing to pieces.

You mind me, son, his father said. It had always been his preferred threat. It had always been a harbinger of violence.

Agnew instinctively flinched, a reaction learned in his earliest years and reinforced ever since. His gaze darted around wildly. There was still no-one else in the room with him.

"What are you playing at?" he muttered to himself, then he almost yelped when his father's voice boomed again in his mind.

You will respect your elders, you little shite.

Agnew dropped the locket on the floor and backed away from it, half expecting the tarnished silver chain to slither across the floorboards towards him like a snake, but it just lay there inert. Several seconds passed, his heart thumping in his chest, and then he huffed a jittery laugh to himself.

"Old dead prick," he said to the empty room, as if daring his father to respond. When no reply was forthcoming, he defiantly walked over and picked up the locket once more, then promptly dropped it again as the voice tore through his mind.

Never did amount to a damned thing. Waste of skin.

"Fuck you!" Agnew shouted at the walls, immediately hunching his shoulders without being aware of it, in anticipation of a blow to the head. It never came, but he did feel something take hold in his mind. Like a hand reaching over the top of his skull from behind, caressing gently at first but then squeezing. The pain was brutal, and this time he did yelp.

I'm going to keep an eye on you, lad, the voice said. *You're going to make something of yourself after all.*

Agnew staggered across to the desk, rubbing his skull as if he'd been physically struck, and for a brief moment he thought he might throw up. He knew — absolutely, without doubt, and with every inch of himself — that the voice was real. It was exactly the way his father had always talked to him, and to everyone else. The fact that the man was dead didn't really seem to matter right now.

"The fuck do you want with me?" he demanded, but it was sullen instead of angry, like a kicked dog showing its teeth but averting its eyes anyway.

There'll be time for that, his father said. *You just keep listening. And hang onto that.*

Agnew knew that he meant the locket, and a moment later he found himself picking it up and putting it around his neck just as his father had done, slipping it beneath his clothes.

Better, his father said. *I'll be back in touch soon enough. And you mind me.*

Another squeezing, crushing, biting pain through the upper part of his skull, and Agnew's knees gave way, dropping him to the floor. This time, he thought he could smell the stink of the old man's aftershave in the air.

The pain passed quickly, and if he was really honest with himself, Agnew didn't even mind.

The truth was, he found it comforting.

Chapter 9

Lewis stood across the street from *The Admiral's Hat*, looking at the place with mixed feelings of both nostalgia and discomfort.

There was something unsettling about a place from so much earlier in his life remaining virtually unchanged. It was like looking through a window into the past. A part of him wondered if he would step through the door to find himself a young man again, and that wasn't a journey he was keen to make.

He looked up and down the street, but there wasn't very much to see. Dunleven was too small to have a midweek nightlife, and most of the local population would be at home already, relaxing after a day's work and doing whatever people did in their own homes. His jacket was open in deference to the mild evening, and he straightened the shirt he'd changed into after dinner. For whatever reason, he'd felt a need to smarten his appearance ever so slightly, and he suspected there was an element of guilt to it.

Lewis told himself that he was looking forward to catching up with Anne, and he found that the sentiment rang true, so he crossed the street in ten paces, pulled open the door, and stepped into a pub he hadn't set foot in for more than two decades.

It was quiet, which he should have expected, but it still made him pause for a moment. The barman didn't even look around at the sound of the door opening and closing, and the handful of other patrons similarly didn't pay him any heed. There was a faint aroma of cigarette smoke even though indoor smoking had been illegal for years, and the smell brought another memory: his mother had started smoking again after her marriage broke down, and Lewis had always hated the stink of it. She had smoked when he was a child — though not when pregnant, she'd taken care to assure him — and there had been a time when he was five years old or so and he'd been curious about what the ashtray would smell like. He'd leaned down close to it on the coffee table and inhaled, and then he'd promptly vomited on the carpet. His eyes had streamed with burning tears for what felt like hours, and his mother had been unusually upset with him.

His nose twitched at the memory. At the time, he'd decided that ashtrays must be what Hell smelled like, and it still seemed like a fair conclusion today.

Movement caught his eye, and there she was. Anne was already there, even though it was still a few minutes before 8PM, and she'd taken a booth towards the back of the place. She was waving at him. It looked like she had a soft drink in front of her, and as he walked over, Lewis could see that she had changed too, and he could also see that she was a little nervous. He smiled and approached the table.

"I can't believe how little it's changed," he said as he reached her, and she nodded, gesturing at the decor all around.

The walls and all of the booths were wood panelled and varnished to within an inch of their lives. Lewis thought that bullets would probably bounce right off the thick and glossy sheen. All the fittings, from the lights to the foot rest on the floor along the base of the bar, were of brass that was cloudy with age and abuse, but still warm and inviting. There were also some new touches here and there, as was inevitable. The cocktail and food menus bore a QR code that would doubtless lead to a digital version of themselves, there were prominent signs on several walls giving the wi-fi information (network "admirals", password "hat123456789"), and the choice of dishes had gained their own linguistic garnish like *pan-seared*, and *aioli*, and *jus*.

As far as Lewis was concerned, fish and chips was still fish and chips, no matter how you dressed it up. Some things stay the same.

He sat down, and gave Anne a proper smile. She looked both more and less relaxed than earlier. A yellow blouse, dark jeans, and just a touch of makeup made her look younger and not at all like the teacher he'd bumped into earlier in the day. She was more like he remembered her, and maybe that was the point. Lewis found himself speaking before he knew he was going to.

"It's really good to see you," he said. "Again, I mean. I didn't realise how much I needed someone to talk to here."

She nodded, reaching across to touch his hand for a moment before withdrawing again. "How are you feeling? What did you get up to in town today?"

Lewis shrugged in response to the first question, and Anne seemed to understand. "I had to see my mother's solicitor to start sorting things out."

A look of realisation crossed her face. "The house. So, I assume it's…"

Lewis nodded. "It's mine now. The whole ridiculous thing. Plus the other family holdings."

"Wow," she replied, lapsing into silence for a few seconds as she processed the news. "I can't decide whether you'd prefer congratulations or more commiserations, but I think that this probably calls for a drink."

Lewis laughed, and it was a genuine laugh, much needed. It had always been like this, he remembered. Even when there had been gaps in their friendship, it was immediately easy and comfortable the next time they met.

Why didn't I keep in touch with her? he asked himself.

"I'm not sure either," he replied instead, "but you're right about the drink. What can I get you?"

Almost two hours had passed, somehow. They were just getting started on their third round, and Lewis was grateful that Anne had also brought back some bar snacks to at least nominally offset the alcohol.

Most of their talk so far had been a combination of catch-up and gossip, about the town, about old school friends, and other safe topics. Anne seemed to know that he needed some inconsequential chat for a while. It was comfortable. It was easy. But there was also something else underneath, just as there always had been. It had taken less than an hour for them to exchange mobile numbers, at Anne's initiation, so that they could keep in touch.

Lewis hadn't even finished his first drink when he noticed she wasn't wearing a wedding ring, or any jewellery at all. And of course she'd caught him looking, and she'd been direct about it. There had been a few serious relationships over the years, but nothing had stuck, and lately life had mostly been about work. Lewis knew what that was like, and he said so.

"I always read your articles, you know," she said as he fiddled with a napkin, and he looked up in surprise.

"Really?"

She nodded. "Not really my area, but I noticed your byline in the paper a few years ago. I read most of them. It's good to know you're writing again."

Again.

Another flash of memory. An old Olivetti typewriter, mint-green with little round black keys, in a carry case with a tartan interior. Lewis had found it in the attic at Pale House when he was twelve years old, and immediately claimed it for his own. At the time, Dunleven actually had a typewriter repair shop, which must surely be long gone now, but in those days he had readily been able to buy a box full of fresh ribbons for the machine and reams of off-white paper. He had loved the mechanical, percussive, noisy, beautiful device in the way that other boys might feel about a first car, or a first girlfriend.

He had written stories. Sometimes a single page, and sometimes dozens of pages, all obsessively kept in a box file in his bedroom. He'd drawn covers for the books he imagined himself writing in the future. He had even showed some of the stories to Anne all those years ago. It had been an intimate thing. And he had completely forgotten about it, for years. Decades.

"You've only just remembered, haven't you?" she asked quietly, and Lewis shook himself from his recollections. Her tone suggested that she wasn't surprised.

"How could I forget something like that?" he asked, not expecting an answer, but she gave him one anyway.

"I think people forget groups of things," Anne said quietly. "Memories that all go together. I think it's the only way to properly leave some of those things behind."

Lewis looked at her carefully, trying to work out whether she was talking about herself or not, and after a moment he realised that it didn't matter. He owed her an apology regardless, and there would never be a better time.

"Listen, Anne, I—" he began, but she waved a hand above her wine glass and gave him a wistful smile. The gesture had the quality of an incantation, or perhaps a banishing.

"That's not what I meant," she said. "And I know. Things happen in people's lives that they're not in control of; not really. Sometimes we have to get away. That's what you did, and nobody has any right to hold that against you. You just… got away."

"You didn't, though," he observed after a pause, and she tilted her head to one side in acknowledgement. She took another sip of her sauvignon blanc, then swirled the pale gold liquid around in the glass, lost in thought for a moment.

"Where would I go?" she asked at last. "My life and everyone I know — knew — was here. Except you, I mean. My mother and father were here. And the school, and everything else. It's not such a bad place."

A bad place.

Lewis frowned involuntarily. He agreed with her: there were far worse places to live than Dunleven. It was a little quiet, and a bit run down now, but just like almost everywhere in the world it was filled with people who were basically kind and decent, and who treated each other well. So why did he feel uneasy?

"Even under the circumstances, it's good to be back," he said. "I should have made more time to visit. For lots of reasons."

"Was time really the problem?" Anne asked, and Lewis saw that she immediately dropped her gaze. He laughed ruefully.

"Touché," he said, and she put her glass back down on the table and reached across to grasp his hand for the second time that evening.

"I'm not trying to score points," she said gently. "I just think you need to be honest with yourself. It's going to be hard enough for a while. The truth always helps, even if you only admit it to yourself."

He knew that she was right, and he could see that she genuinely wasn't talking about the long span of years since he had left and they'd fallen out of contact. And he knew her, no matter how long it had been. She wasn't one to hold a grudge. He sighed, and then nodded before picking up the mostly full pint glass in front of him.

"I'll drink to that," he said.

She didn't reply, but she did take another sip of her drink. Then she asked the question that he'd been asking himself on and off all day since he left the solicitor's office.

"What do you think you'll do about Pale House?"

As always when he heard the name of his family home, the initials were capitalised, and somehow the voice was that of his mother instead of Anne. He saw its outline against the sky, surrounded by trees but set apart from them in a clearing, as if the pine forest was standing guard at a respectful distance all around.

Guarding or imprisoning?

"Maybe now's the time to fulfil my dream of opening a bed and breakfast here," he said, and Anne laughed loud enough to draw a jealous glance from a couple of the customers standing over at the bar.

"Really though, I just don't know yet," Lewis continued. "It's a huge part of my family's history. They built it. It's a landmark around here. But I don't have any family of my own, much less the six siblings and twenty kids that I'd need to actually fill the place. It's a museum up on a hill, outside a town that's in the middle of nowhere."

Anne nodded thoughtfully. "What do you think your mother would have wanted?"

Lewis remembered the letter that Laird the solicitor had given him. Maybe it said something about what she wanted him to do with the house. He would certainly sell the mine and the processing plant, or gift them to the town somehow. Laird could help him with that. But the house was a different matter.

"Honestly I'm not sure. She couldn't expect me to live up there alone, walking through empty rooms and talking to myself like Miss bloody Havisham."

"I find that so easy to imagine," Anne said. "We can get you a wedding dress and a shoe."

He grinned. "I could become the ghost of the mansion. Bring in the tourists for miles around." Then his grin faded. "She left me a letter, you know, with the will. I have no idea what it's about. I'm supposed to read it in private."

"You haven't read it yet?"

"I hadn't really thought about it again until now. I've been putting it off. I'll read it tonight I suppose. Perhaps she'll tell me what she wants to happen."

"You still get to choose what you do," Anne said. "It's not disrespectful or whatever else you might think. It's your life, and your house now. She'd want you to be happy most of all."

Lewis believed that. Fundamentally, his mother had wanted him to be happy, as mothers do. She'd stood in the way of that goal at times, and he didn't think she'd ever quite managed to attain it for herself, but he didn't doubt that her intentions were basically good.

"I know," he replied. "It's just too soon to think about it. I think… I think I'll just see what the letter says, and get through the funeral, and then we'll see."

"When is it? The funeral."

"Oh, it's Thursday morning at ten. Over at Maxwell, of course." It was where his mother's parents and their own parents in turn were buried. Her plot had been reserved for a lifetime. It seemed morbid to Lewis, but it had always given her comfort. "Then to the Boat Shed for lunch. I think Moira is spreading the word."

"That's just what Margaret would have wanted," Anne said. "Familiar places, but not having to clean up her own house afterwards."

Lewis laughed out loud, and he could see that she was pleased with his reaction.

He was lost in thought for a minute or so, and Anne didn't interrupt. At last, he stood up and gestured in the direction of the door that led to the toilets. "Be right back," he said, and she nodded.

Lewis walked away, unaware of the pub door opening to admit a man with a pair of dark eyes that locked onto him immediately.

Recognise him, lad?

Agnew flinched when his father's voice boomed in his head again, but he had the answer to the question already. He had seen the man earlier in town, coming out of the cafe. He'd been talking to a woman. Actually, the same woman sitting over there in a booth. Agnew didn't know either of them.

That's right. Maybe you're not a complete waster after all.

"The fuck does it matter who he is?" Agnew muttered to himself, conscious of the fact that talking out loud to nobody would tend to draw people's attention.

He's the new owner of that big house up on the hill. That's why he's here. Come all the way from the capital. And what have you ever done for yourself?

Agnew didn't see what it had to do with anything. So the man bought a house. Everyone knew about the huge thing at the top of that road, with the trees all around. It belonged to a family that owned a lot of things around here in the past. Not so many of them around anymore.

"So what?" he said, moving past the bar and hovering near the cigarette machine that was switched off and visibly empty.

He thinks you're pathetic. And he's right. Waste of damned skin that you are.

And there it was, the old familiar red mist of anger, filling him up from his boots to his chin in seconds, warming him right up. It was like stepping inside from a cold night, into a place where the heating was already on. It was downright comfortable.

"We'll see about that," Agnew said, already moving towards the door the man had gone through, which he could see led to the toilets.

I'll make something of you yet, his father's voice said, and then there was another bolt of pain in his head for good measure.

Agnew stumbled but didn't fall, and he didn't even notice the stern look of concern from the barman. He was focused entirely on letting the anger out. It was the only thing he really lived for. He went through the door, to be confronted by two further doors at opposite ends of a short hallway. He picked the one with the word LADS instead of LASSIES, and pushed it open.

Lewis finished washing his hands at the sink, and then splashed a little bit of cold water on his face. It had been another long day, and he was more than two pints down after only having a modest dinner. Maybe he'd get a glass of water before finishing his current drink, just to be careful.

He was in no hurry to leave, though. Against all expectations when he'd arrived in Dunleven, or even when he woke up this morning, he found that he was enjoying his evening. Maybe that was something to be careful about too.

He became aware of the man who had just come into the men's bathroom, but who hadn't moved away from the door. Lewis glanced over, and was surprised to see the other man looking directly at him. There was an odd blankness about his face. He was in ordinary casual clothes, nothing very new or expensive, and he looked like he could handle himself if he ran into any trouble.

Or if he caused any, Lewis thought, immediately chastising himself for the ungenerous assumption. He nodded to the man, who didn't respond at all, then turned off the cold tap and took a paper towel to dry his hands.

"Big house you've got up there," the man said, and Lewis looked at him in surprise.

"Do I know you?" he asked, half-turning towards the man, but he received only a shrug in response. There was something both playful and cruel about it, and Lewis was bemused to find himself assessing how quickly he could get to the door from where he stood.

"Dunno," the man said. "Do you?"

Lewis looked at him for a moment, and then shook his head. "Don't think so," he said brightly. "Well, have a good night."

He walked towards the other man, who was partially blocking the door, and reached for the handle. He took an instinctive step back again when the man swiped at his outstretched hand.

"What's the problem?" Lewis asked, suddenly very aware of two things: the door was the only way out, and the other man was about three inches taller and at least twenty-five pounds heavier than him, all of it probably muscle.

The sneer that bloomed on the man's face was a confirmation that this situation had been out of control since the moment he entered the bathroom.

"Big house for a big man, coming up here for a drink with the local women," the man said, and now he took a step forward. Lewis automatically took another step back, inwardly cursing himself for it but unable to think of a better strategy at the moment.

As his brain caught up with what the man had said, a possible explanation occurred to him. This guy didn't seem at all like Anne's type, but maybe he was an ex who thought that women were property instead of people. He looked the sort for it.

"This is about Anne?" Lewis said, but he immediately realised his guess was wrong. The look of confusion on the man's face was momentary, but it had been there. And Lewis suddenly felt tired; tired of feeling jumbled up, tired of feeling guilty, tired of feeling anxious. Tired of this town he'd run away from once before, but still been pulled back to.

"Look," he said, some ancient part of his brain dropping his voice by an octave automatically, "I'm not in the mood for any trouble. I don't know who you are or what your problem is, but unless you want to talk to the police tonight, just get out of the way."

It was bravery he didn't really feel, and honestly he doubted if he could back it up, but he was going to bury his mother in two days and he had a couple of pints of beer in him. And he hated bullies. And Anne was out there. It was a precarious combination, and he knew it.

Somehow, he managed to see the fist coming, and he took the smallest half-step backwards, closing his eyes automatically.

There was a sharp pain and a dull one, both in the same place just above his right eyebrow, and he staggered back against the doorframe of one of the cubicles. Then a shout, in a voice he didn't recognise.

Lewis opened his eyes to see the big barman pushing his attacker out the door. The man who had hit him had an ugly ornate ring on his middle finger, which Lewis suspected was the source of the warm trickle of blood he could feel on his brow. He also suspected it was probably the reason for the man's choice of which finger to wear the ring on.

"You alright?" the barman asked once the other man was gone, and Lewis nodded, touching his fingers to his forehead. They came away wet with his own blood. The barman looked at him disapprovingly for a moment, and then he also nodded.

"Might be time to call it a night," Lewis said, and the barman's expression said that it would be a wise decision. Then Lewis was alone again, and he turned to the mirror above the sink. It wasn't so bad, really, but he suspected it would look worse in the morning. He rinsed his face for a second time, pressing a damp paper towel to the cut until the bleeding stopped, and then shook his head.

Welcome home, he thought, before going back out into the pub's main room.

Anne looked up as he walked over, and he saw the concern on her face even as he glanced around. The barman was just returning to his post, having come from the direction of the front door, so presumably the lunatic with the ring had been thrown out.

"What happened?" Anne asked, and Lewis shrugged as he sat down.

"Did you see the guy who came out? Any idea who he is?"

Anne nodded. "You got into a fight with him? I see him around sometimes. I think he works for the bus company here, or owns it now. It was his father's. He died not long ago. There was a huge funeral, and it was in the paper. His family name is Agnew. I don't know his first name."

Lewis considered this new information. He still couldn't understand the man's animosity, and he was certain they hadn't ever met before.

"Not a fight. He hit me, for no reason I can think of. I'd barely even said a word to him. But he knows me, somehow."

He reached up to his brow again, and he saw Anne wince on his behalf. "It's nothing," he said. "No need to worry. Maybe he'd just had too much to drink."

Anne looked worried nonetheless, and the mood had changed. Lewis was also aware of occasional glances from the barman, who presumably thought that it took two to tango.

Maybe I should leave before he decides to throw me out, he thought. He was considering what to say when Anne spoke instead.

"Dair, you're bleeding a little," she said, suddenly rummaging in her handbag. She produced a tissue, and moistened it with the condensation on the outside of his pint glass before handing it to him. He pressed it to his brow gratefully.

"Listen, Anne, I think I should probably go ho—, I mean, I should go back to the house and get some sleep. Maybe find some frozen peas first."

He hoped the remark would lighten the mood, but Anne didn't smile. "You should report him to the police," she said. "He gets in trouble all the time, I've heard."

"And he's somebody kind of important in town, while I'm an outsider. No, I think I'll chalk it up to experience and let this one go."

"You're not an outsider, Dair," she said, but he was already getting up. Anne sighed, and then she got up too. They didn't speak again until they were standing outside *The Admiral's Hat*. The street was deserted, which Lewis was grateful for.

"Thanks for tonight," Lewis said. "I really needed it. And I can't blame you for arranging for me to be roughed up a bit."

She looked exasperated but also amused, and then the concern returned. "You're sure you're alright? That's going to be sore in the morning if you don't find those peas."

He knew what she was going to say next. It would be something about her having a tray of ice at home, and it not being too far, and he knew that it could mean as much or as little as he wanted it to. Lewis found that it didn't make him feel very good about himself. He reached out and squeezed her hand, and then he impulsively kissed her on the cheek.

"I'm going to go now," he said. "I'll text you tomorrow, if you like. I know you're working, and I've got some things to attend to, but maybe we could have dinner or something this week."

"I'd like that," she said. "And if you don't feel well during the night, just phone. You could have a concussion and not know it."

Lewis laughed. "Pretty sure I'm alright. And you're OK to get home?"

"It's not far," she said, waving off his question. "Are you walking back to the house?"

Lewis nodded. "Clear my head. And I should probably get started." He smiled at her. "Goodnight, Anne."

"Goodnight," she said. It had the same quality it always had, he remembered, but he didn't feel quite the same way he had when he was a young man. That was a thought for another time.

He smiled again, put his hands in his pockets, then turned and set off.

Chapter 10

Only a pair of floor lamps in the hallway were on when Lewis returned to Pale House. He wondered if Moira had been up, but then he saw that both lamps were plugged into old-style rotary timers, set to go on and off at fixed hours each day, just like the exterior lanterns.

Could do with bringing this place into the twenty-first century, he thought.

The house didn't even have wi-fi, so smart home integration was out of the question for now. Mobile signal was thankfully fine, given Pale House's elevated position, but otherwise there was little technology from later than the nineties — and a great deal from much earlier decades.

It had been a long, strange day, but at least the walk in the evening air had wakened him up a bit.

There was a toilet adjacent to the new kitchen, and Lewis guessed that it would be the best place to find some first aid essentials. A check of the mirrored cabinet over the vanity proved that he was correct, and after washing the cut above his eyebrow and rubbing on some antiseptic gel, he felt suddenly tired again. He went back along the service corridor and out into the main hallway, still wearing his jacket.

Whenever he'd visited while his mother was alive, he'd put his outerwear in the cloakroom as she insisted. Now, though, he was aware that he was keeping everything close at hand, treating the place like a hotel or the home of a stranger. His bag still wasn't unpacked, sitting on the bed in the room where he'd spent last night, and he had no plans to settle in at all.

So that I can leave at any time.

It was how it had been for years. The need to be able to go at any moment, without delay, and the corresponding tension he felt if anything got in the way of a potential quick escape. There had been a particular year when he'd visited at Christmas time, and of course had stayed over due to the length of the journey. Against all odds, while Christmas Eve had been dry and clear, the next morning he had awakened to over five centimetres of snowfall, with more coming down every minute. The idea of being stranded at Pale House beyond his planned two nights had filled him with something very like panic.

Lewis went up a level, and along the main hallway before impulsively turning left and entering the library. He couldn't begin to guess at the combined value of the hundreds of volumes that lined the walls of the two-storey room. His late grandfather had loved nothing more than to receive guests here, far more interested in showing his success through his access to fiction and facts, instead of opulence for its own sake. During his long life he had acquired some stunning first editions, rare books, and classics of literature, all immaculately preserved. Lewis wondered if the library's contents had even been properly assessed for insurance purposes.

There was a solitary oxblood wingback Chesterfield chair set near to the fireplace, with a reading lamp just behind it and a small drinks table to one side. The chair had been re-covered at some point, but it was the same one he'd sat in as a boy, ignoring the shadows and sounds of the large room around him as he lost himself in *Treasure Island*, or *Moby Dick*, or *Alice in Wonderland*. He also remembered that his mother had encouraged the activity, and was always willing to obtain any new books he requested.

The thought of his mother made him reach into his jacket and take out the envelope that Laird had given to him. He looked at the cursive script on the front. *Dair*, just as on birthday cards down through the years. And now this, her last ever inscription of his name.

The library was cold, and he considered lighting the fire, but decided against it. He walked over to the reading chair and switched on the light before sitting down. The old and worn leather barely creaked at all, and was shiny and smooth where his mother had obviously spent many, many hours. Lewis sighed, looking down at the envelope again. He flipped it over, carefully unsealed the flap, and drew out a single folded sheet of thick notepaper.

The scent of her perfume again, the same as in the hospital, brought tears to his eyes once more. He swiped them away quickly, lest they fall onto the paper, and with an uneven breath he unfolded his mother's final message to him.

Dair,

I should have tried harder to repair things between us, and I'm trying to put that right. You made the best decision in leaving. I never blamed you; not really.

I hope we'll have the chance to talk, but I'm lodging this letter with the solicitor just in case. I'm trying to find what I need to make you understand, but I don't think he wants that. Perhaps I still have time.

If you're reading this, though, it means I've passed on without telling you the truth that I owe to you. The house will take care of that, I think. It's yours now — and everything in it.

I love you. I always have. That was the reason, if you can find it in yourself to believe me.

Pale House will show you, and then you'll know.

When you do, please forgive me.

It wasn't signed, but it was in her own handwriting and it was certainly in her voice. Lewis read it again, with a growing sense of unease. Moira had outright rejected the idea of his mother suffering from any kind of cognitive decline, but the letter seemed to indicate the opposite. It came across as both vague and paranoid, and he could imagine only too well what the response would be from Sergeant Howarth, or from most of the people in the town.

I can never show this to Moira, he thought. She'd only blame herself for not realising the extent of his mother's distress and confusion. But she had been so certain that there was nothing wrong with his mother's mental state, and she'd been the only person to see her every day.

It felt wrong. His mother wasn't a senile old woman. But she also wasn't the woman he could imagine writing these words, frightened and desperate. Nor did she usually have any interest in riddles, but the letter only raised questions without answering them.

Pale House will show you, she wrote.

"And then I'll know."

The library was colder now, and silent, and the reading lamp only accentuated the shadows all around. And then the clouds must have moved along, allowing wan moonlight to flow in from the large windows on the eastern side, illuminating the fireplace with its ornate stone shelf above. Lewis glanced towards it.

The small dark eyes of Blue Rabbit looked back at him.

Wednesday

Chapter 11

When Lewis woke, dragged abruptly from strange dreams, it was already after nine in the morning.

The images were rapidly fading and losing their meaning, but he could still recall fragments. His mother asking him to forgive her, but blocking his path into the room on the second floor with the clock outside it. There was dread, and the sense that he'd already seen what was in there, but his mind refused to produce the memory. And then tree branches, writhing like tentacles, had sprung from below the closed door, reaching out towards him.

He sat upright in bed and pressed a palm against his face, then winced at the pain on his brow, bringing back the memory of the altercation in the pub the previous evening.

"I've got to get out of this fucking place," he muttered to himself, then he shook his head at hearing his father's sentiment from all of those years ago spoken in his own voice.

Just like your father, Dair. That had been one of his mother's biggest problems with him all along.

He was sweaty from the nightmares and the dehydration, he had a hangover headache, he'd been punched the night before, and now he was dredging up old bitterness. A wonderful start to the day.

Lewis got out of bed, not even bothering to put any more clothes on, and went straight to the bathroom. After relieving the pressure on his bladder, he stepped into the over-bath shower, turned it all the way to cold, and switched it on. Three eternal minutes later, when his body stopped shivering, his thoughts had finally begun to quieten.

A text message was waiting on his phone's screen when he got back into the bedroom, towel wrapped around his waist and yesterday's boxer shorts crushed in his hand. It was from Anne, and Lewis sat down on the bed to read it. He tapped the notification and unlocked the device, then he grinned.

How's the face?

The bathroom mirror showed that it wasn't much more than a cut with a bit of swelling around it, and the freezing shower had probably helped a lot too. He didn't think it would bruise, which would be helpful given he had to look at least presentable for the funeral tomorrow. He quickly typed out a reply.

Slight improvement on how it usually looks.

The message was delivered, but the status didn't change to Read, and he noticed that Anne's own message had actually been sent a couple of hours earlier. He must have slept through the message alert sound.

Lewis stood up again and went over to the pile of his clothes on a chair with his backpack beside it, and he pulled out his mother's letter again. He felt a little differently this morning. Whatever it meant, it had clearly been of overriding importance to her. Even if her mind had begun to decline, he would at least have an explanation. Right now, he had nothing but questions.

So I'll ask Moira a few of those questions, he thought. *I'll even let her see the letter itself, and see what she thinks. But I'm not ready to dismiss it as nonsense just yet.*

He decided to skip breakfast, and instead quickly dressed and headed straight out. He drove down the hill to Moira's, and was unsurprised to find her out in her front garden, no doubt having been awake for hours. He asked if they could speak indoors, and she led him into her charming little home for a second time.

Without preamble, he handed the letter to her and she read it. To her credit, her facial expression didn't change at all, but after she folded it and handed it back to him, she walked across to her living room window and looked out in silence.

"So what do you think?" Lewis asked a couple of minutes later, once she'd had a chance to digest what she'd read. Moira shook her head.

"I think she was a woman who kept too much to herself, son," she said. "And she'd have been all the happier if she'd talked instead."

Lewis nodded. It was a fair point, and it applied to others besides his mother.

"As for what she meant, I swear I don't know, and I feel like a poor friend for it," Moira added, turning to face him again. Lewis smiled at her.

"You were more than a friend to her, Moira," he said. "Like a sister and a mother, I think. She was incredibly lucky to have you, and I'm grateful for it every day. It even makes me feel a tiny bit less like the world's worst son."

Moira looked scandalised for a moment, then she shook her head again. "Look at the two of us, and her up there in the next life probably laughing about it."

"Probably," he replied, then he raised the letter again. "I think there are only two ways to read it, and I know you don't believe the one that most people would assume if they saw the letter."

"There was nothing wrong with her mind," Moira said firmly. "Not in the ageing way. Obviously she was upset about something though."

"Which leaves us with the other interpretation: that there's something I have to find in the house. You already said she was looking for something, and going through old things, so I suppose she didn't manage to find it herself."

Moira scratched her heavily lined cheek for a moment, but she was clearly at a loss to think what his mother could have been searching for. "All I can think is that it's a matter from before my time with her. Or else I would have known, or had some idea."

Lewis thought it was a reasonable conclusion. "Obviously it wasn't that bloody rabbit," he said, and the old woman looked at him strangely.

"You found that then, did you? She had it out a lot recently. I'd find it all over the place. She liked having it around. I never really understood the attraction of stuffed toys, but to each his own."

He saw the image in his mind of his vacant-eyed mother holding Blue Rabbit in one hand, and a knife in the other.

To each his own, he thought, then pushed the image away. There were more pressing matters to deal with.

"I think I have to at least try and work out what she was so preoccupied with," Lewis said. "If nothing else, it'll give you and I some peace of mind. I'm not sure where to start, but if I do find anything, I'll let you know."

"That's good of you, son," Moira said. "If anything springs to mind, I'll be sure to tell you. Are you wanting me to keep coming up to clean the house? Or do you need a few days to yourself?"

Lewis felt guilty to even be asked the question. Moira was too old to be acting as caretaker in a stately home, and probably without being paid for it either.

"I really appreciate everything you've always done for my mother," he said. "I think it would be good to just have a few days to myself, while I take a look around and try to decide what to do next."

She nodded in understanding, and had clearly been expecting the answer. Lewis internally debated for a moment, and then decided the moment was right.

"She made an amendment to her will recently too, to ensure that you'll be able to live comfortably and without worrying about money. I was glad that she saved me the need to instruct the solicitor about that myself."

Moira opened her mouth to speak, and then she was overcome with emotion, turning away as she fished a linen handkerchief from a pocket on her dress and dabbed at her eyes. Lewis couldn't bear to see the old woman cry, and decided to allow her some privacy. He walked over to the living room door, half-turning his head in her direction without quite looking at her.

"I've got some things to do, so I'll be off now, Moira. You take care and I'll see you tomorrow at the service."

She just waved a slender hand at him, and Lewis left quietly and with a feeling that he'd at least carried out one aspect of his mother's wishes.

Once outside Moira's garden gate, he considered going straight back up to the house to begin his search, but something made him turn his car in the opposite direction instead.

Lewis drove aimlessly through town at first, but soon found himself drawing up alongside St. Margaret's secondary school. He checked his face in the rear view mirror, and at least in the heavy shadow of the car he looked alright. The cut on his head was definitely visible, but that was all. It would have to do.

He got out and approached the entrance, expecting to be challenged as to his business in the school, but the doors were unlocked and the reception area was empty. No-one was in sight, and he waited for several minutes to see if anyone would appear. There was no bell or other way to summon attention, and eventually he decided to just seek out somebody to help him.

Lewis had attended this school himself for a few years before going away south to a boarding school for the remainder of his secondary education, so he remembered the layout well. The staff room was in the diagonally opposite section from the main entrance, reached via a connected set of three corridors which ran through an atrium with an internal courtyard bordering the sciences classrooms.

He had just turned a corner into the second corridor when he heard running footsteps echoing on linoleum, coming from behind. It was the sound of a child's feet, perhaps someone late for class, and Lewis stepped to one side and turned to see the source of the sound. There was no-one there.

The footsteps had ceased as soon as he turned, and he frowned. He hadn't heard any doors opening, but it was possible that the child had gone through an open door and into another area. Lewis shrugged, and resumed course towards his destination, only to be stopped by the same sound, this time coming from up ahead.

Again, there was no-one to be seen, despite the corridor offering a clear view for at least thirty metres ahead. Lewis quickened his pace this time, listening as he went, and the sound was definitely getting closer. There was a junction at the end of this corridor which linked it to the final stretch before the staff room. He passed his own old biology classroom, glancing through the glass pane set into the door, but the room was unlit.

Lewis reached the junction in the corridor and looked left and then right, half expecting a child to collide with him and knock him backwards, but both connected corridors were as empty as the one he'd just left. The sound had stopped the moment he looked around the corner.

"Is this someone's idea of a joke?" he said aloud, and he cried out in shock when a hand fell upon his shoulder.

"Dair? What are you doing here?"

It was Anne, clutching an armful of papers with her purse stacked on top, and she looked worried. There was a door open behind her, and she must have just come out of the room it led to. Lewis could feel his pulse pounding, and he looked from Anne to each of the three branches of the corridor junction in turn.

"Did you see someone just now?" he asked. "A student, running along here? I heard someone."

Anne's lips pressed together in a thin line, and he saw her gaze flick up towards his forehead. "It's an in-service day for staff," she said. "This week is a holiday for the kids. None of them are back at school until Monday. Even the staff get tomorrow and Friday off."

He looked at her for a moment, then his forehead creased in confusion, which brought a brief jab of pain as the movement pulled at the edges of his wound.

Could have sworn I heard someone, he thought. *Not a good sign.*

"Dair, maybe we should get you checked out at the hospital," Anne said, but he waved her off.

"I'm fine, honestly. I just could swear that I... but I suppose not."

She looked at him for several seconds, clearly not satisfied with his answer, but he could tell that she was pleased to see him. She adjusted her grip on the pile of papers. "So what *are* you doing here? You're not really supposed to just be wandering around, you know."

"The door was open and there was no-one on the front desk. I wanted to see you."

She smiled, in a way that showed she was clearly trying not to, without much success.

"Oh?"

"You seem a bit cavalier about the glaring security problem at your place of employment," Lewis replied, relieved that he'd managed to distract her from her concern about his health. "I could be a strange man from far away, living in a weird old house, who came here to kidnap someone. And that's actually the truth, too."

"Kidnap? Where am I supposed to be going in the middle of a work day?" she asked, again adjusting the load in her arms. It was beginning to look heavy.

Lewis reached out and took the papers, handing back her purse. "It's an *in-service* day. There aren't even any kids here. And maybe kidnap is the wrong word after all. I just wanted to sort out a time to talk to you about the letter my mother left for me."

Anne's eyebrows shot up. "You read it then?"

Lewis nodded. "It wasn't anything to do with her wishes for her estate. It's strange. I went and saw Moira this morning but she doesn't understand it either."

"Moira is the housekeeper, isn't she? Why would she have known anything about it?"

"Not just the housekeeper," Lewis said. "She was my mother's friend, probably her best friend. She lives at the foot of the hill, but spent most of her time in recent years in the house with my mother."

Anne nodded thoughtfully, waiting for him to continue. Lewis lowered his voice, and leaned closer.

"I don't want to talk about it here. Do you take a lunch break today too, or can I meet you somewhere after work?"

Anne looked back down the corridor that would have taken Lewis to the staff room if he hadn't bumped into her here instead. She thought for a moment, then came to a decision.

"There's almost no-one here anyway. I'll lock these essays up then we can go somewhere and talk. But I have to come back to work later."

"You really don't need to do that, Anne," Lewis said, but she just glanced at him and then went back through the nearby open door, gesturing at him to follow. She made short work of securing the papers, locked the room behind them, and draped the coat she'd retrieved over her arm.

"So where to?"

The park was quiet. Dog walkers took their individual preferred routes, either lost in thought or talking to their canine companions, and a few children were in the fenced-off playground area, but there were fewer than ten people there besides Lewis and Anne. She led him to a bench that sat on a slight rise, overlooking an expanse of frosty grass that should probably have been cut one last time before the weather turned colder.

"I learned to ride my bike here," Anne said, and Lewis glanced at her for a moment, surprised to have a new piece of trivia about her life from the time before their paths had separated.

"I learned at the house," he replied. "Surprise surprise. I can't even remember the last time I rode a bike."

They had walked to the park. It was only five minutes from the school, and the children sometimes had PE here during the summer. Lewis remembered one time when his English class had even put on a play among the trees that lined the whole eastern side.

"You don't have to tell me what the letter said if you don't want to," Anne said. "It's between you and your mother. But I'd like to know how you're feeling about it."

"I'm feeling confused," Lewis replied, retrieving the letter from his jacket's inside pocket. He handed it to her, and she took it without hesitation, but then she looked up at him with a question in her eyes.

"Read it," he said. "I want to hear what you think."

She held his gaze for a moment and then she nodded and unfolded the paper. It took her less than half a minute to read the brief note, and then she looked at him again. She seemed troubled, and Lewis couldn't blame her.

"What does she mean by *that was the reason*?" Anne asked. "And what did she want you to forgive her for?"

Lewis raised one hand, palm upwards, in a gesture that effortlessly said *your guess is as good as mine*, but Anne just frowned and then read the letter again, more slowly this time, before finally handing it back to him.

"So obviously you're going to search the house," she said. It wasn't a question, and Lewis just stared at a dog in the distance, running to fetch a frisbee. It was a big animal, somewhere between red and gold, like a scruffy version of a Labrador. A woman walking her own smaller dog was openly admiring it.

"Obviously I am," he said. "I just wish she'd been more direct. But we didn't really have that kind of relationship. I think it was my fault."

Anne put her hand on his arm. "There's no point feeling that way," she said. "Your mother loved you. She said so in her letter. And she gave you her house and everything else. Try to remember that."

She turned her upper body to face towards him, tugging his arm until he looked at her. "We'll find out what she meant, but it won't change those things. Are you sure it's a good idea to get into this before the funeral tomorrow? Maybe it could wait until afterwards."

Lewis hadn't considered that, and it made good sense, but after a moment's thought he knew it was a moot point. He couldn't change the fact that he'd read the letter, and he couldn't just ignore his curiosity and his guilt-fuelled need to give his mother whatever closure it was she'd been seeking. He would feel even worse if he delayed it.

"I know what you mean, and you're right, but I've got to know. I owe it to her, I think. I definitely owe it to myself to find a way not to feel like this."

"Like what?" Anne asked gently, but her tone suggested she already knew the answer.

"Like… I don't know. Like I let her down," he said, admitting the truth of it to himself. "Like she was up there in that house, trying to find something or do something or whatever it was, and it was connected to *me* in some way, but I wasn't even there. I wasn't there for her, not then and not before."

He was surprised at how quickly the emotion rose up, and he turned his head away from Anne, grateful for the breeze that made him blink. He felt her grip tighten on his forearm, and he was suddenly aware of just how much worse this trip would have been if he hadn't happened to cross paths with her the day before.

"You're not responsible for any of this," she said at last. "I know you weren't as close as you might have wanted to be, and you feel guilty now along with everything else. That's normal. You're going to have to learn to forgive yourself somehow, because you're still here and you have your own life to live. If your mother was sitting here on this bench too, I bet she'd be telling you the same thing."

Lewis knew that it was good advice, and that it was also both kind and true. It would be a while before he could accept it, but he thought he would get there eventually. For now, though, everything was too raw, and the answers he needed seemed to be of paramount importance.

"I bet you're a good teacher," he said, and Anne gave a surprised laugh.

"I'm an excellent teacher," she replied, "but why do you say that?"

Lewis shrugged. "You just really sound like you know what you're talking about, and I find that I really want to believe what you're telling me. Pretty good qualities for someone in your line of work. You might have missed your calling though; you should go into local politics."

Anne rolled her eyes. "Teaching the town's children *is* local politics," she said. "And flattery will get you nowhere today. How are you going to start, then, since I know you'll go straight back to the house after this? Did your mother have a study at Pale House?"

"Sort of," he said. "And I'll go through whatever files she had there, but I don't expect to find much. Moira said that my mother had been searching the house herself, looking for something from the past. I suppose I need to try and work out where she was searching, and from that maybe I can narrow down the possibilities on what she was after. That's my first step."

Anne thought for a moment, and then nodded. "I suppose that makes sense. Just try and be kind to yourself, Dair. There's a lot of history in that house for you, and this is a really difficult time. It's almost the opposite of what you should be doing before tomorrow."

He nodded, and they lapsed into silence for a few minutes. All but one of the dog walkers had disappeared now, with only the elderly lady and her small dog still visible. There was also a woman pushing an expensive-looking stroller that seemed like it might convert into a light aircraft at the push of a button. It had rugged wheels, and Lewis thought it was probably designed to allow for the recent trend of running while propelling your baby ahead of you.

"Do you remember when our school did a fireworks show just before the summer holidays?" Anne asked. Lewis glanced around at her, but she was looking off towards the tree line, arms now wrapped around her midsection.

"Of course," he said. "They almost burned down the rugby scoreboard."

It had been when he was barely seventeen and Anne was sixteen, and only a month or so before he had abruptly left to go south to Edinburgh and attend a boarding school there. He sensed that this conversation was straying towards difficult ground, and he suspected that she had brought the subject up partly to distract him.

But also because I owe her an explanation, he thought. *One that I don't want to give her.*

"That's right," she said, smiling now. "I'd forgotten about the fire. They put it out quickly. What was the PE teacher's name again?"

"Tanner," Lewis replied. "But we all called him Tiger. I can't even remember why. I think it might have been passed down by the older kids."

"And the librarian was Mrs. Crawford." Anne's opinion of the woman was clear from the way her nose wrinkled up, and he also heard her mutter the word *bitch* under her breath.

"Do the kids have a nickname for you?" he asked, and she looked at him in surprise. He studied her face with exaggerated care, but he honestly couldn't tell whether the answer was yes or no. Anne just shrugged innocently.

"If they do, I haven't heard it," she said.

St. Margaret's was both a primary and high school for the area, so its pupils ranged in age from four to eighteen. Anne said she only taught those aged six to nine, but Lewis could imagine that the older boys probably had a few leering nicknames for her nevertheless. If she truly hadn't heard any, then he was glad about it.

More silence, but it wasn't very long before Anne spoke again. "You left soon after that."

Lewis nodded. "I got the train down to the academy at the start of August. Two years of dorm rooms and itchy woollen blazers. Took a bit of getting used to."

Anne looked at him, waiting to see if he'd address the implicit question, and after a few moments he sighed. "Would you believe that I didn't really think of it as leaving, and more as going?"

"What's the difference?" she asked, and he could hear that the question was genuine.

"Perspective, I suppose. I was thinking about me instead of other people. And I was still only a kid, really; it's not like I made the decision myself. But I did go along with it. Willingly."

"You were never really happy around that time. For a while before, either. I sort of held it against your mother, you know. I thought she'd sent you away."

Lewis laughed, but it was a sad sound. "She did. But it wasn't like that."

"Then what *was* it like?" Anne asked. There was a note of frustration in her voice, and he couldn't blame her for it. He knew very well that they had been more than friends, at least from her point of view. He even knew it at the time. The night of the fireworks show was probably the closest they had come to crossing that line, and he'd be lying if he said he hadn't thought about that evening many times over the years.

They had first met at school as young children. Anne's parents lived in a modest house only a ten-minute walk from the foot of Middleshade Road, and once he was old enough, Lewis used to ride his bike along her street in the summer on his way to another friend's house. He would stop and talk to her if she was in her front garden, which she increasingly often was, and it wasn't long before he had invited her to come and see his own home. The young girl had been stunned by Pale House, thinking of it as a castle or a palace, and they had often played in the grounds together whenever her parents would allow her to.

As school wore on, the one-year gap in their ages and thus their class group had began to matter more and more. They had also become aware of the difference in their social circles, even if neither was old enough to really understand the concept properly. Anne had never allowed it to deter her, though, and if Lewis was honest, she had probably harboured feelings for him for years before he even began to suspect it.

The night of the fireworks show was the final night of term, and so it was charged in the way that impending partings often are. The fact that the two teenagers still lived near to each other and could meet outside of school whenever they wanted to didn't seem to matter, and there was a pervasive sense of time slipping away.

Lewis smiled at the recollection. Nothing in adult life ever really compared to how things felt in youth, when the world was so simultaneously complex and simple, full of promise and potential, where almost every experience and emotion was new and vital. It was a time that could never be captured again, and he had learned to be grateful for that, but he was also able to recognise the loss of something unique to a particular phase of life.

The evening had played out like any of a thousand bad movies. Several of the older pupils had secretly brought along alcohol, which was consumed in the usual places like the stands at the sports field, in the beaten-up first cars of elder siblings, and anywhere that patrolling teachers could be evaded for a few precious minutes. Bravado and wilful amusement were all around, as were borrowed aftershave and inexpertly-applied makeup. Kisses were had, and conquests were lied about. Boys leered and girls cried. All of it predictable, inevitable, and with its own strange beauty of the years-long rite of passage towards adulthood and the evaporation of those mysteries.

Lewis and Anne had remained mostly on the periphery of it all, even genuinely watching the fireworks together for a while before wandering away, and when she said she was cold he'd had the good sense to take off his jacket and drape it around her shoulders.

They walked for a while, and they both talked in the way that seemed required of them, where he would try hard to seem interesting and she would try harder to seem interested. They'd come to a place at the western-most part of the school grounds, where a locked side gate blocked the way to a path that led down to the river. There was a bench there just like the one they sat on now, and they had also taken the same positions then. Lewis could remember how clear the night was, and he could certainly remember the warmth of her hand when she had silently reached out to interlace her fingers with his.

He'd looked around at her, and this time he had the good sense to say nothing, and then she smiled shyly and leaned in to kiss him.

The shout of a staff member made them flinch away from each other guiltily even though their lips had never met. The too-knowing eyes of the mathematics teacher had followed them as they did as they were told and returned to the main field for the finale of the show.

The fragile moment had been lost, and there wasn't another moment that night. In the tragically unlikely way that things only happen in real life, they in fact hadn't spoken again once the evening was over. A month later, Lewis was gone.

"Why did you never come back? Properly I mean." Anne asked in a quiet voice, and this time she did look at him.

That's the question, isn't it? he thought. In his mind he saw the Accident and Emergency entrance of the hospital again, and a lone ambulance outside it. There were some things he wasn't ready to share.

"I'm sorry," he said. "I really am. I thought about you; of course I did. But I needed to get away, and when my mother told me I was transferring to another school down south, I didn't argue."

This time it was Lewis who reached out and took her hand, and it felt both the same and different this time. A spark, but without fear. He waited until she was looking at him again before he continued.

"I don't regret it, you know. I never will. But I do regret disappearing on you. I hope you can believe that."

To his surprise, she gave a simple nod straight away. "I do," she said. "But you didn't really answer me. Have you noticed that you sound a bit like your mother in her letter? Asking for belief while evading giving a reason."

Lewis couldn't argue with that, and he considered saying *touché* for the second time in as many days. But he could also see that she wasn't really angry.

Just hurt, which is a lot harder to deal with.

He tried to think of the right thing to say, but Anne gently withdrew her hand from his and checked her slender wristwatch.

"I really need to get back to school. If you're going back to the house, maybe you should stop by this Moira's place again on the way, and see if she can tell you which rooms your mother was looking in."

Lewis shifted position on the bench, trying not to feel chastised but recognising that he deserved to anyway.

"That's a good idea. I'm planning to. Sure you don't want to open creaking doors and rummage through dusty boxes with me?"

It was a half-hearted attempt at humour, but it seemed to be the right thing to say. Anne gave him a small smile.

"I'll pass, but text me if you find anything. Oh, and about tomorrow…"

"What about it?"

"I just wanted to say that if you prefer to have some privacy then I completely understand, but if you want to go the funeral together then I can meet you there before the service. It's up to you. Just let me know later."

She stood up, and Lewis took that as his cue to do the same. Anne looked at the cut on his brow again and frowned, then gave him another smile. Lewis thought it looked a little strained.

"I'll see you tomorrow then," she said, and Lewis nodded, then she turned and walked away at a brisk pace.

He watched her for a full minute, before realising that he'd left his car back at the school and should have accompanied her.

I have a feeling that an old score was just settled, he thought, then he sighed and put his hands in his jacket pockets, and started to walk. By the time he reached his car in its parking spot outside St. Margaret's, Anne had already gone inside.

Chapter 12

Agnew lay on his bed, fully clothed, staring up at the ceiling.

He hadn't gone into work today, but that didn't matter when you were the boss. The company ran itself, and it had to run itself because he had no particular interest in it in the first place. As far as he was concerned, it was a bank that had buses instead of tellers, and the only person making withdrawals was him.

Last night had been interesting. He reached for the locket around his neck, just as he'd done a hundred times since he put it on yesterday, and listened for his father's voice. He heard nothing, but that didn't matter either; the old man would be back in touch soon enough.

Agnew had gone to another pub after being thrown out of the place where he'd punched the new owner of that big house up on the hill. He'd stayed there until closing time, drinking alone, and he'd felt like it was a celebration. One that had been a long time coming.

Finally, he was somebody important.

It wasn't every day that you heard your dead father's voice in your head, giving you a job to do. It sure as hell wasn't every day that the job in question was what he'd always wanted to do anyway: let some of the burning anger out, and make other people understand that they needed to respect him.

What he didn't understand was why it was so important to take that particular guy down a peg or two. Sure, he was probably rich — or at least he definitely was now. Agnew had seen pictures of the big house, and it was more like a castle. He also knew that the people who lived there had damned near employed everyone in the town at one point. They had the old mine, and the plant, and their name was on everything. He could almost remember it.

Starts with an L, he thought. But that also didn't matter.

The locket was cold, even though it had been lying against his body for hours. He had opened it a few times, including during the night, to look at the little photograph again. His mother and his father together, looking as happy as a couple of idiots, cheeks pressed together. They probably had the photo taken just for the locket.

Agnew didn't understand that kind of relationship between people. When you got right down to it, he didn't really understand any kind of relationship between people, unless you counted one person putting another person in their place, with words or fists. You had to care about somebody a lot to hit them in the face, or beat them down onto the ground, without killing them. If you didn't care, why would you even bother to stop?

Another thing he didn't understand was people's obsession with memories. The locket was an example, and so was the tombstone at his father's funeral. They were just things, a little piece of metal and a big piece of granite, that were supposed to remind you of people and what they'd done. Agnew didn't think that people deserved to be remembered once they were gone. They'd had their time, and then they died, and that was all. Being remembered, and being respected, was for the people who were still here. The people who could still hurt you, to show that they really cared.

He frowned. His father could still hurt him, even though he was dead. He was an exception to the rule. It made sense, because his father had always been the one to decide what the rules were, and which ones applied to him. Agnew wasn't even very surprised that the old man had decided that death wasn't the end of him. He definitely wasn't surprised that his father still had things for him to do.

It was a relief, if he was being honest about it. A re-lief to still have the guidance of his father's loving hand, and to know that his own destiny had finally begun to manifest itself.

An image flashed up inside his mind, vivid enough to startle him and make him sit upright in bed.

It was a vast hallway, with a grand staircase stretching upwards and splitting, then splitting again and again, climbing further into the darkness. The space was far too large to be within any building he'd ever seen, with doors spread irregularly along the walls at every level, balconies and landings in strange places, and the sense that the area behind the twisting staircase receded infinitely far back into something that couldn't be seen. Not a real place. Not a place that could ever exist.

But Agnew had been there. He was certain of it.

He could see more snatches of it in his mind now, as fragments glimpsed for a moment and then forgotten. There was a glass-walled place choked with plants, moonlight barely getting through from the night sky beyond. There was a ballroom, its wooden floor moving and rearranging itself like a sliding puzzle. A room with pianos and other instruments, scattered in strange positions, with sheets of music covering every surface like snowfall.

And there were people. Moving too quickly, more like shadows than anything else, whispering through rooms and along corridors, always in different clothes, and of different ages. Most of their faces were blurred, but sometimes Agnew could almost remember what they looked like.

He rolled out of bed, suddenly nauseous, but then he closed his hand around the locket and his stomach settled. In his mind, he saw a bleak landscape, all in muted colours, viewed from the air. Dark earth and grim pine forest, as far as the eye could see. Hundreds of miles of it, with no sign of human beings or their works, and then suddenly a clearing that could have been ten miles across. In the centre, there was the house. The house at the top of the hill, but somehow also the place in his mind, too long and too wide and too tall and too deep to ever be the same building, yet it was. He knew it. He remembered it.

It was *his* house. He had never been there, and at this moment he was sitting on the edge of his bed in the modest home he'd grown up in, but he somehow knew that the place in his mind was also rightfully his. It was his domain. His inheritance.

His hunting ground.

Agnew saw it so clearly, its windows ablaze from something inside, and then he saw the hallway again with the staircase snaking and soaring upwards towards the artificial sky of distant chandeliers far above. At the top, where the stairs met an upper floor that stood like a cliff face above the void, a man was standing, tall and slender, silhouetted in black. His features weren't entirely clear, but there was something very familiar about him. Agnew struggled to recall. It was on the tip of his tongue, but just out of reach. What he did know, though, was that this man was important, and to be listened to — just like his father.

Someone from earlier in his life, maybe. It felt that way. Why couldn't he remember? Why had he never remembered before? But he wasn't worried. It would all come to him soon, he was sure of that.

He lay back down on the bed, no longer feeling like he was going to puke. In fact, he felt even better. Everything was turning around for him.

Maybe the past mattered after all.

Moira had managed to suggest a few rooms that Lewis could begin his search in, but had warned him that she had always been either absent or elsewhere in the house when his mother had been looking for whatever she had been seeking. Lewis had the strong impression that Moira felt his mother had purposely kept her in the dark, and he knew that her intuition was correct.

He arrived back at Pale House around lunchtime, and considered postponing his search to get something to eat, but he wasn't really hungry. He read the letter again, dismayed once more at the tone of desperation, but he felt no closer to understanding what his mother wanted him to know than he was yesterday.

Lewis went to the library first, even though he knew he was delaying the inevitable. Blue Rabbit still sat on the stone shelf above the fireplace. He could readily hear its high-pitched voice in his mind. He could have made it say anything at all, but all he heard was his mother's dying request, over and over. He turned and walked away, scanning the spines of hundreds of books without seeing any that were out of place.

Go to the damned room, he told himself, and a moment later he set off.

The second floor of the eastern wing was bright, and if he squinted, Lewis could almost see it in its heyday. The grandfather clock was the same as it had always been, heavily varnished and marking time metronomically. The sound was hypnotic and comforting, and Lewis rediscovered the same quirk of perception he'd often had when he heard its steady *tick-tock* as a child — that it wasn't just a device for measuring time, but somehow the origin of it. He had imagined that if it were to fall silent, then the whole world around him would be frozen in place, trapped within an instant for all eternity, while he was free to roam wherever he chose.

When he was a child, the fantasy had seemed to be filled with potential and liberation. Now, it unsettled him. He could think of few fates worse than being confined to Pale House forever.

He reached for the door handle and tried it, but it was locked just as Moira said it would be. There was a fire extinguisher on every landing of the main staircase, and Lewis was just beginning to wonder whether he could break the door open with one of them when he realised he was being foolish.

As expected, one of the keys on his mother's personal keyring fit the lock, and the door swung open easily. The light coming in from the tall window at the far side of the room was dazzling for a moment, and he shielded his eyes with his hand.

The room was empty. Not just empty, in fact, but bare. The walls above the wood panelling and dado rails were stripped back to the plaster, with small patches of residual paper in high corners and awkward crevices. The floor was uncarpeted, the floorboards scuffed and dull, but clearly recently swept clean. There was no furniture of any kind, and neither curtains nor blinds in the window.

"Maybe she really was redecorating," he muttered to himself, but that still didn't explain what his mother had been doing in this room. She certainly wouldn't have been up a ladder scraping wallpaper off, or lifting carpet herself. Moira would have known about any work going on in the house because she would have heard it, and seen the tradesmen coming and going.

Could it have been like this since before Moira ever came to the house?

But again, the same problem. He could think of no reason to spend time in a completely empty room, particularly one that had been an unremarkable guest bedroom and then an occasional utility area.

Lewis walked over to the window and looked out, his eyes more adjusted to the light now. The gardens below were still well-tended, and the view beyond was of uninterrupted mown grass stretching to the tree line in the middle distance.

This would make a great office or writing room, he thought, and then he again contemplated the possibility that the room was a red herring in his search. Perhaps she really had just wanted to repurpose the room as a more picturesque place to attend to administrative tasks than the Old Kitchen. It was certainly warmer up here too.

There was a single built-in cupboard, of the shallow style called an Edinburgh Press, which still had its original door. The wood was faded but in good condition, and Lewis twisted the doorknob and pulled it open. There were three shelves inside, and just like the room itself, the top two were entirely bare. The lowest shelf, however, held a large, black leather-bound schedule book exactly like the one on his mother's makeshift desk.

His pulse quickened as he reached down and picked it up. It wasn't dusty, and nor were the shelves, so it must have been placed here or at least used relatively recently. He opened the cover and flipped through a few pages, but they were all blank except for their pre-printed divisions and calendar information.

Lewis frowned, turning more pages, several at a time, until his fingers found a slight gap in the stack of sheets towards the last third of the book. He turned to the relevant page, and he was surprised to find a small pressed flower there. It was a vivid and striking blue that was almost purple, with velvet petals and a butter-yellow centre crowned with five white radials. There was nothing written on the pages which held it either, and the date had no significance to him, but he knew that his mother never did anything without good reason. It was the eighth of September, a little over two years after Lewis had left Dunleven. He would have been in Edinburgh at the time, just about to begin his first year of university, in the middle of a very difficult time in his relationship with his mother. They had gone months at a time without any contact, though things had eased after another year or two.

He took out his phone and snapped a picture of the flower, and then another photo of the diary page it had been placed on. Satisfied, he returned the flower to its page, closed the diary, and tucked it under his arm before closing the cupboard again. With a last look around the empty room, he walked back out into the bright gallery and pulled the door closed behind him. He considered locking it, but there didn't seem to be any reason to, so instead he took his phone from his pocket again and quickly searched its built-in software repository for a certain very specific type of app.

Amazing what they can do these days, he thought.

Even as a technology journalist, Lewis had never lost his appreciation of what was possible now, and the new things that came within reach with each passing year. He found a suitable app, tapped a button to download it, and within a few seconds it appeared on his phone's home screen. It bore the icon of a rose, and when he launched it, a prompt immediately asked for permission to access his camera and photo library.

He loaded the photo of the flower into the app, and it immediately displayed a single word: *Myosotis*. It was apparently the genus of the flower, and it was accompanied by another photo which confirmed that it was indeed the same plant. The app's purpose was to use machine learning and a vast database of species to identify any flower presented to it. Lewis wasn't familiar with *myosotis*, though he vaguely thought he'd seen examples of it often enough when out in the countryside. He made a mental note to ask Moira about it later.

Or Anne, I suppose.

He would see her in the morning, at least, and he could maybe find a suitable moment to apologise again. This ongoing strange and unpleasant week was forcing him to re-evaluate his own past, and Lewis thought that maybe it was time to start revisiting some old decisions. Certainly his life hadn't led to very much so far, and the news in the early hours of the morning two days ago had been a wake up call in every sense.

The screen of his phone dimmed and then went off. He considered texting Anne to tell her about discovering the pressed flower in the empty diary, locked away in a stripped-bare room, and he was sure she'd appreciate hearing about his progress even though nothing was any clearer. After a moment's thought, though, he just slid the device into his pocket. He'd give her some time instead, and meanwhile he had plenty more places to search.

Lewis went back downstairs via the eastern wing's own staircase, which doubled back on itself twice. There were large paintings hung above both landings, one of Dunleven as it had looked in the nineteenth century, and another which he'd never liked very much. He stopped to examine it, having to crane his neck a little.

It was a fiery painting, all reds and oranges and yellows contrasted against black. It showed three horses in abstract form, galloping through a rudimentary land-scape. All of the edges were angular and sharp instead of flowing, and there was an overwhelming sense of threat and desperate motion. Lewis could never decide whether the horses were fleeing a wildfire, or whether they were demonic steeds, separated from their horned masters but still seeking to bring chaos and suffering to the world on their own. The most unsettling aspect of the painting to his young mind was that the two horses nearest to the foreground were drawn in contrasting colours; pitch black for the frontmost, and bright flame-orange for its neighbour, such that it almost looked like a single horse had been cleaved in two lengthwise but somehow continued to run.

For probably the five-hundredth time in his life, he squinted at the artist's scrawled signature at the lower right, but as on every previous occasion, he couldn't make the name out.

Maybe they have an app for that too, now, he thought, but a part of him felt that he would be better off not knowing. He shook his head, vowing to get rid of the awful thing as soon as possible, then he continued down the stairs.

Lunchtime had come and almost gone, and his stomach grumbled in protest, so Lewis began to make his way towards the new kitchen. There was a short corridor that connected the dining room with the kitchen, and it was the most direct way through towards that part of the house. He broke into a jog, another habit of childhood which had irritated his mother no end, and when he was only a few metres away from the dining room entrance, he came to an abrupt halt.

The family room's double doors lay open, and sitting on the wooden coffee table beside an L-shaped sofa was a model of a vintage 1922 Bentley 3-litre Sport.

"My god," Lewis said to himself. "Haven't seen that in bloody years."

It had been his grandfather's model, bought as a nostalgic gift because the man had owned the real thing earlier in his life. The model was a duplicate in every respect of the particular vehicle it commemorated; brown bodywork with silver panels surrounding the engine, and an elaborate heart-shaped boat-tail back, brass headlights to match the exposed horn and the wheels, and a small Scottish flag on the offside engine casing. His grandfather had been delighted with it, and as a young boy Lewis had longed to play with the little vehicle. Only thirty centimetres long but intricately built and with real rubber tyres, he had been allowed to touch it only when supervised. It was a miracle that it had survived all these years, particularly in such immaculate condition. Lewis thought it had been lost or given away decades ago.

His instinctive smile faded as he recalled exactly when he'd last seen the model car. It was the night of the separation. When everything had changed.

It had been a Friday evening. Lewis, not yet changed into his favourite pyjamas, had wandered into this room and found his father sitting in an armchair in silence. The man had been holding the model Bentley, slowly turning it around in his hands, seemingly inspecting every tiny detail of its construction. Lewis had paused in the doorway to watch.

His father had never shown a particular interest in the model, and knowing that it was of great value to his father-in-law, had generally left it alone. Some part of Lewis's young mind had registered the innocuous behaviour as not just unusual but also ominous, but he had pushed the feeling away. After a minute or so, his father had noticed his presence, and then put the model back down. Ross Lewis's expression had been unfamiliar to his son, and too complex to read.

It was only a moment or two later that his mother had arrived, and Lewis could sense the tension that suddenly filled the room. A silent question seemed to pass from his mother to his father, and the latter shook his head. Then Lewis's mother walked over to him and put her hands on his shoulders, then told him to sit down.

Even after the passing of three decades, Lewis felt foolish for not seeing it coming. He'd listened to their fights after he'd gone to bed on so many nights. He'd seen the evidence of their deteriorating relationship. He'd noticed his father's increasing absence from family activities, and even at mealtimes. And then, on that evening, he had been aware of the charged atmosphere, and the odd, subdued and contemplative way his father had been. But for all of that, it had still come as a surprise.

It's time for a family discussion, his mother had said, and at the time Lewis had actually felt excited. He couldn't remember any previous family discussion that had actually been announced as such, so it had to be important. He sat up straighter in his chair, glancing at his father and mother in turn, paying close attention even as part of his mind began to list some possibilities. The list didn't include his mother's next words.

Being told that your parents are getting a divorce, especially when unprepared for it or in denial about it, is an experience that any child will always remember. It remained as clear in Lewis's mind as if it had happened yesterday, and thirty years of life had only recoloured his emotions about the event from shock and betrayal to an overriding sense of pity. He had grown to feel a profound sympathy for his mother and father in that moment, and how it must have been for them to have to break the news to their child. An unenviable task, scheduled for the end of the working week, to be awaited with dread and probably any number of bitter emotions. He had often wondered how they had imagined it would go. He suspected that perhaps the evening had played out exactly as they'd foreseen.

His mother had needed to tell him a second time, because he hadn't believed her. Lewis had even asked if she was joking, and he was sure that her face had paled further at that question. His father had said nothing at all, merely watching at first, and then lowering his gaze. And then, when the reality of the situation had become apparent, Lewis ran from the room.

That part of the evening was blurry in his mind. He could remember the thump of his own feet against wood, and carpet, and marble; all the surfaces of Pale House as he ran along corridors, and up stairs, and through doorways. He had no destination in mind, but his feet knew where to go, and it was twenty minutes later when his mother found him in the enormous attic. She had been compassionate but firm, and led him back to the family room.

The irony of the choice of venue for breaking the news had never occurred to him until now, decades later, and again he was compelled to wonder if deep down he was still that same deluded child, wilfully blind to what would be so obvious to others.

His father had been standing by the unlit fireplace when Lewis and his mother returned to the room, and had turned to face them immediately. Lewis asked the only question that occupied his mind at that point.

When is dad leaving?

Even then, he had held onto a dwindling hope that it wouldn't happen. Even if they didn't want to be married anymore, Pale House was vast. They could both live here and never have to see each other if they didn't want to, but he could still see them both. It was a child's fantasy, unable to survive the cold light of practicality. Ten minutes later, standing halfway up the main staircase, he had watched his father go, the man's belongings apparently already taken away hours earlier while Lewis was at school.

His mother had given him tea, and it had been far sweeter than usual, and then she had taken him to his bedroom and told him that she loved him, and he should get some sleep. Oblivion had claimed him within minutes, and it had been fully ten years later when he realised there must have been more in the tea than sugar.

Standing here in the same room now, alone in the house that had become his own, it was as if he could still see the faint outlines of those younger versions of his parents and himself. He found that he could play back the scene as an observer, with a detachment that was impossible when the canvas was purely memory. Again he felt a burst of pity for his father, and much more so for his mother. She had the aftermath to deal with, and she was the one who had to remain here, within a community that very much knew her name and her face, and for whom this sad development would surely have been the talk of the town for weeks afterwards.

Lewis picked up the model car and idly spun one of its tyres. It moved smoothly, and the bodywork was free of dust, nor had the paint faded.

Did she put this out on display recently? he wondered. *Or did she just make sure it was well looked after?*

He set it back down, and with a last look around the room, he returned to the hallway. His appetite had waned again, but he was going to eat regardless. He knew of more than one friend who had lost a parent, taken time off to make the arrangements and so on, and returned looking gaunt. It was too easy to neglect your own needs when other things were going on.

That wasn't going to happen to him. Both Moira and Anne would scold him for it too. So he would eat.

He had barely taken two steps in the direction of the dining room when the distant but unmistakable sound of a piano being played echoed down the corridor.

Chapter 13

Lewis ran, and in those first moments it was like the night of the separation all over again, except with broad daylight filtering in through high windows and from the gaps below doors.

His feet thumped against polished floorboards as he retraced his earlier steps to reach the lobby which housed the eastern stairwell. The music was coming from upstairs, of course, because that's where the pianos were. He went up the broad steps two at a time, avoiding even a glance at the painting of the hellish horses.

There were two possibilities. One, Moira had come in while he was occupied, and apparently she could do reasonable justice to the *Moonlight Sonata*. It would make sense; his mother had loved the piece, but she had never learned to play any instrument at all. Lewis hoped that it was Moira he'd find.

The other option was that someone was trespassing here, albeit someone with a moderate degree of classical piano training. He was furious already, in anticipation of the possibility, and even though a part of him knew that his anger was just the result of being startled, he quickened his pace.

He reached the second floor, went through the open doorway to the eastern gallery with its view of the gardens, and pounded along the thick carpet. He could see the grandfather clock further ahead, but he wouldn't be going that far. Sure enough, the door to the practice room was open, and the music now filled the whole gallery.

Lewis slowed his pace just enough to avoid crashing into the doorframe, and sprang into the room. The last note he'd heard from outside hung heavy in the air, bouncing off every hard surface. The grand piano was covered, with its lid closed and the stool tucked sensibly underneath, partly concealed by the cover's edge.

There was no-one else in the room.

Lewis knew that there had been no time for anyone to leave the room, and the only exit was the way he came in. He was still standing just in front of the open door, and he spun away from it in case the intruder was hiding behind it, but again there was no-one there. There were a few pieces of furniture in the room, but the only two objects large enough to conceal someone were the two pianos: the grand that stood ahead of him and to his right, and the upright that was pushed against the left wall.

He circled right, moving entirely around the enormous instrument, but he found nothing. Lewis even peered underneath, despite knowing he'd have been able to see at least the feet of anyone who was crouching there. He crossed to the curtains, pulling them quickly away from the bay window in turn, and then he arrived at the upright piano. The far side of it likewise concealed no unwelcome guest.

What the hell?

He looked all around the room, checking again that there were no other hiding spots, then he paused to listen carefully. The grandfather clock along the gallery marked time dutifully. There were no footsteps, running or otherwise. He couldn't hear anyone breathing. He couldn't hear anything else at all.

"Is someone here?" he asked, half expecting a response from just over his shoulder. No reply came. After a moment, he turned his attention to the grand piano again.

Could it be rigged? he wondered. *They have player pianos. I suppose it's possible you could convert one of these to do it too.*

Lewis approached the instrument and pulled the cover off, then lifted the lid. He peered through the opening into the case interior, moving around to check every angle. His understanding of how it worked was rudimentary, but he saw everything he expected to. The felt-clad hammers that struck the strings, and the bridge that coupled them to the soundboard. There was nothing unusual there, and certainly no indication of a mechanism to operate it autonomously. Besides, there was no power source. The piano stood alone in the middle of the floor, with no cabling or power sockets.

He supposed that a battery was possible, or even an old spring-wound system, but again there was no evidence of anything like that. If the piano had been modified for use as a party trick or a prank, whoever was responsible had done an excellent job. But Lewis didn't believe it.

An unpleasant feeling began to creep over him, and it took a few moments to recognise it as the early onset of an anxiety episode. His mind served up image after image from the last several days.

You thought Sergeant Howarth said "forgive her", but he didn't.

You thought someone was running along the school corridors, but they weren't.

You thought you heard the piano being played, but it wasn't.

They all came in the same voice, and it was the reason for the rising tide of panic that seemed to be lapping up around his throat. The voice of a man who chased him from his life in Pale House.

No longer caring about the piano, Lewis lurched out of the practice room, slamming the door behind him as he went, and he didn't stop until he had pushed open the door of the nearest bathroom and clamped his shaking hands onto the sides of the sink.

Anne had said that people forget groups of things, all together, because it's the only way to ensure some of them are locked away. Lewis decided that she was absolutely right about that. He felt sick to his stomach, and he twisted the cold tap until a stream of crystal clear water was running down the curve of white porcelain only to vanish into the brass drain.

He hadn't thought about it. He really hadn't. It had been staring him in the face since the day and hour he arrived back here, and every other time he'd sporadically visited in the past, but somehow he'd managed to avoid looking directly towards the memory.

Donald Spence, his once and would-be stepfather. The only man his mother had ever become seriously involved with, as far as Lewis knew, after the divorce. Spence had even lived here in Pale House for almost five years, moving in when Lewis was a little over fifteen years old.

Lived and died here, he thought.

The room that even his mother had stopped going into decades ago. Up on the fourth floor, barely used even in the house's prime, reserved for the least-favoured guests or perhaps once upon a time for servants. It had been a small bedroom at the time, but it had also been the last place that Donald Spence had looked upon during his life.

Lewis pulled the hem of his shirt from the top of his trousers, lifting it up until it was bunched around his ribcage, and then he turned until he could see a part of his back in the bathroom mirror. It had become an automatic behaviour to never look, or at least to never notice. The occasional twinge of pain was readily ignored.

But he could see and feel that the old scars were very much still there, physical and otherwise.

And so of *course* it was Donald's voice in his mind, telling him to doubt his perceptions, and the evidence of his senses, and even his sanity.

You're imagining things, son. That's what Donald would have said. Lewis could still hear the spite and the dark amusement. *You useless little bastard.*

The man's face had blurred a little in his memory, but not in a way that gave any relief. It only served to distort his features, stretching and exaggerating them, until his eyes were all pupils, and his mouth was only an angry slash. And he was tall, too tall, much taller than a boy, and his arms could reach so very far.

Why did you never come back? Anne had asked.

"Because I was hunted here," he said quietly, making the confession to his own pale reflection.

Lewis wanted to get in his car and drive south and home, without looking back. But he also wanted to do his duty and lay his mother to rest, and to learn whatever it was she had so desperately wanted him to know. And he wanted to talk to Anne.

He wanted to leave, but he knew that he couldn't. He wanted to continue to forget, but here within the walls of Pale House, he seemed destined only to remember. There was nothing else he could do.

Without knowing he was going to, he abruptly ducked his head towards the sink, and for the second time in three days, he vomited.

Lewis had been sitting on a step outside the main entrance of the house, nursing a cup of tea, when he heard the sound of footsteps coming up the main gravel path.

Moira had apparently spared him the trouble of going to find her, and the old woman's kind and almost maternal smile both warmed and pained him. She walked with a stick, but only to aid her on the shifting little stones. Her pace was as brisk as his own, and Lewis found himself wondering if Moira might live to see her hundredth birthday.

She was already rummaging in her fantastically oversized shopping bag as she drew near, and Lewis had to laugh when she triumphantly produced a transparent zip-lock bag containing fruit scones. He had no doubt they were freshly baked that morning, too.

"You didn't have to do that," he said, getting up from his position a little awkwardly. "But I'm glad you did. Can I get you some tea?"

Moira waved the bag of scones whilst shaking her head, in a doubly-emphatic refusal. "I was just going to drop these off for you," she said. "I'm meeting a friend in town shortly."

"Then I'll drive you there," Lewis said, seeing it as a chance both to talk to her about the pressed flower and also to get away from the house for a little while. Moira immediately but politely rejected his offer, but he could see that she was leaning a little more heavily on her walking stick now that she was standing still.

"Moira, I insist," he said. "It's the least I can do. And I want to pick up a magazine anyway."

The lie was transparent to both of them, but the old woman seemed to recognise that the gesture wasn't entirely selfless, so she smiled graciously and thanked him. Less than two minutes later, they were both in his car and headed back down the access road.

After they turned onto the main road back into town at the foot of the hill, Lewis asked if there was anything special about the date in the diary where the pressed flower was stored. She looked at him without surprise, but also without any particular recognition, and shook her head.

"Is it to do with your mother?" Moira asked, and Lewis nodded.

"Then I'm afraid you're asking the wrong person, son," she said. "That was a good bit before my time at the house."

Of course, he thought. *Stupid of me.*

It only took another couple of minutes to reach the place where Moira wanted to be dropped off. There was a small car park two streets away from the oldest and most picturesque part of the town centre, much of which was still cobbled, with historic marker plaques at places of interest. A grid of four streets was zoned for pedestrians only, and had many speciality shops and small businesses.

"Before you go, do you recognise this at all?" Lewis asked, taking the diary from his jacket pocket and opening it to show the pressed flower.

"There's a pot of those in the conservatory," she said. "Other colours too. Pink and purple, and other blues. I think your mother liked them, but I've never seen them in the main house."

Lewis made a mental note to check the conservatory, just in case.

"It's called *myosotis*, apparently," he said, and Moira looked at him for a moment before giving a small shrug.

"My own mother always called them forget-me-nots," she said. "But I'm sure you're right."

Lewis had heard of the flowers after all, just not their technical name. He supposed the same would probably be true for a great many species of plants. The name was suggestive, but for now it was just another question to answer.

Moira took the diary from him, and tapped the page thoughtfully. "Now that I think about it, I can tell you something else about this date after all, but you'll already know it."

"Oh?"

"This was during your mother's illness. I'm certain of it."

He searched his memory, but nothing obvious came to mind. Lewis recalled that she'd injured her shoulder once while gardening, and had to spend a day in bed resting and then a week or so in a sling. It was when he was young, and his parents were still married. He had a vivid memory of his father taking a tray of breakfast up to her. But that was many years before the date in the diary. He felt suddenly embarrassed that he had no idea what illness she meant.

Not the world's best son, by a long shot.

His rational mind told him that Moira would be very unlikely to judge him harshly, but he still felt ashamed. In that moment, he decided to be circumspect about the fact that the date in question fell during a time when he'd been entirely out of contact with his mother for a couple of years.

"How did you know about that? I'm just curious," he said at last, with what he hoped was a disarming smile on his face. Moira just nodded, clearly expecting the question.

"Well there were a few people in town who knew," she said. "It was almost a year, wasn't it? She did make appearances here and there, but she didn't seem like herself. This is all second-hand, of course. I don't recall ever bumping into Margaret myself during that time. But I had a friend, God rest her, who had a niece working at the hospital then. I suppose it would be different in a bigger town or a city, but in Dunleven all the nursing is arranged from there."

She was hospitalised for an illness? Lewis tried to think of a credible question to ask.

"I'd heard that," he said. "Did you ever talk about it with any of the nurses?"

"Oh no," Moira said. "I didn't really know Margaret except by reputation; it was no business of mine. I remember hearing it was just one nurse who was involved, though. In a place this size, they only have one or two doing day-visits."

"Of course," Lewis replied, then he forced a grin onto his face. "Not like the big city."

Moira smiled and nodded again, and then she spotted the person she had arranged to meet, just coming along past the car park. It was another older woman, and Lewis didn't recognise her.

"Well I'd best be going, son," Moira said. "Come and see me whenever you need anything, and I'll see you in the morning at the service. Eat those scones before they go stale. You're too thin."

Lewis laughed to hide the pang of complex emotion he felt at her motherly scolding. "I will. Thanks, Moira. You take care and I'll see you soon."

When he'd watched the two women walk away towards the pedestrian zone and disappear from view, Lewis looked at the empty diary page again, and the pressed flower. He wasn't sure what to think now. His mother had apparently had an illness for a year which at least for some of that time made her housebound, and in need of visits from nursing staff — and he had known nothing about it. She had never mentioned anything of that kind in all the years since, and he had already lost any opportunity to ask her about it.

Was it an injury? Surgery? Cancer? Another nervous breakdown?

Whatever it was, she had obviously made a full recovery, because he'd never had even the slightest inclination that there was anything wrong with her health once contact had resumed between them. He had visited her and stayed at the house for a day or two here and there, and this strange incident Moira had revealed to him had been fully twenty years ago.

He wasn't surprised that she'd opted for home nursing, though. Above almost anything else, his mother had always felt a powerful need to maintain a certain image amongst the people of Dunleven. It had probably stemmed from a sense of responsibility, or even pride, regarding her own mother and father and the position they occupied in the town. Every family had its problems and its periods of turbulence, but for the Lamberts, all of those things had remained locked within the many chambers of Pale House. It seemed that his mother had continued that tradition, even regarding her own son.

There have always been secrets in that house, son, Moira had said. How right she had been. Lewis wondered how much else had happened that he had no idea about. His momentary frustration quickly gave way to the familiar feeling of guilt instead.

He started the car's engine, then drummed his fingers on the steering wheel. It would be a long shot to search for anything in the house that would shed any light on his mother's mysterious illness after all this time, and he knew she would have got rid of any such artefacts or records long ago. He didn't even know if it was relevant to what she had said in her letter either.

Still, if I'm going to play detective then I might as well do it properly.

When people were ill, especially for a long time, they tended to use services that kept records of their own. Pharmacies, doctors, and hospitals.

And nurses.

Moira said that all day-visit nursing in Dunleven was organised centrally, from the only hospital. And the nurse called Kerry had immediately recognised him, and had asked if there was anything else she could do.

"Maybe there is, Kerry," Lewis said aloud as he put the car in gear and began to pull out of his parking space. "Maybe there is."

Chapter 14

By early afternoon, Agnew found himself at work even though he'd had no intention of going in. He had been walking through the town, doing nothing in particular except marvelling at how he could look at the face of almost any passerby and feel that they were hollow shells, without a shred of value or humanity inside.

He felt that way about almost everyone and everything. There had been an adventurous fox foraging in the bins of a back street and he'd managed to get all the way up to it before it noticed his presence. He kicked it as hard as he could, hard enough to break its ribs probably, but he hadn't even bothered to look and see what condition it was in. It didn't matter. The important part was done. He had made his presence known.

Agnew liked how people made room for him. He liked how women took a single look at his face and then avoided any more eye contact, moving to the side to get as far away as possible. He liked how men did the same thing, especially if it was after they took a moment to size him up. He liked the fear on the faces of old people, and children, and all the people in between.

And what he really liked was that his father was back.

Agnew had been about five minutes away from the bus depot when he'd felt a sensation like rotten, overgrown fingernails digging into the surface of his brain. He had yelped, and pitched sideways into a teenager, knocking the kid into a wall. The outrage on the young man's face had died quickly when he took a look at Agnew, and then he scurried off. Agnew shook his head hard to clear it, then loped onwards again, turning left blindly at an intersection.

Still paying attention, lad?

Agnew grasped the locket around his neck, and the pain subsided immediately. He took a breath of cold air that had never tasted so good, and then he spoke quietly to himself.

"Of course I fucking am," he said.

That's good. You'll want to get to the company then.

It was what his father had always called his business, like he'd employed accountants or lawyers instead of drivers and mechanics, and the women who handled the schedules and the phones. Agnew wasn't going to argue, and he realised he wasn't far from the depot at all. He continued at a fast walk, expecting more pain any moment, but his father seemed content to let him make his way without any more encouragement.

Agnew reached the lane that ran behind the workshop, and cut through it. It wasn't used by anyone except the periodic parts deliveries, and mostly served as a shortcut for people looking to get to the community centre down the road on the other side. Someone had parked there once, and when they came back they found that all four of their tyres had been slashed. Agnew grinned at the memory.

He was about to go around to the side gate when he felt something holding him back, and he stopped. There was no-one else in sight. He clasped his fist around the locket again. His father spoke as if summoned.

Somebody coming by soon, his voice said. *Right up there.*

Agnew was already looking in the direction of where the lane joined the main street. Sometimes customers would come out of the office at the front where they'd bought a ticket, and go the wrong way when trying to reach the bus stances. They'd end up in this lane, look confused, then turn around and go back the other way.

He'll be in a red jacket, his father said, and barely a second later, a man in a red waterproof jacket appeared. He wore glasses, was a little overweight and red-faced, and he looked like he might be in his early fifties. He was clearly looking for his bus, and even had one of the distinctive orange paper ticket receipts in his hand.

"So fucking what?" Agnew said to the empty air, and then he felt just the leading edge of that same piercing pain in his head before it receded.

You were never a serious lad, his father said. *You were a waste of skin. Nobody at all. Are you a serious lad now? Because you're no use to me otherwise.*

The anger, rising like the steam from hot metal dropped in water. The hate, and the fury, and the wild joy that they'd always given him.

"Serious as the stroke that fucking killed you," he said to no-one at all, drawing the attention of the man in the red jacket. The response seemed to please his father, and Agnew suddenly knew exactly what the old man was going to say. He was already looking forward to it.

Put him down then, his father said. *Put him right down hard.*

Agnew laughed out loud, releasing his grip on the locket, and the man in the red jacket had only a moment to see the danger he was in before Agnew lunged at him, closing the distance in a heartbeat.

Agnew hit him, breaking his spectacles with the first punch and knocking the man to the ground, and then Agnew fell upon him. The anger was everywhere now, the good kind of anger that shut out all the noise that was outside and also the noise that was inside. The anger that cleaned him out.

Agnew, who was known by everyone in town as Rage, hit the man again, and again, and again.

The hospital was so quiet at first that Lewis wondered if it was an in-service day there too.

His car was one of only four in the part of the parking area reserved for patients and visitors, and the ambulance he'd seen last time was absent. He went in through the main entrance, and found a young nurse who looked like she could barely be out of high school, sitting at the reception desk. She glanced up as he approached, and he was certain that she did a quick visual assessment to see if she could tell what was wrong with him.

Nothing you can fix with pills or a scalpel, he thought.

"Can I help you?" she asked, and he smiled apologetically.

"I hope so," Lewis said. "I'm not a patient. I'm actually hoping you could help me find someone. A nurse here. Her name is Kerry, uh, … actually I don't know her last name. Brown hair, not very tall, and she was on duty two days ago."

To her credit, the young nurse gave no impression that this was anything but a mundane request. "Do you have an appointment with her?"

Lewis shook his head. "Oh, no. It's just that she was very kind the other day. My mother died on Monday, and the nurse brought me to see her. I'd just driven up from Edinburgh that morning. I was hoping I might have the chance to thank her, that's all."

The young nurse nodded and gave a compassionate smile that aged her by at least ten years. "Of course," she said. "She's in today, and Creelman is her last name. Let me just have a look."

She used the computer in front of her for a few moments, then nodded again and pointed down the corridor to Lewis's right. "She should be in radiology, down there to the far end, then left through the double doors and straight on. You can follow the orange lines on the wall too if you like. Don't go into any of the rooms, especially if you see a red light outside. If you wait in the department reception you should see her soon enough."

"I really appreciate your help, thank you," Lewis said, and then he set off to follow the directions he'd been given. He reached the radiology department in under a minute, and as it turned out he didn't have to wait for Kerry Creelman to appear at all. She was standing behind the smaller reception desk there, facing the row of low-level cabinets on the wall, completing some kind of form which was attached to yet another clipboard.

I wonder if she's ever without one of those things, he thought.

He stopped a metre or so in front of the desk, and waited patiently and in silence for her to finish her task. When she did, she caught sight of him in her peripheral vision and turned around, still holding the clipboard. Recognition dawned on her face immediately, and Lewis thought she must be a pretty good nurse.

"Oh!" Creelman exclaimed, genuinely surprised to see him again. "Mr Lewis! Are you here for an appointment?"

There was disbelief in her tone, and she seemed relieved when he shook his head and smiled.

"Actually I was looking for you," he said. "The nurse at the front desk was kind enough to direct me here. I was hoping I could arrange to have a few minutes of your time, whenever it's convenient. It's about my mother."

"Of course," she replied immediately. "Just give me a moment." Creelman checked her watch, scribbled a signature on the form she'd been filling in, and then hung the clipboard on a hook above the cabinets. At that moment, another nurse came out of one of the x-ray rooms with a young woman who had her arm in a sling, and directed the patient down the corridor. Creelman went and said something to the second nurse, who nodded and smiled, then she came back over to where Lewis was waiting.

"I have some time right now, if you'd like," she said, gesturing back towards the hospital's main entrance and reception. "What can I help you with?"

They began to walk, and Lewis considered which kind of white lie would be most conducive to getting the information he needed. He decided on a strategy he'd often found was both the simplest and most effective: tell the truth, but with gaps that the other person would fill in with their own misconceptions.

"Well, first and foremost I wanted to thank you for your kindness the other day," he said, and Creelman gave him a sympathetic smile. "But there was something else too. I visited the solicitor who's handling my mother's will yesterday. She was very grateful to many people here, and this town meant a lot to her. It was quite a while ago — twenty years — but there was a nurse who was responsible for caring for her at home during a lengthy illness. I'm trying to find out if I could get in touch with her. My mother's housekeeper mentioned that those services are all coordinated from here at the hospital."

He stopped there, not asking a direct question but leaving the implication clear. As he'd hoped, Creelman nodded enthusiastically. "That's right, yes. It would be paper records for back then, but they're all kept here. I'm sure we can help you. Bless your mother for her generous nature."

Lewis smiled again, feeling slightly bad for misleading this decent and giving woman, but his mother herself had told him to find out whatever Pale House could tell him about the past. A long illness he knew nothing about would certainly count.

The archived records office was in a wing of the hospital where the surgical suite used to be, and he could see indications of its former purpose as they walked along a corridor that was even quieter than the morgue Creelman had led him to on Monday. No other staff were on duty here, and Lewis felt on edge, as if he would be discovered any moment and escorted out of the hospital empty-handed.

Creelman unlocked the office and ushered him inside, closing the door behind them. The lights came on automatically, which surprised Lewis a little, but he supposed that the areas where operations took place would have been outfitted with such conveniences earlier than everywhere else. The records office was an oppressive institutional mint green colour, and whatever used to be here had long since been ripped out. The only furniture was a large table in the centre of the room with four chairs around it, a wheeled documents trolley off to one side, and dozens of stacked metal filing cabinets all around the walls, spilling over into two half-height metal aisles constructed from more cabinets. They were all labelled with colour-coded cards slotted into plastic-fronted slots on the faces of the drawers. Some of the cards nearest the door were laser printed, but Lewis could see that those in the opposite corner, on older and more yellowed stock, had been created on a typewriter.

He gave Creelman the date from the diary page, and she nodded.

"Let's see now," she said, going directly to a section just a couple of metres away. Its label cards were medium blue, and bore several acronyms Lewis wasn't familiar with. A poster on the wall caught his eye. It said *Data Privacy Is Your Responsibility*, with three exclamation marks. Part of him expected Creelman to pause at any moment, and tell him he'd need some kind of legal document to gain access to their information. She'd probably be right to do that. A second part of him wanted to stop her himself, and confess that his enquiry had nothing to do with any implied bequeathment.

But another, more insistent part of him said that this was his own mother's records, and that for practical reasons she couldn't possibly object. She had also all but begged him to investigate. He chose to listen to this voice over the others, and remained quiet as Creelman thumbed through some faded grey hanging files within a drawer she'd opened, then pulled out a folder. She sat it on top of the drawer's upper rails and opened it, then she tilted her head in a way that made Lewis uneasy for some reason.

"That's strange," she said, and Lewis took that as his cue to wander over to where she stood.

"Strange?" he replied, being careful to keep a short distance between them lest she think he was trying to read the file over her shoulder. Even so, he could immediately see what she meant before she picked up the folder and turned it towards him.

The file was a sheet of squared paper, old and a little faded, but not otherwise discoloured. The ink was a vivid sapphire blue, entirely handwritten, and the header of the page bore his mother's full name, date of birth, and a reference number which didn't match the modern health service format Lewis was familiar with. Below, there were rows of entries detailing dates and times, with a column for locations which was only filled-in for the topmost row, with ditto marks thereafter. The strange thing was the second-last column, which was titled *Purpose/Treatment*. Every entry was empty.

"There should always be something here, to say what the visit was for," Creelman said. "It's part of the rules. Legally required too."

Creelman was still frowning at it a moment later, when Lewis noticed the second strange thing, which explained the first.

This entire page was written at the same time.

All the same colour of ink, without any change in saturation. All in the same hand, with the same attention to detail. Someone had taken their time. There were no borrowed pens, or hurried scrawls, or inadvertent errors and corrections. The file had been copied out longhand from an original that was no longer there, and in doing so the Purpose column had been entirely redacted.

"That is strange, right enough," he said, keeping his voice casual but interested. "Does it happen to say who the nurse was? It had just been so long that I think the name slipped my mother's memory."

Lewis could readily see that there was a signature column in the table, which thankfully was filled in. Every entry was identical. Creelman nodded, tapping her finger on the topmost signature.

"Mary Petty, it says. Doesn't ring a bell, but it was a long time ago. She'd be retired now, I'm sure. I could ask around for you?"

Lewis smiled and shook his head. "You've already been so helpful," he said. "The name should be more than enough. I'm pretty sure my mother paid her solicitor a lot of money over the years."

Creelman laughed and rolled her eyes, then closed the folder and returned it to the drawer.

Getting pretty good at lying without technically bending the truth, Dair, he thought, chastising himself for his dishonesty. *Better not get caught out.*

He was back at the hospital's main reception a few minutes later, having gained another nugget of information from Creelman that he hadn't known before: his mother had also donated a large sum to the hospital years before, and there was a clinic named after her which specialised in counselling and outreach mental health programmes. It certainly explained why the nurse had gone the extra mile to help him, and by extension to help his mother.

Lewis thanked her profusely again and apologised for taking up her time, and then he went gratefully out into the grey afternoon. He walked slowly to his car, and he didn't look back as he unlocked the vehicle and got in. There was no shout, and no sound of running footsteps. No security guards or police officers appeared. He started the engine, and manoeuvred out of the car park and onto the road, initially setting off in the direction of Pale House, but on a whim he indicated and turned into a street that would return him to where he'd dropped off Moira earlier.

He wasn't ready to go back to the house yet, and he needed to think about his next step. The obvious thing would be to check the phone book, or online, for this Mary Petty and hope that she was still alive. Then, the problem would be how to arrange to ask her some questions, and what those questions would be.

The slight thrill of his success at the hospital was wearing off quickly, and he began to feel agitated as he came to a stop at a pedestrian crossing whose light was red. He drummed his fingers on the steering wheel, staring into space until he became aware that the light had changed to green again. Thankfully there was no-one behind him, so he was spared the impatient blare of a horn.

Lewis knew that the only thing to do was keep looking, and he also knew that it was his responsibility. He would take a brief break, stopping somewhere for coffee and to look online for information on the nurse who had tended to his mother so long ago, and then he'd return to Pale House and continue his search. There was nothing else for it.

He also had a growing sense that he wouldn't like what he found.

Lewis parked in the same place he'd been using for the last three days, straight in front of the main entrance to Pale House, and facing back towards the access road.

He stood beside his car, leaning against it and looking at the building's imposing facade in front of him. Once again it struck him how disproportionate the house was to his mother's actual needs, but he also understood the powerful pull of heritage and personal connection. He felt those things himself now, and found that he was reluctant to consider the idea of selling the property.

What else am I going to do with it, though?

Even though his work was entirely remote and could be done from anywhere, spending his time haunting this place alone was absolutely the last thing he ever wanted. Moira had repeatedly insisted that his mother's mind and sanity were wholly intact at the end of her life, but Lewis thought it would probably take less than a month for him to lose his own marbles if he decided to stay here.

It was another uncharitable thought, but not entirely baseless. He'd already been hearing things, more than once, since he got here. Anne would tell him to give himself a break, and to allow for the fact that he'd had the shock of losing his mother without resolving the issues that had plagued their relationship over a long period.

She'd be right about all of that, he thought.

He looked up at the house again, but it offered no clarity or insight. He craned his neck to look up at the roofline, and just like every other time in his life that he'd done so, the movement of the clouds overhead made it seem like the whole building was going to topple forwards and come down upon him. Lewis shook his head, irritated at himself, and then he flinched at the sudden shrill sound of his phone ringing in his pocket.

The caller ID said *Anne Sutherland*, and he felt a wave of relief as he tapped the green button to answer the call.

"Hello?" he said, turning away from Pale House to rest one hand on the roof of the car.

"*Hello yourself,*" Anne replied. "*How goes the detective work?*"

Lewis smiled. "I've made a bit of progress, actually. I was hoping we could talk about it sometime. I could use your advice."

"*Sounds interesting,*" she said. "*I finished up a bit early. I know it's only coming up for five o'clock, but if you're hungry I could pick something up and bring it over.*"

Lewis blinked. It was more than he'd hoped for, and he certainly wasn't going to argue. "That would be great. I just got back, so I'll go in and put the heating on and maybe ask the butler to look out the fine china."

"*You do that,*" Anne said. "*I'll be half an hour. See you then.*"

She ended the call, and Lewis pocketed his phone and immediately headed across to the house. He had already decided to tell Anne everything about what he'd found out today, including his trip to the hospital. She might not be thrilled about his deception with the kindly nurse, but he thought she'd probably agree that the end justified the means. Besides, he really did want to get her perspective on what to do next.

He unlocked the main doors feeling better than he had all day, and for once he didn't glance back at the outside world before stepping into the quiet darkness of Pale House.

Anne got there twenty-five minutes later, her arrival announced by the antiquated doorbell that rang a real bell, both in the entrance hall and in the old kitchen. Lewis had been waiting in the hall and listening out for it, and he opened the door for her within a few seconds.

She was carrying a tied plastic bag, and the smell from it reminded Lewis that he was indeed hungry. He ushered her in, letting the big doors close with a bang that made him cringe.

Don't slam the door, his mother's voice scolded him in his mind.

"It's my bloody door now," he muttered to himself, and Anne looked at him questioningly, but he just shook his head. He took her coat, placing it in the cloakroom before taking the bag of food from her and leading her towards the rear of the western part of the ground floor.

He'd briefly considered setting two places in the dining room at either end of the long table as a joke, but he didn't think it would go down particularly well. He settled for the informal table in the new kitchen that he'd used himself in recent days, and where he suspected his mother had eaten most of her meals in the company of Moira.

Lewis had been kidding about the fine china too, but as it turned out, the dinner-sized plates in the kitchen had been expensive looking ones, and he was satisfied with the look of amusement on Anne's face when she noticed them. She didn't say anything though, and Lewis busied himself with serving up a variety of piping hot Chinese takeout.

They talked of inconsequential things while they ate, including Anne's paperwork at school that day, and the scones that Moira had brought over earlier. Once they'd finished their meal, Lewis sat the dishes in the sink to handle later, and picked up a tray with some of the scones, a carafe of coffee, and two mugs. He directed Anne ahead of him and they made their way to the family room, where he'd lit a fire in the hearth earlier. It was blazing away now, and the room was warm and inviting. He'd debated on using it given its associations for him, but had decided that if he was to be the master of Pale House, however temporarily, then he ought to get comfortable with every part of it as soon as possible.

"I'd forgotten how big some of these rooms are," Anne said, lingering in the doorway as she looked around the space.

"We can play hide and seek if you like," Lewis said. "But fair warning: I know all the best places." She smiled, but it didn't quite reach her eyes. When she walked over to sit down near to him on a large sofa, he kept quiet. Sure enough, Anne cleared her throat.

"I think I was a little short with you earlier, and I wanted to apologise," she said. "I didn't have any right to—"

"Anne, of course you did, and it's fine," Lewis said before she could finish. "Honestly, I was relieved. I've been feeling guilty since we first bumped into each other. A lot longer than that, actually."

She looked at him, listening patiently as he spoke. Always so patiently. Lewis knew that he owed her more.

"You deserve a better explanation, and I'll give you one, I promise," he said. "I just... I'm working on getting to the point where I can share that stuff. It's been a big week."

He wasn't making excuses, but he was worried that she might think so. A moment later, though, he could see that his fears were unfounded. Anne just nodded, and gave him a smile that was smaller than before, but much more genuine.

"So what did you find out today?" she asked.

Lewis had put the blank diary in the family room while he was waiting for her to arrive with dinner, and now he went across to a card table in the corner and picked it up. He returned to the sofa, opened the diary to the page with the pressed flower, and handed it to her.

"A forget-me-not?" she asked, and he nodded.

"My mother's, kept in an otherwise empty diary at that particular page. It was the only thing in a cupboard in a stripped-bare room over on the other side of the house. My mother kept it locked. The key was with her house keys."

Anne listened, then asked the question he assumed she would. "Does the date mean anything to you? This was a long time ago."

"It didn't," Lewis said, "especially because she and I weren't in touch at that point, for a couple of years.

But I asked Moira about it, and she said that it was during a time when my mother was ill for a year, and housebound for at least some of it."

Anne frowned in concern. "What made her ill for that long?" she asked, and Lewis only shrugged.

"I haven't found that out yet, and I think she went to some trouble to make it difficult for anyone to get that information."

He explained his trip to the hospital, and he was honest about moderately misleading the generous Nurse Kerry Creelman to gain access to the day-visit nursing records pertaining to his mother from twenty years ago. Anne wasn't half as scandalised as he'd thought, and indeed she seemed grudgingly impressed, though Lewis chose not to remark on it.

"Your family has always been important in Dunleven," Anne said at last. "I'm not surprised she had the influence to have the records altered. It sounds like you're really on the right track. Do you think this is what she meant in her letter?"

"Maybe," Lewis said. "Part of it anyway. But I won't know until I can figure out what happened to the nurse who cared for my mother here during that time."

"Did you get her name?" Anne asked, and Lewis was confused for a moment before he realised that in his eagerness to tell her of the redacted visitation records, he'd entirely neglected to mention that each entry had a signature beside it.

"Yes, it was a woman called Mary Petty," he said. To his surprise, Anne immediately laughed, and then she shook her head at his confusion.

"Dair, I'm a schoolteacher in a pretty bloody small town in the Highlands," she said with excessive patience, and Lewis immediately knew that she was using her teacher voice on him. "I know virtually everyone who lives here, either in person or by name. Most of us in the staffroom could complete a census for Dunleven if we had to. You really didn't think of asking me about this?"

Lewis opened his mouth to speak, and then closed it again, suddenly feeling foolish. Anne seemed far too delighted at his response, and in truth he didn't grudge her this apparent triumph. He allowed her to have her moment, and then belatedly and somewhat sheepishly asked her if she knew anything about someone with a name matching the signatures on the form. She nodded.

"To me, Mary Petty is a precocious eight-year-old who's wonderful at spelling, so-so at arithmetic, and who wants to be 'a YouTuber who tells people about animals' when she grows up. Which terrifies me for some reason."

Lewis laughed out loud. Of course he'd been an idiot not to ask Anne sooner.

"You know what my next question is," he said, and she grinned smugly.

"And yes, I do believe she proudly told me that she's named after her grandmother, who lives at her house now, and who used to be a nurse at the hospital."

Chapter 15

They'd managed only one of Moira's large scones between them after the excessive meal of Chinese food, and Lewis knew that he should be feeling sleepy, but he'd actually never felt more awake.

There was an urgency to visit this old woman who had once taken care of his mother, and to find out what she could tell him about the concealed period of illness. He hoped that Mary Petty would be willing to speak to him, and that she'd share whatever she knew, because he couldn't think of any other avenues of enquiry that were open to him right now. And given everything that Anne had told him — that she was retired, was a grand-mother, and had moved in with her daughter and granddaughter — he knew that he was lucky that she was even still alive.

He had an internal debate with himself that lasted all of ten seconds, and when Anne returned from the bathroom, he stood up.

"I want you to take me to see Mary Petty," he said. "This evening. Right now. Assuming you know where she lives, which I think you do."

She stopped in the middle of the room, and when she hesitated just a moment too long before speaking, Lewis realised that she'd actually been expecting this.

"I don't suppose I can persuade you to wait until tomorrow after the funeral?" she asked, and he gave a small shrug.

"Maybe you could," he said, "but I feel like I have some momentum going, and I need to know what happened to my mother, and what it has to do with that damned letter she left me. It's important."

Anne nodded. "I know. And I know it won't be any use to point out that we'd be bothering an old lady at —" she checked her wristwatch and frowned "—almost seven o'clock in the evening."

"I don't feel good about that either," Lewis replied. "But I think she'll understand, if she really is the same woman. Besides, you know her granddaughter. You *teach* her granddaughter. That's got to buy us some leeway."

Anne folded her arms in mock indignation. "So I'm just your ticket to get through the front door, is that it? I feel so used."

Lewis pointed to the tray on the coffee table. "I shared one of my scones with you. You think that was no-strings-attached? I'm insulted you think I'm that kind of man."

Anne rolled her eyes, and he could see that she was still uneasy about the idea but putting a brave face on it. He walked over to where she stood.

"Listen, I appreciate this," he said. "I know it's a lot to ask. I don't want you to do anything you're really uncomfortable with. And definitely not out of any misplaced sense of guilt for your perfectly reasonable remarks in the park today."

"I'd be lying if I said I was looking forward to it," Anne replied, but I know how important it is to you. And I read the letter too. I think this is connected to what your mother was talking about, and that means it was important to her too. Your family was always kind to me. I feel like I owe you both."

Lewis smiled. "Well, you really don't. But I'll wait until later to remind you of that, because I really do need you to get me through the Petty family's front door."

She made a sound that might have been a laugh, and Lewis gestured towards the doorway. "After you," he said.

Lewis drove, leaving Anne's car at Pale House for now. It was only a ten-minute drive, so it would be easy enough to collect the vehicle later, and he hoped they'd have a chance to talk about whatever they might find out, or at least come up with a next move if the trip turned out to be fruitless.

Mary Petty the eight-year-old, as it turned out, lived only two streets away from Anne, and they sometimes waved to each other on the way to school in the morning. Lewis followed Anne's directions, and as he slowed when she said they were getting close, she pointed out the exact door when they were still a few houses away. Lewis found a parking space across the street, trying to quell the feeling of nervousness that had taken up residence in his chest.

As they walked over to the small garden gate that led to a path that ended at the dark blue door, Anne put a hand on his upper arm briefly.

"It'll be fine," she said. "I'll explain, and if it's not a good time, then we'll come back again at a more reasonable hour later in the week."

He nodded, going ahead to open the gate and then letting her go through first. He stayed just behind her, reasoning that it would be less threatening for Anne to be the one that the occupants saw first when — and if — they opened the door.

Probably think we're Jehovah's Witnesses or something, he thought, just as Anne rang the doorbell. When the door opened to reveal a woman in her mid-thirties, though, Lewis was relieved to see the recognition on her face.

"Miss Sutherland!" the woman said, smiling widely. "What brings you here? Is everything alright?"

Anne returned the smile and nodded. "I'm really sorry to bother you, Louise, but we think you might be able to help an old friend of mine. Actually, we think your mother can."

Louise Petty glanced at Lewis with curiosity but no concern, and he gave her an apologetic smile. Anne introduced him as the heir to the Lambert estate and the son of the late Margaret Lewis, and for one terrible moment he thought that this woman was actually going to curtsey.

She didn't, though, and he shook her hand warmly, offering an apology for turning up at her doorstep at such a strange time. Anne quickly relayed a sanitised version of what had brought them there, and asked if it might be possible to speak to her mother. To Lewis's surprise, Louise Petty agreed immediately, and invited them in.

They were directed to the rear of the house, where the living room was. The street was of terraced houses, and the rooms were narrow, but Lewis was much more comfortable here than in his family's sprawling home. There were traces of the young girl everywhere, including a pink school backpack in the hall, a scooter beside the stairs, and many drawings stuck to the fridge that Lewis glimpsed through an open door. Louise told them that Mary the younger was already in bed, and Lewis's sense of trespassing on these kind people increased even further.

When they reached the living room, he went inside first, and immediately set eyes upon the girl's namesake. Mary Petty was the elder in every sense, with a heavily lined face and eyes that peered through thick bifocals. She looked like she must be seventy-five at least, but she was sitting in an armchair reading a newspaper, and she looked up immediately when he entered. Her expression was exactly the same one her daughter had worn at the door, and Lewis had to suppress a smile of immediate fondness for her.

Louise Petty arrived a moment later, and explained the basics of the situation before asking if Anne and Lewis would like some tea. They declined, and Louise excused herself to finish tidying up in the kitchen, telling her mother she'd be right next door.

"I was sorry to hear about your mother," Mary said to Lewis once he and Anne had sat down. "She was a fine woman. Good to this town too."

"Thank you," he said. "And I think I owe you a lot more thanks too, for taking care of my mother a long time ago."

The statement was a question of sorts, and Mary seemed to understand that. "I was just doing a job that I loved," she said. "I never really knew why she wanted to hide away up there, but people have their reasons."

Lewis shifted in his seat, wondering how exactly to proceed, and he was surprised when Anne spoke instead.

"There was a letter to Lewis with her will," Anne said, "about something she wanted to tell him. I think she planned to do it herself, but sadly she didn't have the chance. She wanted very much for Lewis to know what had happened. And I know it's a lot to ask, but we knew that you were her nurse at the house, and we think you might be our last hope."

There was anguish on Mary's face now, and it pained Lewis to see it. She looked at him with such compassion, even reaching out to clasp his hand with her frail and twisted fingers for a moment, until the effort of her grip became too much.

"I'm so sorry, son," she said. "Of course I'll help if I can. What is it you want to know about?"

Lewis exchanged a look with Anne, and then leaned forward slightly. "Well, we just wondered if you could tell us why you were there. I mean, what her illness actually was."

Mary looked at him as if he was speaking a foreign language, and then she looked at Anne, and her face paled. "Good lord above," she said, and then she took a noisy breath that panicked Lewis for a moment, but she seemed to recover. Now he could see the woman she must have been during her working life, strong and patient, filled with empathy, and having to often deal with people on the worst days of their lives. She leaned forward and clasped his hand again.

"Son, God help me for being the one to tell you this, but I cared for your mother in her confinement."

The rest of the visit was a blur, and hadn't lasted long. Anne asked Mary all of the remaining questions.

The baby was born at Pale House a week early, and healthy. It was a boy. Mary didn't know what name Margaret had chosen. Her duties ended after the birth.

There was nothing else she knew. She was truly sorry that Lewis had found himself in this position.

They drove back to Pale House in silence. Anne kept looking around at him, but Lewis kept his eyes on the road. As they drove between the stone gateposts and left the public roads of Dunleven behind, she asked if he was alright. Lewis just nodded without replying. His mind was blank, his senses padded with cotton wool, and it was all he could do to focus on keeping the car on the road.

He parked without knowing he was doing it, this time leaving his car facing the house and at a strange angle compared to Anne's vehicle alongside. They got out, and Anne had to remind him to press the central locking button on his key fob.

They went into the entrance hall, and if anything, it was colder than it had been outside where evening was quickly taking hold. Anne decided to keep her coat on for now. She approached Lewis, who was standing very still and completely lost in thought, and she put her hand on his elbow. He barely moved.

"I'm going to make some tea," she said. "You should come back through to the family room when you're ready. I'll be waiting for you there."

She paused for a moment until Lewis nodded robotically, then she set off towards the western corridor, looking back at him more than once as she went.

My half-brother, Lewis thought. The three words had been going round and round in his mind since

Mary Petty's revelation, in an endless refrain that stunned him anew each time.

There were no words for how he felt. He didn't even *know* how he felt. Lewis tried to remember what his mother said in her letter, and he found that he was having trouble bringing it to mind. Something about how she loved him, and that was the reason, if he could believe it. It made no sense.

Who would hide something like this? he asked himself, and the voice in his mind was almost screaming, as if he was addressing his mother directly right now.

Without any forethought, he abruptly ran across the entrance hall and up the main staircase, all the way up until he arrived at the third floor, four storeys above the ground. Then to the end of a short hallway that went straight towards the rear of the house, ending in a door that revealed a final stairway of slatted wood. He ran up these stairs too, feeling the boards creak underneath his feet, until he arrived in the cathedral-like vault of the attic. He was out of breath, heart pounding, and the dust was thick up here.

Must still be on Moira's to-do list, he thought. A small part of his mind remarked that he had no reason for bitterness towards his mother's friend and companion who had also already been so kind to him, but he pushed that rational realisation away. He felt betrayed, and he was furious about it.

The nearest thing within reach was an elegant tulip table lamp that he vaguely recalled seeing in use on a sideboard as a child, doubtless consigned to the darkness and dust here many years ago. Its proximity proved to be its undoing, and its elegance came to an abrupt end as Lewis hurtled it against the stone wall that encased a chimney riser. The lamp shattered spectacularly, and his anger only grew.

"What the fuck were you thinking?" he shouted at his mother, but only Pale House was there to hear him.

The next thing that came to hand was a suitcase, one of the thermoformed plastic kind with four rotating castors. The big grab handle made for an easy grip, and he pitched it towards the same stone wall as hard as he could. Lewis had a moment of vengeful satisfaction when the lid broke into three pieces, two of them flying free of their hinges to land in a corner, then he immediately spun round to seek his next target. He found only Anne, standing about three-quarters of the way up the attic staircase, looking at him with concern and understanding.

"I think that's a presentation set of wine glasses," she said, pointing towards a navy blue box with fine silver lettering inlaid on it. "I won't judge you. I'm angry at her too."

It took about two seconds for Lewis to transition from truly intending to smash every one of the glasses in the box, to letting his knees fold and depositing his backside heavily onto the floor.

"I should never have come back here," he said at last, burying his face in his hands and pressing the base of his thumbs into his closed eyes so hard that he saw flashes of light behind his eyelids. "This is madness. I just… I don't even know what to think."

Anne walked over slowly, and then crouched down beside him before sitting on the floor, facing in the same direction Lewis was.

"I wish I could tell you what to think," she said quietly. "But maybe the thing to focus on right now is that she loved you."

Lewis snorted, knowing as he did so that it was unfair, but he simply couldn't help himself. To her credit, Anne didn't remark on it, and instead just continued speaking in the same soft tone.

"I can't imagine what her reasons were for never telling you about this, but I know that they must have seemed like incredibly good ones to her. Whatever happened, I have to believe that she would never have kept this secret from you if she felt she had any other choice."

"Especially if the other choice was honesty," Lewis said. He didn't like his own tone. It was petulant and spiteful, and on some level he was aware that he was making a damned fool of himself in front of Anne. Right at the moment, though, he didn't give a damn about that.

"Fucking hell," he said, shaking his head.

"Fucking hell," Anne agreed, and that at least seemed to pierce the veil of shock and anger that surrounded him. The sound he made wasn't quite a laugh, but it was obviously close enough to one, because Anne reached over and took his hand, squeezing his fingers for a moment.

"I'm sorry," he said.

"That's not going to bring the lamp back," she said, "but you've got nothing to apologise for. Dair, you just found out something incredibly traumatic, so of course you're going to feel betrayed and angry."

"I just don't understand," he said immediately. "And I can't believe it. But I also can. All these years…"

He tailed off, and Anne pulled their joined hands into her lap. "I know. I'm finding it hard to accept myself. I can't tell you what to feel. But I do know one thing."

Lewis looked round at her, hoping that his desperate need to make some sense of all this wasn't too obvious on his face. Her own expression suggested otherwise.

"I know that now we've got two more questions to answer," she said. "Why your mother kept this secret, and where your brother is now."

They were back in the family room, and Anne had brought the same tray from earlier. Two more scones were on it, plus two mugs of hot tea, and a whisky glass engraved with the logo of a distillery about two hours' drive south of Dunleven.

Lewis had already gone over to the ersatz antiquated globe that served as a drinks cabinet, and poured at least two measures of single malt into the waiting vessel. He'd swallowed half of it in a single gulp.

"We don't have to talk about this tonight," Anne said, sipping her tea. "It might even be better not to, Dair. I don't like to bring it up, but remember we've got the service in the morning."

Lewis noticed her use of the word *we*, and he wondered when exactly they'd become a unified front in the midst of this bizarre chapter of his life. Not that he was complaining, of course.

Probably when we went to Petty's house, he mused. *That's what really sealed it.*

The thought brought another burst of anger, and he found that part of it was actually embarrassment. He was ashamed that his mother hadn't thought him worthy or deserving of learning that she'd had a second child, not then and not at any point in the two decades afterwards, until the very end of her life.

He could be anywhere now, he thought. *He could be at university down south. He could have stayed here, and served me my bloody coffee the other day. He could be at a research station in Antarctica for all I know.*

Anne took another sip of tea and then set the cup down on its saucer. The sound pulled Lewis from his thoughts, and he looked over at her. He was almost certain that she knew exactly what he was thinking, too.

"I'm finding it pretty hard not to take this personally," he said, and she nodded.

"Whatever her reasons, she didn't do this to hurt you," Anne said. "Not that it helps very much. I just wish I knew what the next step was."

"The next step is to check the town records. Births are public information," Lewis said. "I can do that tomorrow after the funeral. Or instead of going to it."

Anne gave him a reproachful look, and he held a hand up in surrender to indicate that he wasn't serious. *Or at least that I'm not actually going to follow through on it.*

He had a brief speech planned; a eulogy of sorts that focused mostly on his mother's relationship with the town. Lewis had been writing it in his mind ever since that early morning phone call. He knew that the best thing to do now was just deliver the speech as if nothing had changed. Funerals weren't for the dead, after all. Their purpose was to comfort the living, and provide closure to allow progressing to the next stage of grief.

"I did insist on talking to Mary Petty last night," Lewis said. "I brought this on myself. It would definitely have been better to wait until after the funeral. But what's done is done."

"What do you think you'll do?" Anne asked. "If you find out what happened to your brother, I mean. Will you try to contact him?"

"I think so," Lewis replied. "Why wouldn't I? I wonder if he even knows that she's passed away. I might end up being the one who has to tell him."

It was a troubling thought, but it wasn't any worse than the rest of the whole mess. Then another possibility occurred to him, and he immediately wondered why he hadn't thought of it sooner.

"My god, he might not even know that I exist. And he wasn't in the will at all. What if she gave him up for adoption when he was really young? Isn't that the most likely scenario here?"

Anne thought for only a moment, and then she nodded. "Yes, I think that's probably what happened, honestly. I think that for whatever reason she decided she couldn't keep him, and she covered it up, and decided never to tell anyone. It's probably a lot more common than we'd like to think."

It made sense at least. And everyone had heard tragic stories of children given up for any number of reasons, only for the biological parents to harbour regrets later in life. Lewis's next thought was automatic.

"I should provide for him," he said. "From the estate, once I find him. Of course I should. It's the right thing to do."

Anne smiled at him. "You're a good person, Dair," she said. "And I think that would be a really generous thing to do. Just... maybe try not to get ahead of yourself. It's been twenty years, and we don't know anything yet. We don't even know he was adopted. He could be anywhere at all, and in these situations sometimes people aren't happy to make connections with the family of their biological parents."

"Meaning that he might resent me, as a proxy for my mother, and want nothing to do with me," Lewis said, nodding as he spoke.

It made sense. He knew that he shouldn't get his hopes up, but already he was picturing a younger version of himself out there, just beginning to become a true adult, and about to embark upon his own life's journey. Irrationally, he already felt protective of a person he hadn't even known existed when he got out of bed this morning.

"It's possible," Anne said. "I just don't want you to get hurt all over again, from both sides of this."

Lewis looked at her, and he clearly saw the spark of anger in her eyes, even though she kept her face neutral. He knew he should probably find it validating and even flattering, but he found that he actually felt only sadness. Anne had known his mother, and had even felt quite at home in Pale House at one point. It was a small collateral tragedy of this situation that another relationship had been damaged.

"I know," he said, "and I really appreciate it, but I promise you that I can be angry enough for the two of us. My mother cared about you too, you know."

Anne didn't respond, but Lewis could see that she understood. She had every right to her own opinion and reaction. It also felt good to have someone on his side.

Teachers probably get to see more of the consequences of broken homes and split-up families than most of us do, he realised. Maybe that was also a factor, in which case he really couldn't blame her for being angry on his behalf.

Lewis picked up the glass of whisky and took another sip, and he'd barely swallowed it before a huge yawn stretched his jaw so far that it actually clicked.

Anne immediately put her tea cup down on the tray, and stood up. It was still before nine o'clock, but it had been an uncommonly draining day. Lewis considered asking her to stay for a while, but he suddenly felt more tired than he had in a long time.

"You should have an early night," Anne said. "Finish your drink then just go to bed, Dair. I think you really need it."

Lewis stood up slowly, putting his glass down on the tray. He wasn't going to argue with her. He didn't know how easily sleep would come, but right now it felt inevitable.

"You're right. I think I will. Sorry to be such crap company."

She smiled again. "At least you have an excuse this time," she said. Lewis smiled at that, and found that he felt just a little bit better.

"Listen, thanks for everything today. It feels like a week's worth of stuff. Or a month. I don't just mean getting me in the door at the Pettys' house. I just… I appreciate you being here."

He ran a hand through his hair, unaware he was making it stick up in odd places. "I'm not saying this very well."

"I know what you mean, and you're welcome," Anne said.

She paused for a moment, her eyes flicking up to the irregular tufts of hair that he'd disturbed, and then she reached up and smoothed them down. It was an intimate gesture, and when their eyes met before she could withdraw her hand, the outcome was inevitable.

Her hand slipped around to the back of his head, and it was Anne who stepped in closer. Lewis felt a gentle puff of her breath against his chin, and then she was kissing him.

She tasted of tea, and of something sweet, and also perhaps of something just a little bit sad. The image in his mind was of the fireworks in the sky over the school playing fields so many years ago, and for a few seconds it was like all the time since then had never happened at all.

It was also Anne who pulled away, letting her hand fall from the back of his neck, and he caught it before she could step back. Her lips were parted and for a moment he was sure she was going to close the distance between them again, but instead she squeezed his hand, and then they both let go.

I could ask her to stay, he thought, knowing that it would be the wrong choice, or rather just the wrong time. *I could just ask her to stay here.*

"Goodnight, Dair," she said, and then she impulsively reached up to touch his cheek before turning and walking over to the doorway of the family room. She stopped there, looking around at him again.

"I'll meet you at the service in the morning," she said. "I'll be there a little early, if you like."

He nodded. "I'd like that."

She smiled, and then she was gone.

Lewis kept looking at the empty doorway for several long moments, then he exhaled loudly and picked up his drink again.

Maybe I could sleep after all, he thought, even though a part of him wanted to chase after her instead. It occurred to him that something good had happened in Pale House, and while he was still feeling a thousand different things, the anger seemed to have faded for now. He had no doubt that this had been her intention, but he hoped that wasn't all of it.

He drained the glass in one gulp, put it back on the tray and left everything exactly where it was, and then went upstairs.

Lewis woke exactly once in the night, startled awake with his heart hammering in his chest.

He had been running, up and down endless stairs and along strange, warped corridors, both indoors and somehow outdoors too, but all of it in a monstrously enlarged version of the house. A young boy was up ahead of him, and Lewis was shouting at him to stop and come back. He knew that the boy was terrified, and he was determined to protect him, but the child only ran away even faster.

At one point, Lewis crossed a gallery and lost sight of the boy, and so he stopped to look both down and then up the vast, other-worldly stairways that branched from the balcony he was on, and it was then that he'd seen a different figure far above. Tall, eerily slender, and silhouetted in black, Lewis nonetheless knew that this being was staring directly at him. He was immediately consumed by fear, the child forgotten, and it was then that he'd woken up.

He pulled the sheets back and took several ragged breaths, willing his pulse to slow. In time, it did, and he rubbed his hand across his face in the darkness. For a moment, he thought he heard something and he froze, but a full minute of listening brought only the sound of the trees in the wind, and the night birds beyond the window.

Pale House was silent.

Agnew awoke from a dream where he was in the house again.

He saw the figure, still at the very top of the biggest set of stairs he'd ever seen. Far above anything else, like something from a movie. The figure had pointed at him, then opened his hand before clenching it shut again, and Agnew had felt more pain inside his head than he would ever have imagined was possible.

This is what killed my old bastard of a father, he'd thought, weeping in pain even inside his dream, but then the pain had gone away. He looked up again, and now all the stairs had moved, twisting away in every direction to leave just a void above him. The figure was still there, so far overhead, and standing on a platform that connected to nothing at all. His hand was outstretched, and then he curled one finger in a gesture that was understood everywhere.

The figure whispered, and somehow Agnew could hear it clearly in his mind.

Come home, lad.

That was when he woke in his bed, knuckles still torn and clothes still bloody from what he'd done to the man in the lane. Agnew was fairly sure he'd killed him.

He'd always wanted to let himself feel his own anger properly. He'd wanted it forever, and now he had no idea what had been holding him back all his life. It had felt like the purest experience he'd ever had. It was what he was meant for. But there was something else too.

He got out of bed, not giving a damn about the bloody handprints on the sheets, and went over to the small oval mirror that hung above a chest of drawers. He flicked the nearby light switch, and the room was thrown into sharp relief.

When he fell into bed a few hours earlier, his hair had been black all over. Now, two streaks of grey, finger width, snaked from his temples towards the back of his head and out of sight. Even the stubble on his chin was lighter.

It was his reward. He had done his father proud, and this was a badge of how well he'd done. He touched his own hair, and he wondered what it would take to make it all as white as snow and death.

Come home, lad, his father said in his mind, and every hair on his arms stood on end.

Another image flashed through his mind, and this time it was the man from the pub the other night. The man who had come here and now owned the big house up on the hill.

My fucking house, Agnew thought.

It all seemed very clear. The other man might think the place was his, but he was wrong. He didn't know the half of it. He didn't realise that when you were special, special things happened to you. You could take what you wanted, and do what you wanted, and god help anyone who got in your way.

Agnew was a serious man now. Serious as a stroke, or a heart attack. Serious as death.

He would sleep for now, and then he'd wake up early and get out of here. A part of him knew that the police would arrive before long, but it didn't matter. They would never catch him. His father would see to that.

Then he'd wait for his moment, and he'd go home, to the place that he was sure was his. The place he'd somehow been to before, even though he'd never been in the big house up on the hill. He didn't quite understand that part yet, but he would.

Things could be simple, if you let them. And there was nothing simpler than dealing with someone who stood in the way of what you rightfully deserved.

He was a special man. A *serious* man. He sure as hell was the right man for this job. He had been someone else before, but that didn't fucking matter either.

Now, he was only Rage.

Thursday

Chapter 16

Lewis decided to walk to the church.

It was a bright day, not too cold, and he very much needed the fresh air and some time to prepare himself. He left at least half an hour earlier than he needed to, but he found himself walking at a brisk pace, ill at ease in the formal clothing he wasn't at all accustomed to.

The tie was too tight, the shirt collar was too high and too stiff, and his black woollen coat was heavy and constricting. He felt like he was dressed to perform the service as well as attend it, and he frowned in irritation as he tugged at his collar yet again.

Better get a grip before you arrive, Dair, he told himself.

He had wakened earlier than usual, but all things considered he'd had a reasonable enough night's sleep despite the nightmare. The house felt subtly different this morning, but he knew it was only his own projected emotions. He had to bury his mother today, and on the eve of that already difficult experience, he had found out that he had a half-brother he'd never met, born twenty years earlier, who could be anywhere at all.

Anne had texted him earlier, and he'd been glad to hear from her. She was meeting him at the church a little while before the service would begin, and he was going to ask her to sit with him at the front, alongside Moira. He expected there to be quite a few other guests, and if he was being honest, he wasn't looking forward to what was expected of him today. It would be tiring enough under any circumstances, but right now his feelings for his mother were more confused than ever. But there was nothing to be done about it.

He pushed on, trying to stay in the moment and enjoy the walk, but he felt as if every pair of eyes was on him, and that everyone knew who he was and where he was going. It was a ridiculous idea, but he hated to be conspicuous and today he would be at the centre of everything that was taking place.

It took about twenty five minutes for him to reach Maxwell Church, and the parking area was blessedly empty of cars except for two vehicles in the reserved area towards the rear, plus Anne's own little red compact that could have fit into the cloakroom back at Pale House. It was empty, and there was no-one in sight, so she must have gone inside already.

Lewis considered walking through the graveyard first, but the last thing he wanted to see was the prepared plot. He knew that these days they threw a green covering over the mound of exhumed earth, to make it just a little more palatable to the mourners, and somehow that seemed even more macabre to him. Instead, he walked towards the building, seeing that one door was propped open with a wedge, and he steeled himself for the day that was ahead.

He saw Anne as soon as he went through the doorway. She was sitting on one of two isolated seats in the foyer that were presumably for older people's use, and sipping coffee from a paper cup. On her lap was a magazine, and Lewis used the brief observation opportunity to peer at its pages, wondering what sort of publication she was fond of buying. The article, at least, looked like a book review.

He stepped into the foyer and Anne looked up immediately, her eyes meeting his. She smiled, folding the magazine and tucking it into her large purse. She dropped her cup into the adjacent recycling bin, then she stood up. When he approached her, she kissed him chastely on the cheek, taking hold of his forearm.

"How are you today?" she asked, and he could hear all the different levels of the question in her voice. He nodded.

"I'm OK. Really," he said. "The walk over here cleared my head a bit. And before you ask, I did get an early night, and I slept pretty well. Considering, I mean."

One of the funeral directors appeared from a doorway at the end of the corridor that led away from the foyer, and the man gave a polite and restrained nod and smile to both of them before going through a different door, clearly busy with his work.

"Have you thought about what you're going to say during the service?" Anne asked, and then she pre-empted him by tapping a finger on his lapel. "And be serious for once."

Lewis smiled for a moment. "I've thought about it a bit, but not too much. It'll be fine. You can drag me off the pulpit if I start losing the audience."

"Just remember that all we have are questions right now, and that she wrote you a letter telling you she wants you to know everything. And that she loves you."

Lewis thought that he could probably say anything at all and Anne would still defend him, but he knew that a funeral was the last place for an angry rant. He would do the right and proper thing, the expected thing, and praise his mother and her long life of generosity towards Dunleven. He'd do everything he could to appear as the son she would have wanted him to be at this time.

He was pulled from his thoughts both figuratively and literally by Anne tugging on his arm.

"People are starting to arrive now," she said, tilting her head towards the doorway. Lewis saw a car drive into the parking area, closely followed by another, and he knew that within a minute he'd meet the first of an unknown number of well-wishers. Nervousness bloomed in his stomach, and he licked his lips without being aware of it.

Some of these people — probably a lot of them — think I'm a terrible son for not visiting my mother more often. They're probably right, too.

He wondered if anyone would actually call him out on it, and what he'd say if they did, but he also recognised the train of thought as a precursor to an anxiety episode. This wasn't the time or the place for that, if there even was such a thing, so instead he placed his hand over Anne's hand on his forearm, which drew a surprised look from her.

"I'm glad you're here with me," he said. "I want to talk later about last night, and about... well, what exactly we're doing here. But for now, just, thanks for not letting me do this alone."

Anne shifted her grip just enough to interlace her fingers with his, and then squeezed his hand. A moment later she gently withdrew her arm and took a half-step away, as they both heard the sound of approaching footsteps on the gravel of the parking area.

Here goes, Lewis thought, and he prepared himself to shake the first hands of the day.

Lewis stopped counting after about two hundred people had arrived, but they kept coming nonetheless.

By the time an usher came to invite everyone to take their seats in the pews within the nave, Lewis could see a police car outside on the main road, and two officers directing traffic towards overflow parking. He was trying very hard not to think about that, and he was mostly succeeding due to the constant flow of people coming over to offer their condolences.

Anne was standing off to one side, beside the chair she had been sitting on earlier, which was now occupied by Moira. The old woman had an actual funeral veil, and Lewis had been able to detect a rose-scented perfume from her when she arrived. Moira embraced him as if he was her own son, and he found himself choking back emotion that he hadn't expected before the service actually began.

The one near-constant of each approach was that everyone told him who they were, and Lewis was finding it very difficult not to read anything into that. They all had some connection or other to his mother, and while many of the women remarked on how different he looked now to when he was a boy, most of the men simply said that it was good to meet him. Some even qualified the sentiment with the word *finally*.

There was a period of about ten minutes when Anne remained by his side, steadfastly greeting and introducing people before they could do the job themselves, and Lewis was now certain that Anne's own funeral service — hopefully very, very far off in the distant future — would surely be even bigger than this one.

The parking area was still packed with people queuing to come in when the minister of Maxwell Church, a man called McNay, tapped Lewis on the shoulder, smiled at him, and invited him to come straight in so the service could begin. Lewis just nodded mechanically, already shellshocked by the experience, and looked toward Anne and Moira.

"We'll see you there in a minute," she said, already taking Moira's arm to escort her. For her part, Moira seemed to have sized up the situation between the two of them within the first five seconds after she arrived, and if anything she seemed more cheerful than usual despite the situation.

Lewis looked at each of them briefly, then turned to follow the minister who was already making a path through the crowd of people.

Here we go, he thought.

There were two equal worst parts of the funeral service, even if you didn't count having to greet everyone before and afterwards. The first worst part was when Lewis was listening to the minister's summary of his mother's life, and he realised that this man knew a lot more about the details of the last couple of decades than Lewis himself did. It wasn't unexpected, but it was certainly uncomfortable.

The second of the worst parts was when Lewis got up to give his own eulogy, reached the pulpit, and had his first view of all the pews behind the one at the front he'd been sitting on.

Standing room only, he thought.

Every metre of every pew, on both sides of both aisles, was occupied. Not only that, but the upper level too, on all three sides. Plus, there were probably fifty more people just standing along the back of the ground level, almost all of them men who had presumably fore-gone a seat in favour of their female partners. All silent, all in black, and all looking straight at him.

Lewis was fairly sure this must be the largest as-sembly of people this church had ever seen, and he had to force himself not to make a nervous and totally inap-propriate joke about this being a great time to pass around the collection plate. Instead, he cleared his throat and risked a quick glance at Anne, then he began to speak.

"Thank you all for coming," he said. "It would have meant a great deal to my mother to see so many of you here today. I'd like to extend my thanks to Rever-end McNay for conducting the service today." Lewis ac-knowledged the minister, and the man nodded with a kindly smile. "You've already heard a lot about her life here, so let me tell you a bit about the woman herself."

The words came more easily than he'd expected. He spoke about his mother's great fondness for the town and its people, including this church and its con-gregations over the years. He talked about how he had always been taught that it was a great privilege to be able to contribute to a community, and that he should never forget that whatever he had, it came not from his parents and grandparents, but from the people of Dun-leven. A few heads nodded in approval, and Lewis warmed to his subject.

He allowed himself to remember his childhood, and the bright times that had remained clear in his memory, using them to weave a picture of a person who had split her concerns between her own biological family, and the extended family of those connected to the Lambert businesses. He spoke of her pride in what they had been able to accomplish during her own generation and that of her parents, and how she had made sure that Lewis understood how important it was to recognise one's own duties. The last part was mostly fabricated, but it was probably true enough nonetheless.

Next he touched upon the causes dearest to his mother's heart, making mention of her contributions to the hospital, and even that she had remembered this church itself in her will. It was a calculated move, and obviously well received, judging by the many smiles it prompted. Lewis could tell that the minister had already learned of the bequeathment, and he was doubly glad in retrospect that he hadn't made the remark about the collection plate. Lastly, he made fond mention of Moira and her steadfast friendship and companionship, which had been an especially bright point in his mother's life. The old woman dipped her head, perhaps embarrassed, but certainly grateful.

"In closing," he said, "I know that my mother would want me to tell you that it was always a point of particular pride for her that her family was able to enjoy the good regard of the people of Dunleven, our home. More than anything else, she would insist that I express her gratitude — to those here, and those no longer with us — for being a part of the community that she cared about so very much. Thank you all."

The applause was a surprise, and to the minister's credit, he joined in without hesitation. Lewis returned to his seat, maintaining a sombre expression and nodding to the minister, and he sat down with a considerable feeling of relief. The part that he could conceivably make a complete mess of was over. Now he just had to get through the rest of the service, and the wake afterwards.

Anne gave him an appreciative look when he took his seat on the aisle beside Moira, and the old woman patted his arm. He had apparently performed his task adequately, at least, but Lewis had already forgotten most of what he'd said. His main hope right now was that the townsfolk would be gentle with him at the wake, and not ask him too many questions. He forced himself to pay attention to what the minister was saying, and a moment later everyone rose to sing a hymn from the printed order of service.

Lewis suddenly remembered a scene from a movie he'd once watched, where a young suitor barged into the wedding of the woman he was infatuated with to steal her away. He imagined a darker version of it, where a twenty-year-old young man who looked a bit like himself would suddenly burst through the doors in the narthex, demanding to know what had happened to the woman that was his own mother every bit as much as she was Lewis's.

Not a good time to be thinking about that, Dair, he chastised himself. *But it would certainly save me from having to look for him.*

Lewis pushed the thought away as the opening refrain from the pipe organ rang through the church, and he began to sing.

The interment was a very brief affair, but it took about twice as long for the mourners to all file into the churchyard and take their places, and the same for them to all leave afterwards.

There had indeed been a green cloth over the excavated earth, and Lewis had been bemused to see that the coffin bore the Lambert family crest on each of the longest sides. He supposed it was understandable that his mother already had her funeral arrangements in place, but he had no idea of the logistics involved in obtaining that sort of decoration. The only reasonable conclusion was that the crests had been made a long time in advance, and then lodged with the funeral director for whenever they were needed. It was a strange thought, but no less so than all of the rest of it.

The Boat Shed was a family restaurant that also served as a function venue and sort of middle-aged nightclub for the town, and when they arrived — with Anne driving both Lewis and Moira for barely one minute down the road from the church to reach it — Lewis could see that the venue had wisely put on extra staff for the occasion. The owner and his battalion of white-shirted and black-trousered foot-soldiers stood lined up outside the entrance, as a sort of food service honour guard. He felt the day take yet another shift towards the surreal.

"Am I supposed to inspect their uniforms?" he muttered as they were parking, and Anne shot him a look in the rear view mirror.

"That's Fergus Nairn over there," Moira said conversationally just as Anne engaged the handbrake, as if introducing her own grandson, and Lewis and Anne followed her line of sight. There was a portly and ruddy-faced man with silver hair, getting out of the back seat of a recent model Jaguar whose door was held open by a chauffeur. Lewis laughed inwardly as he saw Nairn make a gesture to his driver indicating he'd only be ten minutes or so, and he could guess the answer to his own question even before he asked Moira.

"Who's Fergus Nairn, then?"

"He's a politician, and he's the mayor," Moira replied, confirming Lewis's suspicion. "I suppose it's nice of him to drop by."

Her tone strongly suggested that Moira thought it was anything but nice, and was instead the transparent piece of performative public-service political manoeuvring that Lewis had already judged it to be, and he found himself delighted at the usually sweet old woman's obvious ire. Anne turned around in the driver's seat to mirror his grin.

"Then I suppose I'd better go and let him shake my hand and grip my arm at the same time," Lewis said, and he was rewarded with a cackle from Moira. He steeled himself while Anne got out of the car and went around to help Moira, then he tipped the passenger seat forward and stepped out himself. His feet had been on the tarmac surface of the parking area for perhaps ten seconds when Nairn spotted him and immediately marched in Lewis's direction.

The large man's handshake was firm and dry, and Lewis saw Anne duck her head when Nairn really did grasp his right forearm with his other hand.

"Mr. Lewis, I'm terribly sorry for your loss," Nairn said. "Your mother was extremely important to this town and to all of us. It's a true tragedy. I'm Fergus Nairn."

"Thank you," Lewis said. "I appreciate that. I believe my mother mentioned you to me not too long ago, in fact. She spoke highly of you." The lie was unnecessary but diplomatic, and he was sure that Nairn's chest puffed up a little more.

"She was a delightful woman, and certainly a role model to many. She was always generous to Dunleven, and of course your family was in many ways the foundation of this town's prosperity for decades. She will be very sadly missed indeed."

There's the 'indeed' again, Lewis thought.

"That's very kind of you," he said. "There's a lunch being put on for anyone who wants to attend. You'd be most welcome."

"I'd love to, but unfortunately I do have a prior council meeting very soon," Nairn replied. "I just wanted to offer my condolences personally."

"I appreciate that very much, and I know my mother would feel the same."

Nairn smiled in an official sort of way and shook Lewis's hand again before bidding farewell to him, acknowledging both Anne and Moira as he made his way back to the Jaguar.

"Dair Lewis, you shameless liar," Anne said once Nairn had got into his car. "Your mother didn't speak highly of him at all, did she?"

"Costs nothing to be nice, Anne," Lewis said, "and I might want a statue of myself in town at some point."

Moira shook her head. "The only statue *that* balloon of a man would pay for would be of himself."

Anne locked her car, and Moira took her arm once more, even though Lewis knew the old woman didn't need any help. He looked towards the Boat Shed a short distance away, and felt pre-emptively exhausted at all of the close-quarters condolence-receiving that was in store. But it was a necessary part of the day, and he would do well to remember his own words about how his mother felt about the community around her — even if he'd ad-libbed a fair bit of it.

He put on a brave face, and he was just about to gesture for the ladies to precede him, when Anne took his arm. Moira seemed to approve, and Lewis nodded. They walked three abreast towards the restaurant and its patiently waiting staff, just as another convoy of vehicles turned from the main road into the parking area.

The reception part of the wake had taken a little over three hours, all told.

The lunch itself was five small courses with a set menu, and the Boat Shed had done an admirable job of catering to well over a hundred people. Lewis asked Reverend McNay how many people had attended the service, and the man had said he was certain it had been over four hundred in all.

Lewis's mother had put aside money to pay for everything related to her funeral, and even after paying for the entirety of the bill for food and drink, the total came to only about three-quarters of the amount she'd kept in reserve.

At least she knew how much she meant to the people of Dunleven, Lewis thought as he walked in the direction of the administrative centre of town, his wristwatch now showing it was almost four o'clock in the afternoon.

He was full of food, very slightly tired from a couple of well spaced beers during the proceedings, and his tie was folded up and tucked into the inside pocket of his woollen coat. The top two buttons of his shirt were undone, and he was glad of the breeze around his neck.

There had been so many condolences. So many memories of his mother, too; far more than he would ever have expected. Some of the women had become upset when talking about her, and even a couple of the men too. Some had greeted him like a nephew, and others had treated him more like a delinquent ex-husband, especially once the first round of drinks had been consumed. But there were no outright awkward scenes, and for the most part it had been more enjoyable than he'd

been expecting. All the same, by the time he left
— which was only after almost everyone else had bid
him farewell — he had a hell of a tension headache.

Anne offered to drive him home, but Lewis had declined, saying he needed to decompress. Moira was still
there with them at the time, so Anne had refrained from
mentioning that she knew he'd be going to check the
records at the town hall too. She had, however, offered
to come to Pale House later on after she'd been home to
change and attend to a few things. Lewis said he'd look
forward to it, and then he'd walked the women to
Anne's car so she could give Moira a lift back to her
house. Moira embraced him once more, and he smiled
at her, then waved them off before gratefully leaving the
reception venue behind.

His mind was blessedly empty, even given his current destination and purpose. It had been a pleasant and
affirming service, and he was humbled by the number
of people who had nice things to say about his mother.
The onslaught of relentless eulogy had created the odd
effect of splitting his mother into at least two different
people in his mind. There was this public and beloved
woman they all spoke of, who he hadn't known at all,
and then there was his actual mother who he'd been in
contact with sparsely but fairly consistently for all these
years. There was very little overlap between the two.
And then of course there was the third person she'd apparently been, as a mother to someone else entirely.

His headache was a little worse now, but thankfully the sandstone bulk of the town hall and council

building was just ahead. He climbed the wide stairs and pushed open one of the absurdly heavy doors using its brass handle, and he said his first prayer of the day in hope of not bumping into Fergus Nairn again.

The girl behind the enquiries desk was playing with her phone, and to Lewis's eye she didn't even look old enough to drive. When she looked up and politely asked how she could help him, he was relieved to see absolutely no recognition whatsoever in her eyes.

"I'd like to look at the registry archives, if that would be alright," he said, and she nodded without much interest.

"Looking into your family tree?" she asked, not looking at him while she rapidly pressed keys on a computer keyboard in front of her.

"Something like that," Lewis said. "It's quite popular these days."

The girl, whose name badge said *Suzanne*, nodded twice, eyes still on her monitor. "It really is. We get people in here every week."

Her voice made it clear that the subject held absolutely no interest for her, and Lewis had to suppress a smile at her guilelessness. After the day he'd had, it was refreshing. He heard the sound of a small printer whirring for a few seconds, and then Suzanne handed him a piece of paper.

"This is your pass, and the records office is the fourth door on your left down there," she said, pointing down the hall. "Please don't alter, damage, or remove anything. There are copying machines you can use, or your own phone's camera. If you have any problems, just come back and see me."

Lewis smiled and nodded, taking the ticket. He expected to find very little that would require the service of a copy machine or his phone's camera, but it didn't hurt to check. He was trying very hard not to get his hopes up.

The records office was larger than he'd expected, and remarkably similar to the archives in the hospital he'd visited yesterday. Even the filing cabinets might have been the very same model. It took him a few minutes to work out the filing system, which used an indexed system you could look up in two ways. Dates in chronological order was the master organisational system, of course, but there was also a family names archive on the opposite side, with single index cards that referred to particular parts of the master archive. He looked up Lambert first, which led to his mother's married name of Lewis, and a single descendant: himself. His own index card had a paperclip attached to it, and nothing else. His heart sank, but he went to check the date archive nonetheless. The date from his mother's diary had three births, none of them relevant. At this point, he wasn't surprised.

She was an important woman here, and that was even more true twenty years ago than it is now. It would probably be pretty easy, relatively speaking, for her to have these records altered too.

Lewis tried to think who else might have known about his half-brother, but the tricky thing would be trying to investigate without most of the town knowing about it immediately.

He was tired, and he had no idea what his next move was, but he did know that he wasn't able to do anything more today. He left the records office, nodding his thanks to Suzanne at the front desk as he passed, and went back out into the early evening air.

He would go back to Pale House, maybe take a shower and try to have a nap, and then wait for Anne to arrive later on. She might have some more ideas. For now, he could really do with not thinking about all this for a while.

Chapter 17

The police had come by earlier, but Rage didn't talk to them.

He stood silently with all the lights off, holding a kitchen knife in one hand and a cricket bat in the other. The bat had been donated to his father by the local team because the bus company sponsored their matches for many years. Rage didn't give a shit about any of that. He just wanted to break someone's skull open.

There were two coppers, a man and a woman. The man wasn't very big, and the woman was a woman, and Rage knew with completely certainty that he could and would kill them both if they tried to come in. His blood-stained clothes from yesterday were lying on the floor, easily visible from the living room window if the police decided to peek in. Rage didn't give a single shit about that either. If it happened, it happened. They'd use it as justification to break the door down, and then he'd cave in their heads and probably cut them up a bit for good measure. Then he'd drive their fucking car, with the lights and siren on.

The police rang the doorbell again, waited for a minute, and then he heard them walk back to their vehicle. It was three full minutes before the engine started, and Rage wondered if they thought he was a complete idiot. They probably did. A lot of people in this town had underestimated him in the past. It would never happen again.

The police car pulled away from the kerb and drove off down the street, but Rage knew they'd be back later, and that they'd be coming in whether he answered the door or not. There would also be more of them. It didn't matter, because he wasn't going to be here.

Come home, lad, said the voice in his mind, for what had to be the fiftieth time today.

It was his father, but it also wasn't. It had the voice of James Maurice Agnew, and it certainly knew how to hurt him the same way, so he knew that most of the time it was his father he was hearing. There was someone else too, though. Rage knew it was the strangely tall and thin figure at the top of the stairs in the house he kept dreaming of.

It made perfect sense, because the house was two places too, just like his father was two people now. His father, and the figure. The big house up on the hill, and the real house, the vast house, the *true* house, that was hidden inside it. Two and two.

The house was his, even though he'd never set foot in it. That much was clear to him. And that meant that the man who came to town to claim it was a thief.

Rage dropped the cricket bat onto the sofa, but he kept the knife. It felt good in his hand, and he liked the way it whispered in the air. It felt serious, so it was right for a serious man to carry it. He tucked it safely into the back of his belt, and walked into his bedroom for the last time. The top drawer of his dresser was already half open, and he grabbed the first thing that came to hand. It was a navy blue hooded jumper, and Rage thought it would do just fine. He pulled it on, taking care to make sure it covered the handle of the knife, and he put the hood up.

His plan was very simple. He would go out the back door into the garden, jump the fence, and go along the river until he got to the cycle path that joined the main road out of town. Then he'd run along it like a jogger, and go up the hill towards the big house. He'd find a way over the wall instead of going in the obvious way, and then he'd hide somewhere until the thief was asleep tonight.

The next part was even simpler. He'd kill the man, and then the true house would be his forever.

When Lewis finally got back to Pale House, instead of going inside he stood in front of his car, weighing his options.

He could try to find his half-brother. God knows he had enough money now to get some proper help with that. He could hire private investigators, and offer a reward, and even ask Fergus Nairn to pull as many strings as the man could lay hands on, which would be plenty. That was option one.

Option two had the same goal, but he would keep going the same way he had so far, keeping it as quiet as possible. There would still come a time when secrecy was impossible, but it didn't have to be soon. Anne was obviously willing to help him, and perhaps he could make inquiries without arousing too much suspicion. He could also just bribe people to keep quiet, or pay them to sign a confidentiality agreement, which was the legal version of bribery.

The third option was why he was standing there looking at his modest but reliable car. He could just go inside, get his things, lock the place up, get into the car and set out south towards Edinburgh. He would text Anne first to say he needed a bit more time to recover from the day, and then he'd call her tomorrow once he got home, to tell her the truth. Then he might invite her to come and visit him in the city. He could just pretend he'd never read his mother's letter, and never unlocked the empty room, and never found out anything at all.

But of course he couldn't actually do that. Not only could he never do it to Anne again, but he also wasn't capable of letting the matter rest. He had family he'd never known about, and probably someone who needed him, even if they weren't aware of it. He could help this young man, financially at least, and perhaps they could salvage some portion of the relationship they might have had if his mother hadn't kept her secret so well and for so long.

So really there was no decision to be made at all.

Lewis unlocked the main doors of Pale House and went inside, glancing at his phone to see no missed calls or messages, and then he shrugged his coat off and let it fall to the floor just inside the doorway. He could pick it up later. It wasn't like there was anyone to trip on it or steal it in the meantime.

A shower, he thought. *Just have a shower. One step at a time.*

He climbed the stairs, automatically heading in the direction of his childhood room before he realised what he was doing, and changed course for the guest bedroom he'd been sleeping in since he arrived. He was only a few doors away from his destination when he stopped dead in his tracks.

The smell was rich and acrid. Like earth, and wood, and books in a library that was on fire. It was like old machines and engines. It was like—

A dragon's breath. That's how it would smell. It's what a dragon's breath would be like if you were close enough.

That was what he had always thought. He had loved Tolkien's tales of Middle Earth, and the association was natural. But the scent, so awful and familiar, didn't come from a creature of myth. It came from those brown cigarettes, and from brandy, all mixed together in the air. It was the smell of Donald.

Pain flared across the scars on Lewis's back, and in the next moment he distantly heard the scratch of a record player's needle being set into its groove. Then the music, the soft jazz music that Donald would always play when he was going to *relax*, which meant to get drunk, and then to turn his boiling hot anger — his rage — upon the boy that Lewis used to be.

This time, the fear came as it always had, but there was something new: Lewis was furious. He listened again for a moment, and then he ran in the direction of the sound.

The east lounge. Of course it would be. It was where Donald's record player was, and it was the room he'd claimed as his own so early in his time here. Every thud of Lewis's feet against stairs and floorboards and carpets made him go faster and faster. He finally came within sight of the lounge, and both of its doors were lying wide open. Light spilled out from within, and the music was much louder now. Lewis even thought he could see a faint wisp of smoke drifting out into the corridor.

Bastard, he thought. *Bastard. This is my house now.*

Lewis didn't care who was in there, or what kind of sick game they were playing. He was going straight in, and he was going to make whoever it was very, very sorry they'd ever set foot in Pale House.

The lounge was warm, too warm for just the central heating, and Lewis immediately saw why. The fireplace was lit and blazing away, but there was no-one in the room. An ashtray on a table held one of the horrible little cigarettes Donald had enjoyed, its filthy smoke curling up towards the high ceiling. The record player was there too, and it was the same one; the exact same machine, because even from the middle of the room Lewis could see the marks on the right side where Donald's fist had once broken through the faux-wood finish to reveal the primed plastic beneath.

That's not possible, he thought. He'd been in this room himself a number of times during the years since Donald died, and he had been pleased that his mother had evidently got rid of everything connected with the man. Surely she would never have kept something like this in storage, either.

"Who's here?"

He didn't wait for a reply before going over to the table with the ashtray. He had to know whether he was just imagining all this, even though all the evidence said he wasn't. Lewis reached out for the cigarette, closed his fingers around it, and picked it up. It was real enough.

He lifted it up awkwardly, turning it until it was suspended over his palm, and then some hot ash fell from the smouldering tip and he felt a burning sensation. Lewis used his other hand to flick the residue into the ashtray, and then stubbed the cigarette out there too.

Definitely real, he thought. *But nobody's here.*

He turned, and that was when he caught sight of it. At first, he thought it was a snake, of all things. Lewis had only ever seen one snake in his life in Scotland, not counting the zoo, and it had been a tiny thing. He took a few steps towards the shape, and saw that it was long, dark brown, and when its head glistened in the firelight he finally understood what he was seeing. His blood ran cold.

It was Donald's belt. The same one. There was no way that anyone would have kept it, yet here it was. He had used it as a weapon of punishment for the slightest infractions, and Lewis's body bore the scars to prove it.

There was something very, very wrong here.

The music was still playing, and then Lewis spun around as he heard the clink of glassware. There was a glass of brandy on the table now beside the ashtray, its rich and somehow threatening scent reaching his nostrils immediately. It hadn't been there a few moments ago.

You useless little bastard, Donald's voice whispered, and it might have been in Lewis's mind but it also might not have. His earlier anger-fuelled bravado was gone. He ran.

There were lights on in the house that hadn't been on before. He could see flashes of illumination from beneath closed doors and from the edges of open ones. Lewis even thought he could hear sounds coming from some of the rooms, but the blood roaring in his ears and the thud of his feet muffled his surroundings to the point of uncertainty. When he got back to the main entrance hall and wrenched the front doors open, he had the presence of mind to grab his coat from the floor before he hurried outside into the rapidly cooling evening.

Lewis bypassed his car and kept going until he was at the far side of the turning circle, and then he came to a stop. He was breathing quickly, he could still feel phantom pain in the scars across his back, and his first instinct was to just leave.

I could get into the car and go. There's nothing to stop me.

But he knew that wasn't true, and it wasn't just about Anne. Something strange but also wondrous was going on here, and it was all connected to his own past, and his mother and her secrets. The house was his now, and it couldn't be a coincidence that this was all happening now that his mother had been laid to rest.

He turned around, and saw lights in many of the windows, some flicking on or off even as he watched. Despite himself, he wanted to go back in and see what was going on in each of those rooms, but the scent of his dead stepfather's cigarettes was still upon him, and the belt was firmly in his mind too.

Pale House will show you, his mother had written.

Lewis took his phone from his pocket, selected Anne's contact card, and dialled. She picked up after the second ring.

"Dair? Is everything alright?"

"I need you to come over here right now," he said.

Lewis didn't tell Anne anything over the phone, but he did insist that she come to the house immediately if she could. She told him she'd be there in ten minutes, and she was as good as her word. When her car drove in between the gateposts, Lewis was still outside the main doors, leaning against his own vehicle.

She was in casual clothes now, hair down, and wearing softer makeup than at the service and reception. He could see that she was worried, and he regretted that, but he needed her to see this with her own eyes. He needed someone else to give him the final five or ten percent confirmation that he hadn't, in fact, lost his mind.

Anne locked her car and walked quickly over to where he was standing, not even glancing at the house. "So what's wrong?" she asked, and Lewis nodded towards the building towering before them.

She looked at Pale House in confusion, and after a moment she noticed the lights, then she nodded.

"Something's gone wrong with the electricity? You could have at least told me that before I rushed over here, Dair."

He stepped forward, and gently grasped her elbows. "Anne, I have to tell you something," he said, "and it's very important. Then I need to show you something that you're not going to believe at first."

She frowned, but she clearly decided to hear him out first, so she just nodded.

"There's a question you've very pointedly not been asking since we found out that my mother had another child," Lewis said. "And I appreciate the tact. But I think you can probably put the pieces together regarding the timeline. You must remember that my mother was in a long-term relationship by the time this child was born."

Anne nodded. "I do remember seeing him around. He lived with you. What was his name again?"

"Donald Spence," Lewis said, his eyes closing involuntarily when he said it. "The child must have been his. But that's not the key point right now. You asked me the other day why I didn't come back, and you also wanted to ask me why I was sent away to boarding school, and why I agreed to it. Those are all actually just one question instead of three."

Understanding dawned on her face. "Because of your stepfather. Or your mother's partner, rather."

Lewis nodded, and Anne looked distant for a moment, as if she was trying to remember something. "You never spoke about him back then," she said. "I assumed that you two didn't get along, so I never brought it up."

"And I appreciate that a lot," Lewis replied. "But it was more than not getting along. He was an alcoholic. A Jekyll-and-Hyde sort. He hid his problem at first, but he became much more comfortable with it later on. He would drink in the house a lot, and when he did, he would get angry."

Anne's brow creased, and she nodded at him to continue.

"I would always know it was coming," Lewis said, looking off to one side now. "He would put on his music, light up these stinking cigarettes, and start into the booze. He got a taste for expensive brandy from my grandfather's cabinet, but anything would do. And if I crossed his path, it… didn't end well for me, put it that way."

Anne reached for him, but Lewis had already stepped back and shrugged off the woollen coat again, having put it on to ward off the chill of the evening while he was waiting for her. He draped the coat over his car, then untucked his shirt and lifted the hem, turning around. He heard her gasp.

"There's more than that, and a lot that healed up completely," he said quietly. "And there were worse times. One of them was the night after the fireworks. I was taken to hospital in an ambulance. He knocked me unconscious, and my face was a mess for weeks. That's why I never got in touch, and why my mother arranged for me to move away, and why I went willingly and didn't look back."

"My god," Anne said, watching him as he straightened and re-tucked his shirt, then she closed the small distance between them and put her arms around his neck. "I'm so sorry."

Lewis put his hand on the small of her back. "It's alright," he said. "It's really alright. I wasn't even planning to ever tell you. I deal with it myself, mostly by not thinking about it."

She leaned back to look at him, not letting go, and again there was confusion in her eyes. "How could you think I wouldn't believe you, though? Of course I do."

Lewis smiled sadly. "That's not what I meant. I haven't shown you that part yet. So here's the bit that's hard to believe."

He took a deep breath, and then told himself that there was only one path open to him now: the truth. If he was insane, at least Anne would break it to him gently and make sure he got professional help. But he knew that he hadn't imagined it.

"That night I told you about, it started a lot like other nights. He would drink in the east lounge. He had this stupid fucking record player there, even though everyone else had CDs by that point. He'd drink, and he'd smoke, and he'd listen to his records, and work up a head of steam. Then he would take off his belt and wind it around his fist."

Anne winced, moving one hand from his shoulder to his cheek, but she didn't interrupt him.

"I learned to stay away — to hide, even. Lots of places for that here. But sometimes he'd come to find me. The belt had this big fancy buckle on it. That's what gave me my ambulance ride that I still don't remember. Anyway, after he died, my mother got rid of every trace of him from the house. Everything. I never saw any sign of his presence there again."

Anne nodded. "Well, that's good. It was the right thing for her to do. But she should have protected you."

"No argument there," Lewis said, "but here's the thing. I came home a little while ago and I found a fire lit in the east lounge. One of his cigarettes was burning in an ashtray. His brandy was in a glass. His record player was playing. And his belt was there, ready and waiting."

Anne's gaze moved all around his face, her expression at first puzzled, then shocked, then shifting towards disbelief. Lewis didn't blame her. He gave her a few seconds to process what he'd said, then he nodded towards the house. The lights were blinking on and off in the many windows seemingly randomly, and at a leisurely pace.

"There's nothing wrong with the electricity," he said quietly.

He watched as she looked at the house, then back at him, and then at the house once more. She shivered. When she met his eyes again, she looked frightened.

"My mother wrote that Pale House would show me," Lewis said, "but she didn't think he wanted that."

"Dair, you can't be—"

"There's something wrong with Pale House, Anne," Lewis said. "I think there's been something wrong with it for a long time, and it's been getting worse. I think that maybe she knew."

Anne grasped his upper arms this time. "Dair, listen to me. You've had one of the worst weeks a person can have. You lost your mother, and you found out that you have a half-brother you never knew about, and you had to come back to a place that has incredibly traumatic memories for you. And you're tired, and you had a few drinks during lunch. It's perfectly normal to be... having a reaction to all of that."

They were good words, sensible and reasonable, but her voice was just a little too shrill. She wanted to believe what she was saying, and he didn't blame her.

"The grand piano played itself yesterday," he said. "One of my mother's favourite pieces. I opened it up to see if it had been converted into one of those trick ones. But it hadn't. It's just a piano. The day before that, I chased my childhood self up a staircase until he disappeared."

Anne's eyes were wide, and when she tore her gaze away from his face to instead look at the house again, he felt just a little bit of hope. She at least wanted to believe him, too.

"You're scaring me," she said without looking at him, and he nodded. "When people are under a lot of pressure, this kind of thing can happen. I've read about it. Once I was up all night worrying about a promoted post I applied for, then when I was in the shower I thought I heard my grandmother calling me."

Lewis smiled. "I'm not seeing and hearing things, Anne," he said. "But that's exactly what a crazy person *would* say, I know. I'm asking you to believe me."

She smacked his shoulder in admonishment, looking genuinely hurt. "Of course I do. I believe that *you* believe what you're saying. But how can it be true?"

"There's only one way to know for sure," he said, and this time it was his turn to shiver.

They both turned towards the facade that soared up from the ground a short distance away, blocking out part of the rapidly darkening sky. The lights still pulsed in their strange rhythm. The night birds in the surrounding pine forest were silent.

"Alright," Anne said, taking his hand.

They walked slowly over to the main doors, and went inside.

Chapter 18

Within Pale House, it was Christmas.

Lewis and Anne both stopped in their tracks just inside the doorway, mouths hanging open in shock. An enormous Christmas tree that Lewis hadn't seen in years dominated the space to one side of the master staircase, festooned with tinsel, coloured lights, and every kind of ornament.

At its very top, there was a silver-coloured angel, peering down at them with unblinking eyes. Lewis had always found it unsettling as a child, but his mother insisted that it was there to make sure no-one could sneak into the house and steal his presents from beneath the other tree in the family room.

"My god," Anne said, her face paler than it had been a moment before. "Was it like this when you got home too?"

Lewis shook his head. "It wasn't even like this when I ran outside to call you."

But why Christmas? he wondered.

Anne reached out and took his hand, and the two of them just looked around in silence for a few moments before she spoke again. Her voice was shaky, and full of both fear and wonder.

"Where do you think we should we go first?" Anne asked, and Lewis thought for a moment.

"I suppose I should show you the east wing upstairs. The practice room is there, and the room I found the diary in."

"Alright," she said, "but… I mean, should we take something with us?"

Lewis looked around at her, unsure what she meant. "Like what?"

"I don't know," she said. "Something we could use to defend ourselves."

It was a logical question, but for reasons he didn't fully understand, Lewis didn't feel like he was in danger, at least not for the moment. He tried to think how to articulate the instinct.

"My mother… she said that the house would show me," he said. "I think that's what it's doing. I have no idea how that can be, but it seems to be what's happening. I think that if it wanted to hurt me then it could have done it any time after I arrived. Besides, these Christmases were a happy time for me, back when we still had this tree up."

"So you think it's something we have to just allow to play out?"

"I don't think we have much of a choice about that, unless you count choosing to leave right now."

Anne nodded slowly, not entirely convinced, but apparently less apprehensive than before. "And it's all real. The Christmas tree here, it's your mother's actual one?"

Lewis shrugged. "It was, at least. I've not seen it in a long time. It's possible she had it stored somewhere, but I also wouldn't be surprised if she got rid of it years ago. Even if it stayed here, I think we'd still find it exactly where she left it. This is… it's like what I saw in the lounge before I called you."

"A memory," she said, and Lewis knew she'd hit the nail on the head.

"Exactly. Which is another reason why I don't think we're in danger."

Anne frowned again as she tilted her head back to look up towards the floors above, just visible through the balustrades and handrails of the master staircase. "Which leaves us with another question," she said. "Are these memories all yours, or will there be others?"

Lewis looked at her, suddenly unsettled by the idea. It wasn't something he'd considered while he was waiting for her outside. But she was right: even though he recognised elements of what he was seeing, it didn't mean they were being shown from his perspective.

"I guess I'll have to keep that in mind," he said. "You ready for this?"

"No," Anne said immediately, "but you need someone to tell you whether you've lost your marbles, so here I am. Unless it's contagious."

Let's hope not, he thought, leading her to the foot of the stairs. They began their ascent simultaneously, and they hadn't climbed more than five or six steps when piano music began to issue from above. It was *Silent Night*, as played by his grandfather before his arthritis became too severe and forever separated him from the instrument he'd enjoyed so much.

Anne glanced at Lewis, but they kept going. When they reached the first floor, Lewis stopped, making a low whistling sound. A few metres away, unmissable in brightly-painted plastic and polished metal, was his baby walker.

"This was mine," he said immediately, dropping her hand to walk over to the squat metal frame with castors attached, and a tray on top bearing various simple toys. "I can just remember scooting around in it. This house was great for that kind of thing."

He thought for a moment. "Oh, I know exactly when this was. I almost killed myself at the stairs there." He turned back to face Anne, pointing past her at the top of the stairs they'd just come up. "I must have got away from my mother, and I went full-tilt along here. I nearly went straight off."

Anne winced. "What stopped you?"

"Our dog at the time," Lewis said with a smile. "A protective big boxer bitch called Maisie. Ran right for me and put her teeth around the back of the walker. She didn't let go until my mother came and grabbed me."

The walker suddenly shot across the floor, barrelling past him and heading directly for the top of the stairs. Anne lurched out of the way, eyes wide, and then at the same moment they both heard the staccato drumbeat of an animal's claws on the wooden floorboards.

Maisie ran past him, as large as life. Lewis felt the air moving as she went by, and he heard her breathing, and even smelled her canine breath. Her docked tail twitched from side to side, and it was plain to see the power in her lean and muscled shoulders and neck. She caught the walker effortlessly, fastening down onto the top of the plastic backrest that was suspended within the metal frame. The walker came to an abrupt stop, still a metre or more from the precipice.

The big dog gently tugged backwards, pulling the empty walker away from danger. Lewis, his eyes suddenly filling with tears, moved slowly towards the animal, and when he drew level with her, Maisie looked up at him with those liquid brown eyes he remembered so well — and then she was gone.

He made a sound of grief that caused Anne to come to his side immediately, and no matter where he looked he couldn't see the dog anywhere. The walker remained, empty and solid, but Maisie was nowhere to be found.

"Dair, are you sure you should be putting yourself through this?" Anne asked, holding tightly onto his arm, but a moment later she realised that he was actually laughing softly to himself.

"Tell me this isn't incredible," he said. He reached for the walker and grabbed hold of it just where Maisie had, and his hand came away slightly damp with her hot breath and a trace of saliva. "Tell me this isn't the most incredible thing you've ever seen in your life."

"It is," Anne said, "but it's also the most frightening thing I've ever seen. I don't even know what's going on here. How can any of this be happening? And what does it all mean?"

Lewis looked back down the hallway, seeing the door that led to the upper eastern gallery. He could still hear the soft and melancholy piano music. He tried to think about all the other rooms of the house, and all the moments of his life that had been defined in part by those places, but there was too much of it.

"I think the point is to find that out," he said. "I think that's what my mother meant."

He reached out a hand towards her, inviting her to join him so they could keep going, but she hesitated. "What's wrong?" he asked.

Anne drew her arms around herself. "You said something outside about your mother's letter, and I read it myself. She wrote that she didn't think *he* wanted the house to show you whatever it wants you to know. And you think she was talking about your stepfather."

Lewis nodded, already uneasy. He knew where she was going, and he'd been stubbornly refusing to acknowledge it himself.

"She used the present tense, Dair," Anne said quietly. "Wants. Not wanted, or would have wanted."

"He hanged himself almost twenty years ago," Lewis said. "I could show you where it happened. He's dead."

"Five minutes ago you would have said the same thing about your dog."

You know she has a point, he thought. *Maybe it's not so clear cut anymore.*

She was looking at him with her usual patience, but Lewis could see that she was still frightened too. He was beginning to realise that maybe she was right to be.

"This isn't just a picture, or a hallucination," Anne said, pointing to the baby walker. She stepped over to it and then reached down and gave it a push. It rolled away on its little wheels, rattling and turning as it went. "At least for now, in here, it's as real as we are."

Lewis looked at the walker, and listened to the piano music, and he rubbed his thumb across the fingers he'd used to grab the walker himself. They were still ever so slightly damp. The implications were obvious.

"We'll be careful," he said, trying to sound more confident than he was. "But maybe you should go home, just to be safe. I don't think that this… *whatever this is* wants me hurt or dead, but you're right; I can't be sure. I've never done this before."

"I'm not going home," she said immediately, walking over to where he stood and taking his hand again. "I just wish I'd brought… I don't know. What would it be in a film? A gun or something."

The idea would usually have made him laugh, but Lewis really didn't find it amusing right now.

"I don't think that would help here," he said.

Rage had seen the man arrive back on foot a while ago.

The temptation to kill him immediately had been very strong, but the voice in his mind who was his father, and also wasn't his father, had hurt him for that thought.

There'll be a time for that, lad, the voice had said. *And you already know the right place.*

So he waited, sitting beneath a tree on a blanket of pine needles, listening to the forest. He would occasionally lean over and look past the trunk and in the direction of the house, but he didn't need to keep watch. The voice made sure he knew what was happening.

It told him that the man was going to run back out the front doors. It told him that the woman from the pub was going to arrive ten minutes later. It didn't need to tell him that they were going to go back inside together. Back into his house, that the man had stolen from him.

They were in there right now, both of them, and if the woman was in Rage's house then she belonged to him every bit as much as the building did. That was one of the oldest rules in the world.

He could see that it had started. He could see from the lights in the windows, and he could see from inside his own head, too. It was all beginning to open up. Soon enough, the true house would show itself, and then it would be time for him to finally come home and get rid of all the trespassers. Rage was looking forward to that.

It wouldn't be long now.

The windows all along the eastern gallery gave a view of the gardens, and tonight, at least when seen from inside Pale House, they were covered in snow. It was falling steadily, already fifteen centimetres deep in places, and the opalescent sky promised much more to come.

Anne asked Lewis if it would still be snowing outside the front doors, where their cars were, and he said he didn't think so. Then she asked what would happen if one of them went outside and around to the gardens while the other waited here to watch for them. He had no idea, and he told her so.

All I know is that I don't want to find out, he thought. *In case one of us goes missing somewhere along the way.*

The practice room had changed since the last time he went into it. The grand piano was in the dead centre of the room, the cover gone and the lid propped open, and the stool was now the one that had broken years ago and been replaced. The piano was playing by itself, keys moving without a visible hand to depress them.

After watching the strange spectacle for almost a minute, Lewis had an idea. He opened the storage compartment beneath the stool's seat cushion, and found his old musical notebook along with sheet music for pieces he'd had to practice as a boy. He was standing flipping through one of the pieces, marvelling at the pencil annotations his piano teacher had made so long ago, still fresh and crisp.

"This Christmas was a long time ago," he said. "I was still young when I had these music books."

Anne was nearby, to one side of the piano, watching him. "But a lot older than a toddler," she said, and Lewis nodded before he understood what she meant. "The walker," he said. Anne nodded.

"It's not all from the same night," she said. "Maybe there are places in the house where it's summer, or lunchtime, or yesterday."

He instantly knew that she was right, and he also knew why. "Because that's how memories work. You remember different things from different times, all at once, just depending on what you see."

"Is it too late to ask you to try and think happy thoughts?" she asked, and Lewis looked over at her.

"Only by twenty years or so," he said. "Let me show you where I found the diary. The room was totally empty when I was last in it."

They went down the hall and Lewis turned the handle, but the room seemed to be locked again. He took out his mother's keychain and inserted the appropriate key, but it wouldn't slide fully into the keyhole.

"That's strange," he said. "This is definitely the right key."

"Was the lock changed at any point?" Anne asked, but he didn't know the answer. He could see what she was implying, though — the door could be from an earlier time. The grandfather clock was no help, indicating that it was twenty past six, but it had also stopped. The pendulum hung motionless, and the clock was silent.

They both flinched when they heard a sudden creaking sound from underfoot, and there was a strange sense of motion, just for a moment.

"Was that... an earthquake?" Lewis asked no-one in particular, looking up at the high ceiling to see if there were any cracks, but everything seemed to be intact. A moment later, they felt the same odd sense of motion. The lights in the gallery flickered and went out, plunging them into darkness, and the piano music stopped abruptly. He felt Anne grab hold of his arm.

"We should go back outside," she said. "I have a bad feeling about this, Dair."

Lewis hesitated. He wanted to know what the house seemed so desperate to tell him, and that wouldn't be accomplished by falling at the first hurdle. He turned to face her in the gloom, putting his hands on her waist.

"It's going to be alright," he said. "I can't be certain, but I think we're safe. And if that changes, we leave. I don't think it's coincidence that this is all happening tonight. I think, maybe, that if I come back tomorrow—"

"It'll just be an ordinary house." Anne said. "That you'll have missed your chance?"

"That's what it feels like," Lewis replied. "So I have to stay here, at least for a while longer. You really can leave right now if you want to, no questions asked. I wouldn't blame you for a second, and I can call you later if I learn anything new. I'll even take you to the front doors myself. But I have to stay."

As if the house had been waiting to hear it, the lights came back on, making them blink in that sudden brightness. The eastern gallery looked exactly as it had yesterday. The practice room was silent, but the grandfather clock was ticking again. The gardens outside the gallery windows bore no trace of snow, and the weather was cloudy but dry.

Lewis and Anne exchanged a look, and then he reached again for the handle to the room where he'd found the diary. The door opened easily, onto the same bare room Lewis had first discovered.

"I think it's today again," he said. "Tonight, I mean. The same day."

Anne nodded, understanding what he meant. She looked around the gallery first before she stepped into the room and ran her hand along the rough surface of one stripped wall. "And you don't know what she was planning to do with this place?"

Lewis shook his head. "No, but I've started to wonder about that. It was locked a few minutes ago, with a different key or something."

Anne looked at him and nodded, urging him to continue.

"I wonder if maybe she already did what she wanted to do. Maybe that's what the house just told us. She stripped it bare to get rid of something, not to create it."

She glanced over towards the window, but it was too dark to see very much outside except the distant sky over the barely discernible tree line. She bit her lower lip, and Lewis could see that she was debating whether or not to say something. He waited for her to make her decision, and after half a minute or so she looked at him again.

"But this room, it's not where Spence…"

"Oh, no, not at all," he replied, surprised by the question. "It was upstairs, and over at the other side. It wasn't here."

Anne seemed relieved. "Alright. Well, I suppose we should move on then. If you still want to explore."

Lewis nodded slowly, but he wasn't entirely sure. They went back out into the gallery and he closed the door again. The house felt quiet, in a way that went beyond the lack of musical accompaniment and manifestations of a long-gone Christmas. It felt normal for now, as if this had all been a prelude.

"It feels like intermission at the theatre," he blurted out, and then he cleared his throat in embarrassment. Anne looked delighted.

"That's *exactly* what it feels like," she said. "Especially the part where you're waiting around in a fancy corridor with a guy who's overdressed."

The quip broke the tension as intended, and Anne took his arm once more. "I could actually do with getting changed," he said. "Mind if I drop by the room I've been using before the stage curtain goes up again?"

She shook her head, and they both began to walk down the gallery, heading south towards the rear part of the building. Lewis knew every route through Pale House, and while this one wasn't the most direct path to reach his backpack and a change of clothes, it would let him at least see if anything else had changed along the way.

They'd been walking in silence for a minute or two when Anne nudged him with her elbow, not breaking pace. "There's a part of you that's OK with everything that's happening here, and I'm not sure I understand why," she said. "Is it just because you feel a duty to your mother to find out what she meant?"

"That's part of it," he said, opening a wood-panelled door at the end of the gallery which led to a landing connecting three corridors. He led her towards the middle one, which would cut straight across towards the west wing. "But it's also, hmm. It's hard to describe. It's kind of like coming home."

He thought for a moment, not satisfied with his own answer, and then tried again. "When I think about this house, I don't really think about the actual place we're in right now, as a building. Nobody does, do they? Instead, I think of it in terms of my memories here."

Anne nodded. "That's normal," she said. "Everything has a context."

"And my context here has got some good, and some bad, and all of it at different times," Lewis added. "It's like I've come home to *that* house. The Pale House I remember, not the one that sits up on this hill today."

Anne was silent for a few moments as she considered his words, then glanced all around them as they continued along the corridor. "So it's a museum for you, then. A personal museum of your memories."

Lewis smiled, and there was both admiration and sadness in it. "I think all houses are, at least for somebody," he said.

A little further on, his step faltered as he saw Blue Rabbit sitting on an ottoman bench between two vases, but he chose not to draw Anne's attention to the stuffed animal.

Patrons should remain in the theatre lobby between acts, he thought. *The performance isn't over.*

"I suppose the big question is why this is happening, in this way I mean," Lewis said. He was speaking mostly rhetorically, but Anne answered anyway.

"I think things happen for a reason," she said. "And the bigger the thing, the bigger the reason. I think that a person passing away is just about the biggest thing that can happen, to other people or even places. It leaves a vacuum. That's why we have funerals, to try and accept the change and start to move on."

She glanced at him and saw that he was listening intently, so she continued. "I also think that sometimes people and places can react to each other. You've got a lot of history here, and some major parts of it were bad for you. So maybe you're like—"

"A lightning rod," Lewis said, then he frowned, unsure if it was the right analogy. "Or a catalyst? Something like that."

"Something like that," Anne agreed, squeezing his arm. "I think maybe this was inevitable. Maybe it's been coming for a long time."

They walked on in silence, and a few minutes later they reached the room Lewis had been sleeping in. He could see Anne noticing how tidy and un-lived-in it looked, with the bed neatly made and his backpack sitting on a chair as if he'd only just arrived. He didn't feel much of a need to explain, knowing that she would understand.

"I won't be a minute," he said. Lewis opened the backpack and pulled out a t-shirt and a pair of jeans, along with the brown leather loafers he usually wore. He'd chosen this room partly because of the en suite shower and bathroom. He left the loafers on the floor, and had taken a couple of steps towards the connecting door when Anne spoke.

"Dair, just take your time. Nothing's happening right now," she said. "I'll call you if anything changes out here. It's been a long day, and I think there's probably more in store for us later. Have a shower or whatever you were going to do when you got back here." She sat down on the bed, seemingly content to wait, and after a moment he nodded.

"Alright," Lewis replied. "Thanks, I will. But I won't be long. Let me know if it starts snowing in here or anything."

Anne waved him off, and he went into the bathroom and closed the door. It was only a couple of minutes later when he was ready to step into the shower, and realised he'd left his toiletries bag in the backpack.

Every damned time, he thought. He'd had to make the same trip back into the main room to get shampoo each morning this week, and each time he cursed his own apparent need to be ready to leave the house at any moment. He wrapped a towel around himself and momentarily considered knocking on the interconnecting door before opening it, until he realised how bizarre that would be. Instead, he took a frustrated breath and went back out, cursing his mistake.

"Sorry," he said, pointing to the backpack, "forgot my bloody toilet bag. Stupid."

Lewis crossed to the chair where his backpack sat, and began to rummage through the bag to find his toiletries. Anne hadn't said anything, but he was aware that she was looking at him, and he found that he was self-conscious about the marks on his body. It was an old feeling, a companion throughout his life, and while there was very little shame anymore, there was certainly a reservoir of bitterness and sadness. He'd been uncomfortable with his body for that reason ever since the events that marked him, and had generally preferred to keep himself covered.

He flinched when he felt her cool hand against the worst of the scars.

Anne traced the outline of the raised line of skin, with such care and attention that Lewis almost couldn't bear it. A part of him wished he'd never shown her, and another part of him was relieved that she finally knew.

"It's ugly," he said, and he found that he was surprised at himself for letting the thought escape so easily.

Anne shook her head, visible in his peripheral vision. "What happened to you was ugly," she said quietly. "This isn't. It's part of you, and it shows that you survived, so it can't be bad."

It helped a little to hear it. He knew they were the right words, and that it would take more time — maybe more time than he had — to really accept them. But he was glad that this wasn't still something that stood between them. Lewis gave up on searching for shampoo for the moment, and turned to face her. He put on a small smile, for her sake.

"Sometimes I even forget they're there," he said. "Maybe I should get a big tattoo like a biker."

Anne ignored the quip. "You shouldn't have had to deal with any of it," she said. "And you definitely shouldn't have had to do it alone and far away from your home, even if it was the safer option. It's completely OK to feel angry about that."

Lewis nodded.

"You're not doing *this* alone, either," Anne added. "Whatever happens, I'm not going anywhere."

He felt profoundly unworthy of the sentiment, and of this woman's capacity for forgiveness and compassion, but he knew she would tell him to stop being foolish if he said so out loud.

"I should have stayed," he said instead. "I wanted to."

"Just stay now," she said, putting her hand on his cheek. This time, when she kissed him, there was no-one to interrupt.

Chapter 19

Show's about to start, lad, said the voice in Rage's mind, squeezing hard enough to make him fall onto the grass with tears of pain in his eyes.

"About fucking time," he said, patting the handle of the knife in his belt before rolling over to look up at the dark canopy of trees overhead. He didn't know how long it had been, only that his legs were numb from sitting on the cold ground, and he was so much angrier than he had ever been before.

They had made him sit and wait outside his own house. The house that had always been his, ever since he'd been here before, so long ago. But Rage knew that he'd never been here before, and that was confusing, and he also knew that it didn't matter because his father was the one who made the rules. His father, and the other man; the figure up high, at the top, in the true house that was inside the walls of the place he could see from between the trees.

Clouds covered the sky, and the pine forest was all just black outlines, but Rage could see the house just fine. It had its own glow, marking the edges and the windows and the big doors at the front, like a picture projected on the big screen at the cinema. Something to cover up something else behind.

The images in his mind were constant now, and they all seemed so familiar even though he hadn't seen any of them before tonight. He saw a woman, and a boy, and he saw room after room after room. He saw a piano, and a dining table, and a rose garden. He saw framed paintings on walls, and stairs that climbed to the sky.

There was a child's toy, an ugly cloth rabbit that was blue, and he saw a record player and a blanket and a diary with a flower pressed inside its pages. He saw a belt, curled like a snake, and oh how he wanted to hold it. He wanted to feel its weight in his hand, and by *fuck* he wanted a drink and a smoke.

You'll find it all inside, the two-man said. *Now get on home, you little bastard.*

Rage leapt to his feet, racing between the pines and running low, like an animal. He broke from the cover of the tree canopy with a wild anticipation, and it took him less than half a minute to reach the gravel access road and the turning circle.

The lights behind the windows of Pale House flickered to life to guide him in, and the main doors swung silently open to welcome him.

Lewis was pulled from dreamless unconsciousness by Anne's palm rapidly tapping his chest.

"Dair, wake up! Something's happening."

He blinked, his pulse responding to the alarm in her voice, and it took him a moment to realise that he was lying in his bed in the guest room. They had been there, and they had been in the shower next door, and then they had been in the bed again, and at last they had both drifted off to sleep. He could feel her thigh still hooked over his, and her hair had fallen haphazardly over her bare shoulders.

"What's happening?" he asked, but Anne didn't answer. The room lights blinked off and then on again, and a moment later they were almost thrown from the bed by an extended tremor that he could feel in his bones.

"Get dressed," she said, kicking the covers away with enough force to deposit most of the duvet on the floor, and Lewis couldn't resist looking at the line of her naked body again as he pushed himself up from the mattress. They dressed quickly, becoming aware of a growing sound coming from all around them, as if the building was under profound stress.

"We should go outside," Anne said for the second time that evening, and Lewis nodded.

"No argument this time," he replied, grabbing her hand as they both hurried over to the door. He grasped the door handle with his free hand, wondering whether to bring his bag too but deciding against it. "It's not far.

There's a side door downstairs that goes out to the conservatory. There's a staff stairway we can use just along the hall."

He twisted the handle and pulled the door open, and they both stepped out and then stopped in their tracks.

"My god," Lewis said.

The hallway was a travesty. Everything was in motion, floorboards running like a river as they expanded and twisted. Doors sprang into existence as the walls stretched sickeningly, with the hall spreading in width and length and height all at once. It was nauseating, and Anne clutched at Lewis and at the doorframe at the same time. The floor under their feet had a vibration to it, and Lewis's ears popped as the hallway doubled and then tripled in length while they watched.

"Dair, what should we do?" Anne asked, her voice shrill with fear, and he couldn't think of a good answer. Instead, he clamped an arm around her waist and pulled her tightly against him.

We could go back into the room, he thought. *Maybe we can ride this out in there.*

Anne seemed to have the same thought because they both turned around at once, but they immediately saw that it was no use. The ordinary and solid room they'd spent the last several hours in was there one moment, and gone the next. It became a storeroom, and then a bedroom again but a different one, and then it was the room they knew, and then it was bare planks and rough pink plaster yet to fully dry. For an instant, it was a ruin of a room, windowpanes gone and frames rotted, showing an overgrown landscape beyond which had been left untended for decades. And then it changed again.

"We have to move," Lewis said, steadying himself with one hand against the wood panelling of the hallway, refusing to look at how everything flickered and warped. "Stay beside me."

He pulled her along the corridor with him, already completely disoriented. After they'd moved what should have been only a few metres, he could already no longer tell which door led back to the room they'd been in. The windows had also stretched out and multiplied, showing a pine forest even more vast than the one that existed around the house in reality. The weather fluctuated as Lewis watched, changing abruptly from day to night, rain to snow to clear skies, and the overall effect was so profoundly disturbing that he had to tear his gaze away from it.

Lewis looked ahead to where the discreet doorway to the staff stairs should have been, but it was gone. In its place, there was only an unstable procession of wood panels, some with portrait or landscape picture frames filled with a blank, cloudy grey that he found unaccountably sinister.

Where the hell can we go?

A moment later, the wall across the gallery split neatly in two, expanding to reveal a new corridor that looked similar to the one downstairs that connected the morning room to his grandfather's drawing room, but it

was also wider and darker, with an unfamiliar arrangement of doors beyond. It was like something constructed from a template of parts taken from elsewhere in the
house. There was no way to know where it led.

"We can't stay here," Lewis said, then he guided
Anne across to the newly opened route. "Just… tell me
if you see anything you remember. There has to be a
way out somewhere."

Anne nodded, an anxious but determined look on
her face as she kept pace with him across the gallery.
They dashed into the new corridor, and the pace of
change around them seemed to slow, accompanied by a
lessening of the sounds of structural strain. They were
now in a part of the house that hadn't existed just a few
minutes ago, but it felt entirely real.

With no other option available, they both ran head-
long into the unknown.

As soon as Rage stepped through the front doors,
he knew that he was finally home.

The house's transformation erupted around him,
the sane and quiet spaces stretching and multiplying before his eyes. The entrance hall had been grand before,
but within moments it was the base of a man-made
wooden canyon of impossible size, strewn crazily with
paintings and light fixtures.

Rage walked confidently towards the bottom of the
staircase, ignoring the floor that seemed to ripple and
warp beneath his feet. He was past the outer walls that

hid the real house now, the true house, and this was his welcome ceremony.

"Back home now," he said. "Back where I belong."

He could remember much more clearly. He had lived here years ago, before he had died to get away. There was a woman that he lived with, but she was dead too now, so there was only the boy left to stand in his way. The boy that was now a man, after all this time, who had come back to steal Rage's property.

Rage's, or someone's. It was something he felt confused about, a feeling that had been growing in his mind since he killed the man yesterday. He could feel that he was himself, but he was also something much more. He was Raymond James Agnew, and his father who lived inside his mind now was James Maurice Agnew, so really Rage was both of them together. Father and son, united at last.

But there was the figure too. The thin man. The serious man. The man of the house, who had called him in, and shown him so many things. Rage knew that he was here somewhere too. It would be rude not to say hello to someone who had held onto your house for you until you were ready to take it back. Rage didn't generally give a fuck about rudeness, but his father had taught him that there were some people who deserved respect, and if you didn't give it to them then they'd hurt you, over and over, out of love.

So that's my first stop, he thought. He could feel the house responding, and he wasn't particularly surprised to find that when he set foot on the first broad step of the stairway, he was already far above the entrance, in a dark space that stretched out further than he could see. He craned his neck and looked upwards, and it seemed like the stairs climbed towards the night sky. And there was something far up above that just might have been a slender figure, lit from behind.

"Let's be fucking having you, then," he said, taking the knife from his belt.

Pale House complied, lifting him silently skyward as he squeezed the knife's handle in anticipation.

Rage didn't know how large the house was now, but he had a feeling that it didn't matter. It could change from one moment to the next, and it would always be what it needed to be at the time. That was just fine with him.

There was a breeze as he was lifted through the darkness, and he watched with a detached sort of satisfaction as he saw floor after floor stretching away from him on all sides. Corridors formed and stretched and changed, and a part of his mind that he was only distantly aware of found it all so familiar, as if the house was returning to a shape it had been in before, when Rage was last there.

But he had never been there. But he had *definitely* been there. It was a question to which maybe the figure had the answer. And if he didn't, that was alright too.

It took nearly a minute for the landing he stood upon to first begin to slow, and then come to a stop. He was certainly there now, in the place from his dreams, up at the highest point where he'd seen the shape of a person standing. He could feel the presence now, deep down in his bones, but he seemed to be alone. He looked left and right, and there was no-one, but then he looked straight ahead as the floor beneath him ceased to move at all, and sure enough, there he was.

The outline stood motionless and about ten metres away, features hidden by its hood, but when Rage took a step forward, the figure apparently decided to come to meet him. They approached each other in the dim light, the house around them falling silent in respect for these most serious of men, and Rage felt a dark excitement building within him. A kind of long-suppressed realisation, and one he was eager to make.

Let's be fucking having you, he thought, knowing there was no need to vocalise the sentiment this time around, and when he came within arm's length of the man before him, he reached out towards the figure's waiting hand.

Rage also wasn't particularly surprised to feel the cool surface of the glass under his fingers, seeing his own eyes reflected back at him from the grand mirror.

He reached up and pulled the hood of his sweatshirt even further forward, obscuring his eyes once more. He heard his father's voice in his mind, and the voice of the man who had lived and died in this house years ago, and his own voice. They were all the same. They all belonged here, in his house. In his head. The differences between the three men no longer mattered, because they had all come home.

"Time to teach that little bastard a lesson," they all said together, and Rage nodded. He still had the knife in his hand, and he knew that plenty of other options would become available if he needed them. Or wanted them.

He turned around, looking down at everything that lay below, and he saw a man and a woman exit from a corridor much further down. They would try to escape, but he wouldn't let them. This was his house, after all.

They were going nowhere until he was finished with them.

Lewis and Anne both flinched when a door on their right swung violently open and banged against the wall. It let in a freezing blast of air which staggered Lewis for a moment, but they kept running. As they went past, he glanced in the direction of the room that had been revealed, and he had a terrifying impression of someone inside, outlined against a window, watching him. He tightened his grip on Anne's hand and propelled them both onward even faster.

There was a corner ahead, forcing them to slow their pace to go around it, and then they almost ran directly into a wall. Not even wood panelling or stone, but unfinished brickwork, the surface messy and patched. Lewis slammed the base of his fist against the hard surface in frustration, then he spun around, only to see that they now stood at the top of a vast staircase that hadn't been there a moment earlier.

"Finally," Anne said, and after only a second's hesitation, they both began to make their way downwards.

That damned thing, Lewis thought, seeing that the painting of the hellish horses was on the wall above the landing they were descending towards. The painting was in motion, horses running endlessly in place, and the background was indeed flames. It was something he'd dreamed of once, or rather saw in a nightmare, and he realised that this, too, was a manifestation of a memory. He could see Anne's panicked look as she noticed the foreboding and haunted-looking artwork, but he just shook his head. Their priority was escape, and explanations could come later.

Then everything happened at once.

The sense of vibration and movement, the sound of creaking floorboards and straining timbers, the shocking change in air pressure as the walls around the staircase shot away into the darkness, revealing the appalling height they had reached. Anne cried out, grasping for a bannister and clamping her hands onto it, and Lewis fell backwards into a sitting position just a handful of steps below her.

My god, it must be fifty stories down from here, he thought. He was suddenly consumed with a feeling of utter dread, every hair on the back of his neck standing on end, and he scrambled to his feet, but it was too late. He reached up towards Anne just as the staircase ruptured above him, and for a sickening moment he was certain he was going to plunge through the gap to his death. Then a wet mouth with warm breath seized the waistband of his jeans from behind, and he felt himself hauled backwards and away from the precipice.

He gasped, twisting around, but there was no sign of anyone or anything on the stairs below.

Maisie again, it was Maisie, she's saved me on the stairs twice now, his mind chattered even as he turned back around to find Anne. She was still there, still clinging to the bannister, but she was now out of reach. The section of the stairway she was on was at least ten metres away and above him now.

"Stay there!" Lewis shouted, "I'll try to find a way around."

And then Lewis saw him.

The figure was outlined against a light source that came from far above. It was a man, slender and wearing something dark, his face obscured by the shadow of a hood. He was on a landing far above Anne, coming down towards her with something in his hand, and Lewis watched in awed and horrified fascination as stairs sprang into existence beneath his feet, forming a direct route towards her.

Anne turned to follow his gaze, and then she screamed.

Lewis couldn't see who the man was, but he instinctively knew what the subtle gleam of reflected light from the object in his hand meant. And there was something else; something about how he moved on the stairs.

A person's gait was almost like a fingerprint, and he'd seen this movement before.

Can't be, he thought, but he knew that in this house it was not only possible but likely. This was exactly the place for it, and who even knew what day or what year it was within these walls at this moment?

It's Donald. He's here for me.

"Anne, just stand aside," he called up to her, but she only glanced at him for a moment before fixing her eyes on the apparition above them again.

It was coming towards them even faster now, and Lewis had a moment of chilling realisation that whatever was going on here, the house was doing it, and it was by no means just a passive display of memories anymore. This was real, and he had every reason to believe that he was in genuine danger. Donald had never come at him with a knife, and he'd never been dressed like this, so they were seeing something new. The implications were terrifying.

Anne shrank back against the bannister at one side of the stairs, nowhere else to go as the figure above reached the landing they'd been on. All too late, Lewis saw the man look not at him, but at Anne herself, and at that moment some property of the shifting light caused just a sliver of the hooded man's face to become visible.

His eyes seemed to shift in colour from one instant to the next, and Lewis thought for a fraction of a second that it really was Donald. But then he recognised the angular chin, and the cruel slash of a mouth, and even the look on the man's face.

Agnew. The man from the other night. How is he here?

Then the head within the hood turned, and Lewis felt a cold hand close its fingers around his heart, because somehow it really was Donald too, unmistakably, with that same pinched look of caged fury that he'd learned to dread as a teenager. It was Donald, but it was also Agnew, and Lewis had no idea what that meant, but he knew it was a very bad thing.

Anne screamed again as the man reached for her with his empty hand, and Agnew caught her hair and dragged her brutally back up the short stretch of stairs to the landing. Then he took another look back down at Lewis, and there was no triumph in it, only raw, unfiltered hatred. He made no sound when he spoke, only mouthing the words, but Lewis could understand perfectly.

My house.

Anne was hitting the man with her fists, but it seemed to have no effect at all, and Lewis was agonisingly aware of the knife that Agnew held in his other hand. Suddenly a different corridor burst into existence, connecting to the landing that Agnew and Anne were on, and the man wasted no time in releasing her hair only to throw an arm around her waist and lift her off her feet as if she weighed nothing. Then they disappeared from view, taking the entire corridor and the landing with them a moment later. Lewis felt his stomach lurch, and his pulse was drumming in his ears.

Anne was gone.

Chapter 20

The stairs above Lewis began to fall away, dropping one by one into whatever lay at the bottom of the void they floated above. In desperation, he looked first one way and then the other, but there was nowhere to go that was at his level or higher. With a curse, he turned and ran downwards instead.

He had a sick feeling in his stomach, the sense of being up too high and no longer being connected to firm ground. It was the lurch of reorientation when an aircraft left the runway, or the nauseating twist of perspective when lying face-up on the ground at night and realising you're clinging to the face of a sphere suspended in the infinite darkness of space.

Like a lamp suddenly switching on in a dark room, there was suddenly a landing ahead of him where none had been a moment ago, and he leapt down six steps in his haste to reach it. He landed awkwardly, having to drop and roll, and for a terrifying moment he thought he would overshoot and tumble down the endless stairs beyond. But he caught hold of a newel post and hauled himself back onto his feet.

The stairs were still dropping away above him, the chasm they made getting nearer now, and Lewis knew he had no choice. The landing had a single feature, only a couple of metres away from the connecting stairways: an ornate set of double doors that he recognised as originally leading to a reception room in Pale House's physical reality. He had no idea where they led here, in this place, but he knew that it had to be better than a long fall to his death. He darted forward, grasped both brass doorhandles at once, and wrenched the doors open.

Somehow, Agnew was in the chamber beyond, and Anne was with him. They'd previously been at least one floor above him, but they were here now, and there were others too. Agnew had Anne by her upper arm, at the opposite end of the room from Lewis and just beside the closed door of a closet. He was watching Lewis with a sickening stare, filled with bile and hatred and predation. But Lewis's attention was entirely consumed by the two new people who formed the centrepiece of the scene.

My god, Lewis thought.

The room was his own, from his childhood, but much bigger. A vast empty floor stretched between his bed in one corner, his desk in another, his wardrobe, and the few other items of furniture he recognised immediately. Standing in the middle of it all was Donald, and he had Lewis's younger self gripped by the upper arm in exactly the same way that Agnew grasped Anne. As the dead man wrenched at the boy's shoulder, Lewis felt the phantom pain of it, and he knew that this was a genuine memory. Only the surroundings were distorted. This had actually happened.

This vision of Donald from long ago seemed to notice him, and met his eyes for a moment to sneer in disgust. It was a familiar expression, chilling in his recognition of it, and at the same moment Agnew mirrored the look, movement for movement. It was then that Lewis understood.

Agnew is Donald. Somehow they're the same here.

Donald wrenched the boy's arm yet again, and he was moving his lips now. He seemed to be shouting, but there was no sound, and the boy that Lewis used to be cowered from him, raising his free arm to protect himself against a blow that never came. Donald had always been far too careful for that. It took the very extremes of his—

Rage

—anger for him to actually leave a mark, or do anything that couldn't be denied. Even then, there were the lies and the accusations, of course, but for the most part he had been the cunning sort of monster. The kind who plays off ever-ready geniality and denial in equal measure to conceal their work.

The memory played out in Lewis's mind simultaneously with what he was seeing. Angered by the boy's act of raising his arm defensively, Donald said something — still silent, like television with the volume all the way down — and then drew back his arm and slapped the young Lewis on the top of the head with his open palm.

It had always hurt like hell, even through his hair. Donald had large hands, and the force reverberated through his skull. His scalp was always tender for days afterwards, and he had learned to hate combs for that very reason. But there was never any bruise to see, and the redness was hidden away. His erstwhile stepfather had always taken care to use his right hand, so that the ugly ring he wore on the middle finger of his left hand couldn't cause a wound that would be far harder to deny.

The boy crumpled to his knees, and Lewis felt an explosion of fury and shame and powerlessness. He tensed, readying himself to spring forward and kill this vision of Donald with his bare hands, but then the man and the boy were suddenly gone, leaving him looking across the distorted expanse of the chamber towards Agnew and his own captive.

Anne was aghast. Silent with big, liquid eyes, and even at this distance Lewis could read everything in them. He could see the realisation, the pity and the sympathy, the disgust and the horror, the anger at the event from the past and still more anger at him being forced to see it again here, brought back to life to hurt him once more. What he didn't see right now, though, was fear, and a small part of his mind that could still reflect calmly on things felt a burst of admiration for her.

"Insufferable little bastard," Agnew said suddenly, and the sound of it echoed across to Lewis as if they were in a cathedral or a museum.

Which I suppose we are, in a way, his mind whispered.

It was what Donald had always called him, but there was more to it than that. With a leap of intuition that might also just have been the product of a panicked and frantic mind, Lewis thought he could see something deeper than just a mirror of Donald's own distaste in Agnew's face.

Lewis's heart stuttered when he heard his mother's voice.

It was coming from somewhere nearby, and there was a man's voice too, which he immediately recognised as Donald's. This time, though, the event was entirely new to him, and he realised that he was hearing his mother appeasing the man.

I really don't know what you're so upset about, his mother's voice said. *Dair is a good boy. There are teenagers who are far worse. You two should spend more time together.*

Then it was the long-ago Donald's voice, exactly as Lewis remembered it.

He's never accepted me here, Margaret. Still pining for his useless father, I expect. I swear he's trying to infuriate me.

The words chilled Lewis even now. His mother responded but the words were becoming harder to hear, not that he really needed any more than the tone. It was the sound of a woman making allowances and keeping a veneer on things that she knew were very much worse than she was admitting to herself. It was probably a sound heard far too often, everywhere in the world.

Lewis turned to look again at the thing that was partly Agnew, and partly Donald, and whatever else. The man's eyes seemed to glow from across the stretched room, and Lewis was certain they were shifting colours restlessly, from blue to green to brown.

Anne lashed out at Agnew, but he deflected the blow easily, bringing the knife to her throat. Lewis ran forward, but came to a stop after only a short distance when Agnew shook his head and grinned ghoulishly. The disembodied voices continued, and Lewis had no choice but to listen to them.

Donald became angry, decrying the lack of respect he was shown as the man of the house. Lewis's mother talked him down. Donald said that a young man should know his limits, and that he had never signed up for being a surrogate father. Lewis's mother remained silent on that point. And then the voices faded away.

Suddenly the scene around them changed. They were now at the upper landing of the main staircase of the entrance hall, with the front doors of Pale House visible down below. They were open, and a man stood there — Lewis's father. He was much younger, and the thinnest he'd ever been. Lewis knew exactly what period of his life this particular vista was from. His mother stood within the doorway, and she seemed to be relaying unpleasant news.

Sure enough, Donald marched into the frame, made bold by the cowardliness of being the one who had a right to be there within the house, and Lewis's father made a valiant attempt to ignore him before Donald began to speak.

"He's not available tonight, and he won't be available until you catch up on the child support payments the court ordered you to pay."

There was unsuppressed malice and triumph in his voice, and Lewis had no doubt that the event had taken place in just this manner. He remembered being told that his father had missed two consecutive weeks of what he had to pay, and Lewis had pleaded with his mother that he didn't mind and he just wanted to see his father, but then Donald had been there and made it very clear that it wasn't going to happen. Lewis had watched his father's car arrive, and then depart a short while later, but he had never heard the actual conversation at the door. It was easy to see how his father had felt.

Ross Lewis of the past stood down there, body tense and hands clenched into fists, as emotions cycled across his face: surprise, indignation, fury, and finally an icy calmness that was clearly the product of sheer willpower.

He knew that any reaction would only provoke something worse, Lewis thought, and sure enough he watched as his father turned without a word and walked rigidly back to his car.

Donald threw a comment after him, but the sound of the scene was already beginning to fade and Lewis couldn't quite catch it. It didn't matter; he hated Donald doubly much now, regardless of whatever the man had said. He watched as his former stepfather slammed the doors of Pale House and turned to Lewis's mother with wicked pride on his face. To her credit, Margaret walked away without so much as a glance at him, and then the scene lost cohesion completely.

Lewis was back in the stretched, distorted version of his childhood bedroom, and now the closet door on the opposite wall was open, with Agnew already pulling Anne inside it. There was a corridor there now, and it seemed to be built on an incline, going downwards into shadow. The two figures vanished into the gloom, leaving Lewis standing alone in this pocket of memory.

The only other option was going back, and he didn't consider it for even a second. Anne was ahead, and so apparently was whatever parts of the past that the house wanted him to relive. The only way was forward.

Ready or not, he thought, then he ran across the room and plunged into the darkness of the closet and whatever lay beyond.

"Why are you doing this? Let me go, you bastard," Anne spat, refusing to give the man — the thing — that held her the satisfaction of pleading or tears.

Agnew looked at her briefly, but it was an empty glance, almost devoid of recognition as he marched her relentlessly onwards. The corridor sloped down and down, and they were going fast enough that she feared tripping and falling forward. His grip was too firm, though, and he kept her moving relentlessly onwards.

He didn't respond, and she thought about trying to break free by attacking him, but no sooner had the idea entered her mind when he fastened a much more attentive gaze on her without breaking his stride. Anne's blood froze as she saw the incessant colour change of his eyes, and the sense of him somehow being more prominent against the background than everything else, like there was a faint illumination all around him.

"You'll want to be a respectful young lady," Agnew said, and his voice made her want to scream. It was *wrong* in a way she couldn't articulate or fasten her mind onto, as if it came from more than one place at once. Even his face seemed to shift from one moment to the next, as the play of light and shadow across his features gave emphasis first to one feature and then another, making it seem like there were several men there at once, taking turns to look out through a shared pair of eyes.

It was a relief when they burst through into the light of another room, and Anne saw that it was in fact a gallery like the one with the grandfather clock, but warped in length and especially in height. There were still large glass windows looking down to the nighttime ground below, but these windows might have been a hundred feet high, and she couldn't even tell whether she was standing on the second floor or the twentieth.

Everything was untrustworthy, and everything felt like a trick of the light.

Agnew, or whoever it really was now, released her and stepped over to the handrail running along the edge of the gallery towards the tall windows, and laid his hands on the polished wood. Anne spun around and searched for the doorway they'd just come through, meaning to run back up the corridor as fast as she could and find Lewis, but the door was gone. In its place was a portrait of Donald, the man she'd seen in the false entrance hall minutes ago, staring out at her with the same eyes she'd seen blazing from Agnew's face.

"I remember this too," Agnew said aloud to himself, startling her. She turned slowly to look at him, fists clenched, but he was facing away from her, his gaze directed downwards. He seemed to be looking out of the lowest panes of the soaring windows towards the moonlit ground outside. It was covered in snow, though the sky was clear for the moment, and then Anne really did scream as a huge explosion rattled all of the vast expanse of glass.

Colours bloomed against the black sky, streamers and particles and rings of light, and she realised that she was looking at a fireworks display. Everything was pale blue, as if it was the only colour that the world outside had ever heard of, and she suddenly very much didn't want to see the light reflected on the face of the man over at the bannister. She flinched again at another bang, but this was much closer, and it took only a moment to realise it as the sound of a door being throw open against the wall.

Despite her revulsion, she ran to the gallery's edge too, keeping a wide distance between her and Agnew, but he paid her no attention. Below them she could hear footsteps thudding on the thick carpet, and after a moment her pulse quickened again as Lewis came into view.

"Anne?" Lewis called, expecting to see her just ahead of him, but he seemed to be alone in this strange version of some part of Pale House, stretched and re-assembled from areas glimpsed elsewhere without any real understanding or plan.

"Dair!"

He heard the cry and he turned around, craning his neck, and caught sight of her immediately. Less than a second later, he saw Agnew too, only a few metres to one side, and now the man's eyes were their own source of light.

Then a muffled boom from behind him, beyond the windows, and so he spun back around and saw the patterns of falling light in the sky. He recognised them immediately, and he felt his stomach clench with shame and anger.

He walked over to the windows, letting himself dredge up the memory and the feelings associated with it, because he knew he had no real choice in the matter here. Lewis reached the glass, and watched as the perspective shifted like a focus-pull, lifting his viewpoint so that despite having appeared to be on the ground floor a moment ago, he was now looking out from the vantage point of being several storeys high. And sure enough, the small figure appeared outside, moving out from the cover of the tree line.

It had been the town's winter festival, not long before Lewis's seventeenth birthday. The winter before the summer of the other fireworks display, with Anne. This one had been part of national celebrations of the country's heritage and cultural identity, and there had been a week of coordinated events nationwide, including an evening of simultaneous fireworks in most settlements across Scotland. It had been on the news around the world, at least in places where nothing more important was going on, and to ensure that the message of pride in the country was clearly conveyed, the government had supplied the fireworks all in blue.

Lewis remembered that it had felt more eerie than patriotic, but it was certainly unforgettable. And it had also coincided with one of his lowest points in the closing months before he had finally left Dunleven for good.

He didn't bother to turn and look up to see Anne's expression. She knew nothing of this night other than the festivities, which she'd surely remember as well as he did. She had no idea of its special and poignant significance for him. But she would soon, because the small figure outside had moved far enough across open ground now to finally escape the shadow of the forest and be caught in the pale glare of the moon.

Even from here I look too thin, Lewis thought.

He remembered that it had snowed again later, and he'd been glad of it as a cloak and as a reason for others to go straight home, but for now the sky remained clear. The moon was a crescent, enormous and yellow instead of silver, and to Lewis's eye it seemed like the blade of a scythe held by something impossibly huge and hidden beyond the horizon.

As Lewis watched, he found that he could actually feel what his younger self was experiencing, outside and all those years ago. He could feel the cold, and he could smell the faint traces of acrid smoke from pyrotechnics. He could smell the pine forest too, fresh and heavy and crisp, and then he could smell that particular sharpness of the air over a snow-covered landscape. Those smells should have been pleasant and invigorating, and perhaps even tinged with the unblemished excitement of a night such as this when seen through immature eyes. But those weren't his reactions at all, because he could also feel what the younger Lewis was feeling inside.

It was to have been the final night of his life, at least according to his fogged and desperate mind at the time.

This was how far I'd fallen, he thought, feeling the eyes of the monster that was an avatar of his persecutor, boring into him from above and behind. Then he heard the man's voice, and Lewis wasn't surprised to hear that he spoke now almost completely as Donald.

"Should have minded your elders, you little shit," his dead stepfather said through the mouth of Agnew, from up on the gallery's balcony. "Or had the courage to go through with it."

Lewis glanced back over his shoulder and up towards the sound, in time to see Anne looking from one man to the other, confused and wary.

"It's alright," Lewis said to her, aware of the ridiculousness of the statement but feeling a need to comfort her nonetheless. "If this is what he wants to show me, then so be it. It's part of my past, and I don't deny it." Lewis shifted his attention to the thing standing just a few metres to Anne's side.

"I was a child, and you were supposed to be a man. This only reflects on you."

Agnew only sneered, but of course it was Donald's sneer, twisting the unfamiliar features of his face into familiar shapes.

"You'll miss the good bit," Donald said through Agnew, nodding in the direction of the large windows, and so Lewis turned in that direction once more.

The adolescent beyond and below the glass wasn't dressed warmly enough for the weather, and his breath was clearly visible in plumes as he trudged through the thickening blanket of snow. Lewis remembered leaving Pale House that evening, and deliberately forgoing a jacket because he saw little point in it.

The scene hadn't taken place here, of course, adjacent to the house. It had been farther out, on the other side of the pine forest that stretched across much of the

Lambert land that crowned the whole hill, with the house at its centre. He'd had to walk for what seemed like half an hour or more to break through the far tree line and see the town laid out before him. It had all been orange sodium street lamps and warm yellow light peeking from behind curtains, lighting up hundreds of rectangles of condensated glass like the panes of a cathedral. And then the strange bloom of blue light in the sky above, coming from the park near the centre of Dunleven, enlarging the cold sky and drawing the eye upwards.

The river down below the hill was fast-flowing, with many a jagged rock, and the temperature alone would be lethal enough. Lewis had known all that at the time. A jacket would only have prolonged things. And so he stood there, shivering already, looking down at the scene before him just as his older self was looking down upon him now, and he had experienced what many people do when they're about to take their own lives: everything was so agonisingly beautiful.

In a melancholy and out-of-reach way, yes, but on this particular night it had been close to spectacular. A perfect winter's evening, in an isolated pocket of natural paradise, with a spectacle up above. A night to enjoy with a cold nose and a hot drink, sharing the experience with loved ones. A night not to be repeated, because even if the circumstances came again, the particular moment in time never would.

The worst part was that it had been so beautiful.

Lewis could hear the gasp from the balcony that indicated Anne understood what she was seeing, and he was angry with himself for feeling shame about it all over again.

Because it wasn't me, he thought. *I was standing there, but I wasn't the one who put me there.*

His mind had finally been made up by a well-meaning teacher asking how he was doing, as he wandered the school's corridors one lunchtime. He had sought solitude, but had found compassion instead. It had seemed like another example of his terminally bad luck at the time, though he had been grateful for it in the years since. A mathematics teacher whose eyes were a little too wise, asking if he was OK, really OK, and telling him that it was always wise to talk about how you were feeling.

Lewis had felt only the panic of discovery, and his carefully blank and neutral expression had probably only caused additional concern. The teacher had allowed him to go on his way, though, and for Lewis it had been a sign that his vague schedule would have to be accelerated. The thought of a concerned phone call or letter home was unbearable; it would have been fastened onto immediately by his faux stepfather, and then things would only become much, much worse. Escape was the only option — but from life, not just the house.

"You don't even understand why I didn't go ahead with it, do you?" Lewis asked aloud.

"You were a coward and a waste of life," Donald said through his puppet, and Lewis turned around.

"That's what I thought on this night," he replied. "But no. That describes you, not me. And you know that, don't you?"

Donald didn't reply, instead stalking slowly over to where Anne stood, still holding the knife in his hand. She backed away, but there was nowhere to go. The thing that was Donald and Agnew together came to a halt, his point already conveyed, then he looked down at the present-day Lewis for a moment, before directing his gaze out beyond the glass again.

The past Lewis was still standing there, sometimes looking up at the sky, and sometimes at the town below, and sometimes to the river that was nearer still. His plan had been to throw himself off a particular over-hanging area of the hillside, knowing that he'd hit the river at the bottom and be swept away in the current. The season would ensure hypothermia set in quickly, and he'd lose consciousness and drown. A bad fate, but one without the need for any action other than stepping off the edge.

As they all watched, the younger Lewis became distracted by the fireworks, which at that moment seemed to exist for this sole purpose. The tempo in-creased, and seemingly the volume of the explosions too, creating a hypnotic effect that was only enhanced by the monochromatic colour scheme. The rhythmic spectacle had probably saved his life.

After a few minutes, all sound and light outside the windows vanished, as if the glass had been painted black in an instant. Lewis faced his tormentor once again.

"What's the point of all this? Why did you choose this to show me?" he asked, and he was surprised to see the flash of confusion on Donald's borrowed face.

Rage existed in a state that was like a dream that you know is a dream, but can't wake up from.

He knew that someone else — the stairway figure, the older man, the person from before — was directing his movements and his words, but it felt so completely right that he had no intention of resisting. He could still feel the pressure in his skull that warned of the pain he'd suffer if he tried to push back against his master's wishes, but he also understood that this other man was not his father. It had used his father's voice and manner and punishments, yes, but it wasn't him. It was something else.

The intruder standing below him, the spoiled brat of a child now grown up, the bastard who got between him and his wife… but Rage had never been married either. His thoughts were softening around the edges, blending into other thoughts and feelings, like blown leaves swallowed by a dark tide. It felt like he was being discouraged to even think at all.

That suited him just fine.

But the other presence within him, the master and the puppeteer, the man that the little grown-up shit had called Donald, had just hesitated for the first time. There had been a flash of confusion. Rage knew exactly what it was about, because he could see the thoughts in his mind just as easily as he could see his own thoughts and memories. Donald had thought that the man called Lewis was responsible for these scenes they were all chasing through. He believed it was unconscious, but definitely the little shit's fault. But now he wasn't so sure, because Lewis had asked why *Donald* had chosen to show him the night of those strange fireworks that Rage himself could distantly remember. Rage had spent most of that night smoking and breaking the wing mirrors off parked cars while the town was distracted. You didn't forget a great night like that.

But it hadn't come from Donald, and apparently it hadn't come from Lewis either. Rage could feel that Donald wasn't happy about that. There was a distrustful bitterness and hatred welling up inside their shared body that Rage found so familiar and so thrilling and so sickeningly comforting. It was the same feeling he had when his father would decide the time had come around again to show him how much he loved him, using his fists and his belt and his boots.

Something wasn't going according to plan. That was always the cause for his father's anger, and it was the same for this man Donald. Rage himself didn't care at all. All he really knew was that whatever was happening, it was his destiny to be part of it. He was important, and he mattered, and this was the biggest night of his life. He could feel the knife still in his hand, and he knew for certain that the man who was pulling his strings intended for him to use it before the night was through. So he could wait.

You're right about that much, the voice boomed in his mind, and Rage tried to flinch but found that his body was held rigid. There was pain, though. That came through loud and clear.

"Because you're in my house again, and you're going to regret coming back, boy," Rage found himself saying. It was Donald's voice, and he knew that Donald was looking out of his eyes.

What Rage really wanted to do was put the knife through the woman cowering nearby, and to his surprise and delight, he suddenly found himself lunging towards her.

Chapter 21

Lewis clenched his fists when he saw Donald-Agnew suddenly spring toward Anne and grab a fistful of her hair, pulling her painfully towards him. The incandescent man held the knife up to her throat, and Lewis felt his pulse accelerating out of control.

"No!" he shouted, unable to tear his gaze away from the two figures above for long enough to look for a way to get up there. "Leave her alone! It's me you're here for."

There was anger and hatred on the blended man's face, and Lewis felt his stomach turn over as he saw that there was actually more of Agnew in him right now than Donald. His stepfather had loved nothing more than cruelty, but had drawn the line at anything conspicuous and undeniable. He had been a cowardly bully and a psychological torturer. Agnew seemed to be more of a sociopath.

To Lewis's relief, the man above didn't make any more moves. He could see the tears on Anne's face from the pain of how she was being restrained, and in that moment he swore that he'd kill Agnew as soon as he had the chance. Not if, but when.

The windows were still pitch black, and Lewis suddenly understood that the man above was temporarily at a loss as to what to do next. As if he'd lost control of the situation somehow, or was reconsidering his options.

But why?

There was something he was missing. Some insight or conclusion that he should have made earlier, but which the stress of the situation was preventing him from seeing. He felt that whatever it was, it was the key to his own next move, but he was damned if he could extract anything more specific or useful from his frantic mind at the moment. The advantage was clearly Donald's, since Lewis himself could do nothing from down here, and he also apparently couldn't go anywhere except where the man wanted him to. Through his own worst memories, stretched across the framework of Pale House as a canvas for them all, towards an unknown purpose.

If he wanted to kill me, he could have done it by now, he thought. *A dozen times at least. Whatever his goal, it must involve me seeing all of this. Is it just cruelty?*

It would be a believable conclusion given the character of the man when he was alive, and also the apparent nature of the still-living man he'd somehow merged himself with. A parade of painful recollection, replaying the least-great hits of his early life. But why bother? Donald could hurt him far more by killing Anne, and he hadn't done that yet either.

I should keep him talking, he thought. *Find a way to engage him. If he's focused on me, he won't get any ideas about Anne.*

"This is about you and me, isn't it? Our history together, here in this house? You were a bastard then and you're a bastard now."

Lewis shouted the words, finding that he didn't have to manufacture the bravado at all. It came directly from the fury that so readily rose up within him, and he felt an animalistic triumph as he saw the dark hatred twisting Agnew's features from within. In the same instant, Lewis knew exactly what he'd say next.

"I didn't jump in the end, no matter how much you pushed me towards it. But you did. Right upstairs. Who's the real fucking coward here?"

The volley hit its mark, and Donald used Agnew's body to throw Anne to the ground, forgotten. She crawled backwards and away from him on the thick carpet, still without an exit that didn't involve a dangerous drop over the bannister, but at least she wasn't his target for the moment.

It seemed like Donald would explode with anger, but then he abruptly became still. Lewis's blood ran cold as he watched it happen. The man's piercing eyes focused on him, still shifting constantly from green to brown to blue and then back again, and when he spoke it was with a voice like ice.

"I"m going to add you to this place, boy," he said.

Lewis didn't know what he meant by that, but he did know that he didn't like it at all. His arms broke out in gooseflesh, and he made a conscious effort not to look towards where Anne was crouched at one of the pedestals holding up the bannister further along the gallery's balcony.

The windows cleared as if a cloud had moved aside, and Lewis turned around, startled. It was full daylight outside now, and he could see the turning circle outside the main entrance to Pale House. There was a car there, the one his mother had driven years ago, and he watched in silence as his younger self walked into view, heading away from the house, and got into the car without looking back. Again, he knew immediately what day it was.

When I left this place for good, he thought. *She drove me as far south as Inverness, then put me on a train to Edinburgh. I pretended to read a book, but I ended up crying in the onboard toilet.*

As he watched, he saw the back of his mother as she once was, dressed plainly and in light clothing befitting the summer's day and the long drive ahead of her. Her posture was admirably upright and steady given the circumstances. Lewis remembered beginning the car ride hating her, but by the time they reached the railway station later in the morning, he no longer felt anything at all. That latter feeling had persisted for weeks, or maybe even months.

The car started and then moved off, going through the same gateposts and vanishing from view, and then everything else outside was drained of colour. Lewis felt his ears pop, and then at last he heard the creaking that meant the house was going to shift once again. He looked up quickly, to see that Donald had already grabbed Anne again, and Lewis saw that a passageway had opened behind them.

A doorway also lay ahead of him, wood panelled like all the rest, but a full set of double doors this time. He pulled them both open to reveal a short staircase, and his pulse accelerated as he actually saw Donald-Agnew pushing Anne ahead of him just past the top of it. He finally had an opportunity to catch up, and he ran up the twelve or so steps as quickly as he would have when he was twenty years younger.

"Dair!" Anne called out when she caught sight of him, and Donald gave him a baleful glare before urging her forward even faster. They were all in a twisted hallway, gently spiralling away ahead, and Lewis couldn't see what lay at the end of it. The curving walls were decorated with endless copies of the flaming horses painting, but without the horses themselves. Just fields of fire, all in motion, giving the disturbing impression of being windows looking out from the corridor into some hellscape outside.

Suddenly the picture frames all went blank for a moment, and then Lewis saw his mother in each of them, but not as a portrait. It was a scene playing out, as if each frame was a television tuned to the same channel as all the rest. Anne caught sight of it too, and Lewis did his best to pay attention to the images as he chased after Donald and his captive. Somehow they were getting away from him, though, and it took Lewis a moment to notice that Agnew's and Anne's feet were only occasionally touching the floor. Donald was taking great moon-leaps now, just like in a dream, and Lewis could feel a correspondingly dreamlike sense of being weighed down and held back. He struggled all the harder, sweat on his brow.

There was sound in the framed scene now too. His mother had walked into one of the rooms of the house that Lewis recognised as her own father's old study, and was dialling a number on a landline telephone. A few moments passed and someone obviously picked up at the other end, and it only took a couple of sentences to realise that she was talking to Lewis himself. He even thought he recognised the conversation.

I was in Edinburgh by then, he remembered. *I hated hearing from her, but she called regularly for that first year or two.*

She was saying that she was fine, and asking how he was enjoying his new school. She asked a series of questions about his schoolwork, and the living arrangements in the dormitories, and it was obvious that she was interested not in the answers but just in hearing his voice. She cradled the phone like a precious thing, holding it close as if she was losing her hearing, and her eyes were clearly seeing none of her immediate surroundings.

Lewis found that he did indeed remember this conversation. It had angered him, in fact. She'd said that maybe it would be best if he boarded at the school over Christmas, and she could make the trip down to see him in the new year for a few days. She would stay at a hotel in the city, once things had quietened down after the festivities, and they could catch up properly without the crowds and the distractions. Lewis remembered sullenly agreeing at the time, and inwardly viewing it as a kind of rejection. All the same, he had been very glad of the reprieve from a trip back up north to Dunleven. The very last place he ever wanted to return to was Pale House, for as long as Donald was there.

I always wondered if he listened to the phone calls, he thought, but the idea had always been petulant and foolish. Donald would have had no interest at all in how he was doing, and wouldn't want to be reminded that Lewis was even alive. Sure enough, Margaret was alone in the room of this memory, with the door closed for privacy.

Something flashed across his mind. Something significant. But with the exertion of trying desperately to catch up with Anne and the puppeteered Agnew who drew her deeper into the house, he couldn't quite follow the train of thought to its conclusion.

He felt like he was making more progress now, picking up speed and feeling less restrained, but Donald was much further ahead than he had been when Lewis had reached the top of the stairs a couple of minutes ago. The corridor twisted onwards, and seemed to be tending slightly downwards. Within the picture frames, the long-ago conversation was ending, and when his mother placed the phone handset back on its base, the scene faded out to be replaced by a stranger one.

It was a fractured image, like something viewed through a broken kaleidoscope, showing a place that was clearly one of the bathrooms here in Pale House — or at least in the real, physical version of the house that might remain somewhere within the labyrinth of stairways and corridors and rooms and memories that Lewis and Anne seemed to be trapped in. There were dark tiles on the floor and bright white tiles on the walls, with pipework and porcelain and glass. The viewpoint shifted, and then Lewis saw something that made his step falter. It was a towel, one of the pale green ones his mother had always liked, lying on the bathroom floor as if discarded. There was blood on it, and too much for just a nick from a razor or similar minor injury.

He thought he could hear breathing, and the pitch suggested it was female, but then the scene in the frames shifted again. Lewis glanced ahead just in time to see Agnew's head turn away from the images, and there was no triumph or sneering vindictiveness now. If anything, the expression that Donald wore through Agnew's face was one of alarm.

Anne's shout surprised him.

"There was no-one else there!"

It all clicked into place in Lewis's mind. His mother's phone call to him had been in private, just as they all probably were. Whatever the scene in the bathroom had been, it was in private too. Bathrooms were places of privacy by default. Lewis himself was hundreds of miles away, and Donald was at least elsewhere in the house or even outside of it at those times.

So some of these memories aren't either his or mine, he thought.

He had thought that Donald was somehow making him relive his own memories, with some of Donald's thrown in — like the incident with Lewis's father at the main entrance — to maximise the trauma of the experience. But that wasn't the case at all. Donald wasn't in the driving seat of these scenes any more than Lewis was. There was something else going on.

As if on cue, Donald seemed to lose some of his buoyancy or whatever it was, and he and Anne hit the corridor floor harder than before, almost falling to their knees, but he gripped her arm and pulled her onwards with him. The carpeting ahead gave way to polished floors, and then they were all spilling out into the ballroom, or at least a place that had clearly been inspired by it. It was enormous, like a grand carousel with the mechanism and horses removed, and far more of the walls were covered in mirrors than was the case in the real room. Lewis could see a hundred copies of himself at least, and he raised a hand to shield his eyes from the light of the vast chandelier hanging over it all. Disorientated and blinking, he lost track of where Anne was for a moment, and then heard her gasp echoing off all of the hard surfaces.

Lewis saw himself standing nearby.

The apparition was within a mirror, somehow not further reflected around the room, and was perhaps two years old. The child looked up at him in calm recognition, and then darted out of sight beyond the edge of the mirror's frame. He reappeared at an adjacent mirror, but hesitant now, unsteady on his feet with arms outwards and upwards at an angle. He moved with difficulty from one side of the next mirror to the other, stumbling the last few steps, and then vanished again.

Younger, Lewis thought. *He's younger than a moment ago.*

Anne was only a few metres away now, and she pointed. Lewis saw the child a third time, still behind glass, but on its hands and knees, crawling slowly and without much coordination. At the next mirror, it only sat before being snatched up by pale and slender arms whose owner couldn't be seen. And at one further mirror a moment later, there was a bassinet that Lewis recognised well. It had been his own, and was probably still in the attic somewhere, if the attic still existed here.

A procession of visions of himself, younger and younger. He had no idea what it meant, but from the look on Donald's borrowed face, he wasn't at all happy about it. He snarled, still outlined from his surroundings by the strange light, and his eyes were cycling in colour even faster now.

"Nosy, disrespectful little bastard," Donald said, letting go of Anne to fully face Lewis, knife still in hand. Instead of fear, Lewis felt only rage, perhaps for the first time fully accepting that this somehow *was* the man who had tormented and bullied and brutalised him years before. He felt the hate rise up within him, and before he had time to consciously acknowledge the decision, he was running towards Donald.

Lewis was peripherally aware of Anne's face contorting in horror, and she shouted something, but he didn't care. No argument or plea could have stopped him in that moment — he only wanted to kill the thing that had no right to be back alive again, no right to be back in this house, and who never had the right to be here in the first place.

The entire floor of the ballroom abruptly tilted on its axis, throwing Lewis from his feet while he was still a few metres away from Agnew and Anne.

He collided with the sprung floor painfully, jarring his shoulder, then rolled over several times before managing to get his arms and legs spread out to keep him in place. The floor still felt like it was at a strange angle, and for the moment he couldn't lift his head to seek out Anne again. He could hear her, though, crying out somewhere close by — but it was the sound of aggression, not fear.

Lewis finally managed to flip himself over and at least draw himself up onto his elbows and knees, his head reeling with nausea at the shifting and uncertain surface beneath him. He felt sure he would slide off the floor at any moment, plunging into darkness below, but as he looked around frantically he instead felt the floor begin to return to a level position below him.

His surroundings had changed. The ballroom had expanded, moving the walls further away without stretching the floor too, so now there was a cliff-edge of polished wood on all sides, then a large gap before the walls hovered in empty space. The floor itself had also broken in two, in a great jagged and ripped line that he was amazed he hadn't heard happening, and the two approximate halves were further apart than he had any hope of bridging with a leap.

Anne and Agnew were on the other half, and Lewis was about to curse this new setback when he realised the absurdity of what he'd been about to do. The man across the gulf of empty space from him was most certainly Donald, but Donald was also dead and gone. He may still have life here in this perversion of Pale House, but beyond its ultimate and physical walls, he was a footnote in history. The human being that Lewis was looking at was actually a local man — a lunatic and a threat and most likely a criminal, yes, but still just a living and breathing person from the present-day town. Lewis didn't like this man Agnew at all, but killing him for the actions of his dead stepfather who now somehow animated him? It was unjustifiable. And if Lewis was honest with himself, probably damned unlikely too.

Doesn't look like it's the first time he's held a knife to someone's throat, he thought. *Or maybe even killed someone.*

He would kill Agnew only if he had to, but he would get Anne out of this place safely. Somehow, he would get her out. He didn't have long to begin pondering how exactly he might do that before all the mirrors on the now distant walls sprang to life with images, exactly as the picture frames had in the warped corridor that led them all here.

It was Donald again, younger and alive, and the look on his face was almost like the expression that he now had stretched over Agnew's features. Darkness and anger and hatred, emanating from a pinched and red-cheeked grimace that still had the power to turn Lewis's stomach. It wasn't clear at first what he was looking at, but the perspective shifted a moment later, and Lewis audibly inhaled.

My god, that's him.

The child was beautiful. Clearly only a handful of months old, still with just wisps of dark hair over a large pink head, wrapped tightly in a yellow knitted blanket. Lewis could see the Lambert genetics in the shape of the little boy's face around the eyes, but the eyes themselves were closed, and as more of the scene became visible, it was obvious that the baby was in the same bassinet he'd seen in these same mirrors a short while ago.

In the mirrors, Donald reached down and prodded the child roughly in the face.

When the boy didn't wake up immediately, he did it again, and this time the baby was startled from sleep, blinking with its strange and unfocused eyes, and then the piercing tone of its cries filled the disembodied ballroom.

Lewis felt a murderous protectiveness, and was unable to look away as the image of Donald from years ago actually used his bunched fingers to slap the child repeatedly, muttering *Oh shut the fuck up, you hideous troll.* When the baby continued to cry, Lewis was horrified to see Donald reach down and clamp his palm over the boy's face, blocking both mouth and nose. The baby began to writhe ineffectively, and then suddenly Margaret Lewis rushed into view.

What's wrong with him? she asked, and Donald shrugged casually, giving an easy and indulgent smile that utterly maddened both Lewis and Anne.

I think he just woke up too suddenly, Donald replied, and Margaret gave him only the briefest glance as she gathered the child up in her arms and began to rock him, pressing her nose to his cheek and whispering inaudible words of comfort.

"You bastard," Anne spat, wrenching herself away from Donald or Agnew or whoever he was. "Dair wasn't your son, but that child was. What's *wrong* with you?"

For a moment it looked like she was going to attack the man herself, but instead she turned to look across at Lewis. She seemed to struggle for words, but he could read her facial expression well enough regardless. It chilled him.

I think we have to prepare ourselves for the possibility that—

But Lewis never managed to finish the thought, because the mirrors flashed again and suddenly they seemed to be windows, because the scene beyond showed the exterior of Pale House. It was the real house, not a reconstruction or interpretation like the chambers they had been in tonight, and Lewis recognised the rose garden and the beginnings of the small orchard beyond it. It was night, and Donald was there again, but it was too dark to see what he was doing against the pitch black backdrop of the forest, but Lewis could see that he was at the marker tree.

Agnew screamed.

It was a hellish sound, borne of pain and rage and betrayal, and then his clenched-shut eyes snapped opened again and he fixed an expression of utter madness on Lewis. His eyes glowed almost as bright as the lights of the chandelier that still hung overhead without being attached to anything anymore, and for a few seconds that felt like an eternity, Lewis considered trying to make the jump across the broken floor to reach Anne even though he knew it was too far.

There seemed to be no other choice. Whatever sanity Agnew had once possessed had clearly been consumed by his merging with Donald, and now he was just the machine driven by whatever had brought

Lewis's stepfather back for one more night in Pale House.

Anne, I'm coming, he thought, tensing every muscle in preparation — but the next moment he was on the floor on his back again as the ground beneath his feet tipped and spun. He tried to hang on, but it was too sudden and too fast.

Lewis heard Anne scream too, and an instant later he felt himself slide straight down the inclined ballroom floor and fall off the edge into darkness.

Chapter 22

This is wrong and it's your fault, roared the voice in Rage's head.

The pressure inside his skull was enormous, and he couldn't switch off or ignore the images he saw because they were in his mind. An endless parade of flashes, all showing scenes of violence. Sometimes his own father against him, sometimes his own acts of fury and hate and punishment against anyone who had made the mistake of crossing his path, and sometimes the man who was inside him, and who was somehow inside this house.

Rage knew that the intruder called Dair who was here with the woman had once lived in the house with the man called Donald. He knew that Donald hated Dair, then and now, and he knew very well that Donald had brought Rage here tonight to kill the other man. And the woman too, but ideally in the opposite order so that the man would suffer the most. Rage understood his own role all too well, and he longed for it, lusted for it. It was his only remaining purpose.

But things had changed. They'd got messed up, and changed around, and now the serious man was still angry but it was the afraid kind of angry as well as the usual and good kind that drove you to punish people and beat people and kill people. Someone else was pulling some of the strings, and now it had all gone really wrong, because Rage at last saw that this roller-coaster ride they were on had gone to a place that the man called Donald didn't want to go. Whatever they were going to see in the dark place outside, with the trees, it had driven the man in his mind to reach out and tear the image away. He was scared of it. He didn't want it seen, but they'd almost seen it anyway.

That gave Rage pause, because the single most defining thing about Donald was that he had no doubts at all about being right. Just like Rage's own father, which was why Donald had been able to convince Rage that's who he was, at least for a while. He was absolutely certain of being right, and anyone who thought otherwise could go to hell. Or more likely, they could learn why it wasn't wise to disagree at all. Men like that didn't make mistakes. They didn't end up in situations like this.

And now they were falling. It was cold, and it was dark, and he caught occasional flashes of pieces of the house that weren't connected to anything else, like they were waiting to be put together. He could feel Donald's fury, and then the pain bloomed in his head again, making him flail his arms and legs in a wasted effort to make it stop. Rage was sure he was going to pass out, and he was actually glad for it, but his hopes were dashed a moment later when he crashed onto a floor he hadn't seen coming, knocking the breath out of him.

Donald could see before Rage could, somehow, and Rage felt the anger give way to something very close to fear.

So here we are again at last, Donald thought in his mind, and Rage opened his eyes.

Lewis landed on his feet, more or less. The shock vibrated up through his shins and knees and hip joints, but it was far less than it should have been, given the length of the fall.

He glanced upwards, but there was just a perfectly ordinary ceiling with a light fitting, and then he immediately became aware of how claustrophobic the surroundings were. A small room, within the house, just as it was in real life. He was sure of it.

Because I know this room, he thought. *And I know what we're going to see.*

It was laid out exactly as his mother had once described it to him. The small guest bedroom, chosen for an unknown reason or maybe no reason at all. The single bed, neatly made up but with a thin layer of dust on everything. The modest bedside table. The bare dressing table. And the chair, moved now to the middle of the room.

Donald was there, but so was the Donald from before.

The past version of the man looked haggard, unshaven for at least a few days, and the smell of alcohol was evident in the enclosed space. Lewis took it all in within a second or two before a warm body crashed into him.

"Anne!"

He had his arms around her in a second, scanning the room at the same time and locating Agnew nearby, but the other man seemed transfixed by the scene in front of him.

No wonder, Lewis thought. *Donald is watching himself die.*

The details were prosaic and clichéd in the aftermath, but they were so much more powerful here. The chair was of the basic wooden type, with four sturdy legs, and it was almost but not directly below the light fitting. Lewis saw a detail that made immediate sense, but which had never been revealed to him before: Donald had drilled through the ceiling into the joists above, and mounted a small metal ring. It would support the weight of a man far better than the cord of a pendulum ceiling light could. Especially when the load was sudden.

Lewis immediately knew that his mother must have had the macabre thing removed between the event and the present day, probably very soon after the police investigation had concluded, and she had never mentioned it to him. The rope was already set up, tied securely in a tight nautical knot at the ceiling end, and in a wrapped slip noose at the other. Donald had apparently been taking no chances at all.

Lewis cradled the back of Anne's head, keeping her in the embrace, but after a moment she gently pulled away and looked around, and he could sense the moment that she understood the scene.

"Oh god," she said. "This was…"

She never finished the sentence, because they both knew it was unnecessary. Lewis just nodded, taking her hand, and they both instinctively moved back as the past version of Donald approached them with unseeing eyes, coming to a stop in the middle of the room. He just stood there, shaking his head occasionally, lost in his own thoughts. His eyes were red-rimmed but dry, and there was more of bitterness than of despair on his face.

"Why did he—?" Anne asked quietly, and Lewis shook his head.

"We never knew," he replied, "or at least I didn't. She said he'd been struggling for a while. I never managed to draw her out on it, and she got angry when I tried. Not that I tried very hard, to be honest."

Anne squeezed his hand, and Lewis returned the gesture as Lewis watched Agnew warily. The blended man was standing completely still, his strange and shifting eyes fixed on the vision of himself in the centre of the room. The knife was still in his hand, but held limply at his thigh. Lewis wondered if he could take it from him, but he knew it would be exceptionally risky, and Anne would probably pull him back if he tried. He looked around the room to find anything else he could use as a weapon, but it was as spartan as in the real house, and he had no reason to think that any of the surroundings would remain permanent after the memory had played out.

Donald the younger seemed to reach a decision, and he stepped up onto the chair in a manner so casual and normal that Lewis was physically sickened by it, unable to help feeling a burst of sympathy for the monster in his final moments. It looked for all the world as if he was just going to change a lightbulb, and Donald's facial expression betrayed no more emotion, even when he carefully stepped up onto the arms of the chair, one at a time with his hand on the backrest to avoid tipping over, then straightened up and slipped the noose over his head, then tightened it.

The length of rope above had perhaps twenty centimetres of slack in it, enough for a drop but with no hope of his feet contacting the floor, and Lewis knew he'd measured everything carefully. Carefulness had been one of the man's most prominent traits, after all.

It was as if the scene had paused, but Lewis could see that the younger Donald was still breathing. And then he shifted his weight, allowed the chair to begin to topple, and finally kicked it out from under himself.

Anne flinched at the short drop, and Lewis's stomach churned at the small noises of mechanical and human strain that came when the rope snapped taught and immediately changed the shape and the colour of the man's face. Donald in his final moments, unable to stop himself writhing as his eyes began to bulge and his cheeks reddened, looked not entirely unlike the child he had began to smother in its crib. Anne looked away after a moment, but she didn't cover her face or show any emotion other than disgust. Lewis, though, watched the entire thing.

It took longer than he expected. The thrashing and twisting, and Donald gripping the rope above his own head fruitlessly, and then the lapse into twitching as his suspended body described strange arcs in the air, projected in a hideous shadow on the floor by the light above. His face looked like it would burst open, and his neck was a livid, purple mass, cut deeply by the rope. His eyes were full red with every capillary broken, and Lewis thought that it might even have been his true look.

The red became scarlet and purple and blue, and the movements became those only of the interplay of momentum and gravity. Lewis could see the moment that life fell away, and he could swear that he saw something leave the corpse, just for an instant. Something black and shapeless, gone in a fraction of a second into the walls. Then something about the scene abruptly changed.

The window. The light.

The brightening made Anne turn around again, and she saw that it had become daylight outside the single small window in the space of a moment, when it had been pitch dark outside before. Time had moved forward, and only a few seconds passed before they heard footsteps, and saw the door swing open.

Margaret Lewis stood there, and while she gasped upon seeing her then-husband's body hanging there, her expression hardened almost immediately. There was no real surprise there, other than the shock of discovery. And there were no tears. She didn't approach the body, and she didn't make any effort to cut him down. Instead, she just took a long look at the scene before her, and then she nodded to herself, and left the room.

"She was… expecting it, or something like it," Anne said. Lewis tilted his head to one side.

"She sure as hell didn't care that you were dead, did she? Actually she looked relieved."

He was talking to Agnew and the Donald within him, and the man across the room finally turned his attention away from the spectacle of his own end years ago. There was a disturbing blankness to him now, and one that Lewis recognised. He had seen it on the face of his own younger self, and he even remembered how it felt. It was when you were forced to endure something, and could only wait for it to be over.

Because this is my house, he thought, and as if in answer, he felt and heard an ominous creaking and shuddering from every part of the room.

"I couldn't understand it before," Lewis said, "but now I do."

Anne grasped his forearm in a silent question, and he turned to fully face her.

"We thought he was in control of all this, but he's not. He never was. He has some influence — he brought this bastard here to be his eyes and ears, and probably to kill me — but this isn't his show at all. That's what my mother meant. Do you remember?"

"*Pale House will show you,*" Anne said, and Lewis nodded. He turned his attention to Agnew, but he was speaking to Donald.

"You're not in control of any of this, not really. And you don't know why you're here again. But I do."

"You're going to die here tonight," Donald said, the voice from Agnew's lips now sounding raspy, like something long-silent and having to learn to speak all over again. His eyes had stopped cycling through colours and had settled on dead grey.

"You *did* die here tonight," Lewis said, nodding towards the upended chair, one of its legs now resting on the midpoint of the single bed. "But this isn't the night I'm interested in."

Agnew's eyes widened with Donald's fury, and Anne drew back while still gripping Lewis's arm tightly, but Lewis didn't flinch even when Agnew raised the knife and pointed it at him.

"That's the missing piece," Lewis said, "and it's the answer to two questions at once, isn't it?"

This is mine, Lewis thought. *This is all mine. And Pale House wants to tell me its story.*

Lewis lifted his gaze to the ceiling, not focusing on any particular spot.

"Show me," he said.

And Pale House responded.

Chapter 23

Wood panelling and floorboards fragmented into thousands of pieces, blowing across the room in a storm of splinters.

None of them touched Lewis or Anne, but Agnew was nicked and slashed dozens of times until his face was a mask of blood. He fell through the void of the shattered floor, and far beneath it there was a pine forest. The branches tore at Agnew as he dropped through them, then he crashed down onto hard and half-frozen grass, his knife lost in the darkness. Donald used Agnew's lacerated arms to swipe at his face, and looked up to see Lewis and Anne drifting down like leaves on the breeze, touching down soundlessly a short distance away.

There were on the border of the rose garden, where Lewis had often played as a child. The orchard was behind them, with Pale House ahead in the middle distance — but somehow they were also still inside the house, with soaring interior walls dimly visible as a backdrop to everything, forming a vast chamber both outdoors and in. And the marker tree was there, of course.

The sole pine from the forest that was allowed to grow past the orchard line, it had always been an oddity. Perhaps an accidental oversight when the orchard was first planted decades ago, it had always delighted Lewis for its conspicuousness and incongruity. It formed a sort of boundary between the fruit and the flowers, standing like a sentinel to guard one or the other, depending on which you preferred. It was the same tree they had seen in the mirrors of the ballroom before Agnew's outburst had heralded the collapse of the floor.

Lewis's stomach turned over again. In his heart of hearts, he already knew what he would find here, and he thought that Anne probably did too. He also knew that despite this memory taking place months before Donald's suicide, it was ultimately the end of the story that Pale House had needed him to experience.

With Agnew lying wounded on the ground, eyes blazing with Donald's hatred but also fear now, Lewis took Anne's hand once again and looked towards the marker tree. The night was dark, but they could both easily see the younger Donald there, and when the clouds moved away from the moon and allowed its spotlight to fall on everything, they could see that he had the baby boy with him too, cradled in his arms. The child was crying, clearly too cold and in distress, but all

Donald was doing was rocking him back and forth, far too hard, teeth gritted and pressed to the infant's head.

"Shut the fuck up and go to sleep," he snarled. "It's two in the fucking morning. You useless little shit."

Anne lunged forward, and Lewis didn't try to stop her, but she passed straight through the figure of this Donald from the past, almost stumbling to her knees. Lewis rejoined her where she now stood, and put a steadying hand on her shoulder.

The younger Donald was becoming more and more angry, and at last he resorted to shaking the child cruelly, rattling the boy back and forth, again and again and again, drawing piercing and heart-shattering sounds of anguish and alarm from the baby. He continued for what must have been half a minute stretching into an eternity, until at last he pulled the child against his chest in a sudden movement. He clasped his arms tightly around the boy's back, shaking with rage and exertion as he crushed the tiny form to him, never letting up the pressure.

A minute passed, and then another, as Donald stood there. His face was a mask of indignant fury, teeth still gritted, snarling in silence, holding tight. Another cloud passed over the moon, and then moved away again after a long moment.

Gradually, the man's arms relaxed, and then he jerked the baby away from him to hold at arm's length, peering at the small face in unconcealed disgust. Then his expression slackened, and his face paled. Anne turned her head away and pressed against Lewis, but Lewis forced himself to keep watching.

Your own son, he thought, powerless to do anything but at least pay the tribute of his attention. He accepted the consequences that would come from witnessing what had happened, knowing it was in a very real way his destiny to do so.

Donald's brow was slick with sweat, and there was panic in in his eyes. He pulled the child to his chest again and patted its back harder and harder, then lifted him away and shook him, but it was clearly already much too late.

Tiny features, snow white in the moonlight but also blue and what might have been purple and red, without breath or life. Then the scene froze in place, all movement stilled, with even the sound of the forest now silenced.

"He killed his child," Anne said at last, her voice little more than a whisper in the night. "Your mother's child."

"My brother," Lewis said, and then he staggered back from her, fell to his knees on the cold grass that wasn't really there, and he wept.

Anne was crouched beside Lewis, holding onto him as he cried. She was saying something, but none of the words registered in his mind. He could only keep seeing the image over and over, filling his thoughts, and when he looked up it was there in front of him too, frozen in place just a few metres away.

He could feel the trauma of it taking root in his consciousness, and he gripped Anne's forearm with a panicky tightness. She reached her other arm around his back, holding him in an awkward embrace, throwing occasional looks of utter malice towards the motionless form of Agnew just across the clearing.

Lewis wasn't sure how long he knelt there, but at last the shaking subsided and he drew his sleeve across his face. Squeezing Anne's arm once more, he released his grip on her and got to his feet, then slowly took a few steps towards the frozen figure of Donald from the past. Lewis was breathing heavily, his exhalations visible in plumes in front of him, and his eyes were locked on the silent bundle in the figure's arms.

Never got to grow up, he thought. *Never got to know he had a brother. Never even got to learn his own name.*

"Show me what became of him," Lewis said, and Pale House responded.

The scene around them sprang back into life, the breeze rustling the branches of so many trees, and the sky darkened. The figure of the long-ago Donald vanished into the snowflakes now beginning to fall, and in his place a small void of removed earth opened up, just in front of the marker tree. There were all the dressings of a funeral, but there was no-one there, and Lewis knew that it would have been attended by only his mother, and perhaps Donald, and someone to perform the funeral rites. Someone trusted by the family, sworn to secrecy by both loyalty and decorum.

The coffin was there, though, waiting to be interred. Beautiful polished wood with brass handles and hardware, and a plaque bearing a single word. A forename without a family name, somehow fitting for a life barely begun when it had already ended.

Hugh

Lewis remembered the sound of a child running in the school corridor, and then seeing a boy he had thought was himself, moving through the mirror-places in the distorted ballroom, getting younger and younger as he went from pane to pane. He understood now that he hadn't been encountering himself at all, but an echo of the child that his half-brother had never had the chance to become. The life he had never been allowed to live.

That was all it took. Lewis felt the pressure building in his chest, and he expected another torrent of grief to overtake him. But it changed when it reached his sternum, and before he even knew he'd made the decision, he had already exploded across the frozen grass away from Anne. He crossed the whole distance in a handful of heartbeats, and he hauled Agnew's battered body up from the ground amidst the trees with a dark strength he never knew he possessed.

Donald's glittering coal-black eyes still burned in the other man's skull, and Lewis threw him against an aged trunk and then fell upon him. He hit the merged pair of monsters once, then again, then again and again and again. Agnew was smiling back at him now, enjoying the pain of both of them, and the part of him that was Donald actually looked like it thought it had won a victory.

The man's face, already lacerated and streaked with his own blood, lost its shape under blow after blow, from fists and elbows and tearing fingernails, and Lewis thought that he might have been making a wordless sound of anger and hate the entire time. Anne stood nearby, but she didn't try to intervene.

Agnew reached down for a thick fallen branch and swung it with the single intention of killing Lewis, but it glanced off the rear of his shoulder when he turned, a broken section tearing Lewis's jacket and ripping the skin beneath. Lewis barely acknowledged the blow, breaking Agnew's nose with his forehead in pure, animal hatred.

They danced drunkenly beneath the alternating light and shadow of the tree canopy, Donald and Agnew both taking turns to move their increasingly battered body, and in a moment of carelessness when Agnew clumsily dodged to one side, Lewis suddenly felt the other man's hands close around his throat from behind.

He could hear and feel the rotten breath on the back of his neck, and Agnew was brutally strong. All muscle and sinew and rage, cold fire without moderation and mercy, wanting only to kill for the sheer joy of killing. But Lewis had gone beyond fear for his own life, and the only image in his mind was the child's motion-

less face in its death mask, a thing of innocence pro-
faned and violated in an affront to everything it was to
be a parent and a human being. There was no limit to
his own fury, and in that moment he and Agnew were
equals.

Lewis seized Agnew's fingers from around his own
throat, crushing them together until he had the satisfaction of feeling at least two of them break, and the human part of the thing behind him howled in pain. Lewis
grabbed one of his wrists and spun around using it as a
lever, dragging Agnew from his footing and driving
him hard into rough bark shielded by a hundred thousand pine needles. Then he pulled him back and
smashed his skull into the lacerating and unyielding
surface again, and again, and again, his mind only seeing Donald shaking the child over and over as he did
so.

It took only a minute, and at the end of it Agnew's
body fell to the ground, with Donald's eyes as the only
thing still alive in him. Lewis kicked him in the chest
with the last of his grief-fuelled fury, and even when
darkening blood came from Agnew's mouth, Donald
still looked at him with murderous and gleeful spite.
The monster spoke, animating a shattered, ruined jaw
only with great difficulty.

"She never told you."

"She was protecting me," Lewis replied, hands
clenched into fists, nails digging into his own palms.
"You took her child's life!"

"AND SHE TOOK MINE."

His roar of rage dislocated Agnew's jaw, and it hung strangely in his ragged mouth.

"You… you killed *yourself*, you fucking bastard."

"I wanted nothing to do with her damned children, you or him. But I'll make you show respect the way she never did."

Like the puppet that he was, Agnew jerked upwards, unfolding unnaturally into a warped standing position, as Lewis fell backwards in surprise. The thing's head hung at an angle, a locket dangling lopsided from its neck, but somehow it had found the knife again, and Donald's black eyes burned with vengeance and madness. Agnew's dead arm raised the blade, and in a moment of heightened perception, Lewis could actually see snowflakes falling onto the blade, and resting there like jewels.

"Time to join your brother," the thing said, and it flew at Lewis faster than he would have believed was possible.

It reeked of death and blood and sweat and human waste, and something else that made Lewis think again of the too-small rectangular hole dug in the earth in front of the marker tree. The first slash of the blade missed his right ear by what felt like a centimetre, and a voice in the back of his mind screamed that no matter the source of everything else they had seen tonight, the knife was real, an object from the sane world outside of Pale House, and it could most definitely kill him.

The thing that had been two men, one dead long ago but also both dying in this house tonight, screamed at him, and the sound threatened to unhinge his mind. Lewis could feel his hands shaking, and everything was rapidly taking on the disconnected feeling of a dream. Donald brought the blade down in a vicious slashing motion, and somehow Lewis caught hold of Agnew's wrist, stopping the tip of the knife only a moment before it would have pierced his throat. The thing was hideously, nauseatingly strong, and Lewis could already feel his own muscles weakening after so much exertion. Adrenalin roared through his system, but his vision had started to close in.

Pale House will show you, his mind whispered in his mother's voice, *and then you'll know.*

Donald sneered through broken teeth smeared with blood, hanging at a sickening angle. The knife was so close that Lewis could see his reflection in it.

When you do, please forgive me.

Pale House wanted the story to be told, not just to anyone, but to him alone. It had wanted the record to be set straight, and it had succeeded in that — and yet they were still here in this nightmare. Because the proper order of things hadn't yet been restored.

"None of what you did was her fault," he gasped through gritted teeth, and Donald's eyes widened by only a fraction. "And I do forgive her."

The light was blinding.

It was like a sunrise, but not at the horizon. Light filled the forest, and the orchard, and the rose garden with the marker tree, blinding Lewis and Anne for several seconds. With his eyes squeezed shut, Lewis felt Agnew's body torn away from his as if the thing had been struck by a wave and dragged along with it. When he recovered enough of his vision to lower his head and search the area around his feet, he saw the knife lying there — on polished floorboards instead of frost-rimed grass.

Lewis glanced up, reaching for Anne who was already hurrying over to him, and he was awestruck by what he saw. The remembered recreation of the outdoor areas was all gone, leaving them standing in a chamber almost too vast to comprehend. The far-away walls were like cliffs climbing towards the sky, the ceiling was hidden beyond atmospheric haze, and the floor was a wooden plain that seemed to stretch for miles around them.

It was definitely Pale House, but the entirety of the real building would have seemed like a tiny outpost within the room. Agnew's broken body lay nearby, Donald's eyes looking around in helpless frustration. He had lost something, Lewis could see. Some force of will or strength that allowed him to overcome the limitations of the once-living shell he'd inhabited, and now there was only his malice left trapped behind the windows of the dead man's eyes.

One wall of the ethereal chamber was close by, behind them and rising to dizzying heights above. It was dotted with thousands upon thousands of picture frames, each one an image from the lives of those who had lived in the house, and set into the vast wall there was a single door. It lay open, and the light had come from that direction, still filling the doorway and obscuring what lay behind. And then they heard footsteps approaching.

Anne drew close to Lewis's side, and she was about to crouch down and reach for the sole weapon they had available, but Lewis shook his head. He knew the sound well, and a moment later his mother came into view.

The woman he saw recognised him immediately, but she was still Margaret Lambert, too young to have married and borne any children. But as she took further steps, he watched in amazement as her face subtly changed. With five steps she became the woman he'd seen in old wedding photographs, and with another five she was the young mother portrayed in a recognisable image far above his head on the towering wall. Older still as she began to draw close, and she looked at him with such understanding and acceptance that his heart was pierced all over again.

Margaret moved past the two of them, ageing faster now, and already she was the woman he most associated with her; the mother of his childhood, and then at high school, and during the darkest times of those years before he left. She had passed beyond where he stood and he turned with Anne to keep watching, and even from behind he could see the changes in her hair and her stature. These were the years after, when she found herself pregnant again in her early forties, in a relationship she surely knew was poison, and forced to face that experience with only resentment and bitterness for company.

His mother's destination was the thing on the floor, and Agnew's limbs twitched feebly. Donald's eyes had reverted to their true colour, and when Margaret arrived at where he lay, she reached down with a kind of tenderness that Lewis found chilling. Her frail hand, surely now as it was at the end of her own life, touched the torn cheek of the human monster that held something far worse, and then she moved to take its hand.

When she stood, Agnew's body remained where it was, but Donald came up with her, pulled from his avatar like a shroud, ripped uniformly out and away to stand beside the woman who had been the mother of his child.

He's so small, Lewis thought, and somehow it was true despite the man standing at least a full head taller than his mother. Donald was diminished, and faded, and Lewis knew that he had no more power here. If he ever really had any in the first place.

Donald opened his mouth, but he had no chance to speak. Lewis and Anne never even saw where it came from, but the neatly tied noose was already in Margaret's hand, and it was over Donald's head and cinched around his neck in an instant. He was lifted from the floor, just as in the small guest bedroom, even though there was nothing above him. He thrashed and kicked out, but there was nothing he could do.

Margaret turned around, and her eyes were large and liquid. They were filled with apology and affection and compassion, but there was also something terrible in them. Something of the world in which this nightmare version of Pale House existed, and in that moment Lewis knew exactly what Donald's fate was to be.

His mother looked directly at him, and then at Anne, and then back to him, and then the impossibly vast chamber was filled with the sounds of an apocalyptic rending and screaming of timber, and the breaking of glass, and everything began to vibrate. Margaret's gaze never faltered, and when she spoke there was no sound, but Lewis understood anyway.

Live, she said.

With that, she turned, rising from the floor, and caught hold of the flailing end of the noose that held Donald aloft, and then she hurtled away from Lewis and Anne, dragging Donald behind her until they were lost in the growing shadows that were racing out from the distant perimeter and towards them.

"Dair…" Anne said, taking a step backwards involuntarily, and he nodded.

"Run," he said. She didn't need to be told twice.

The light receded from the single doorway as if a dimmer switch had been dialled down and then turned off entirely, and beyond it Lewis could see the stairway again, the soaring and fragmented one from before. They burst through the portal onto a landing and dashed downwards hand in hand, trying not to look at the flux all around them but unable to avoid seeing it.

There was a maelstrom of fragments of the house, rearranging and distorting and reforming even as they watched.

Their feet thudded on the wide stairs, and they could see that the path ahead was being created in front of them, leading them downwards into structure even as all that lay behind and above them flew apart and re-assembled then flew apart all over again.

A window shot upwards out of the void, attached to nothing, but still showing a part of the boundless exterior of this place. It showed a dog, one that Lewis had never seen and perhaps a neighbourhood stray, sniffing and pawing at the base of the marker tree. And then a doorway from empty space opened ten metres to their right, and inside it sat Lewis's father on a chair, young and nervous-looking, dressed in a suit that looked brand new and one size too big.

Meeting the family as the new boyfriend, Lewis thought, and somehow he knew his intuition was correct.

The portion of the stairway they were on came to an end as carpet unrolled from its base, creating an alarming bridge above blackness. He and Anne hesitated for a moment because the carpet didn't appear to rest on any kind of solid surface despite being completely flat, and a pair of matching chests of drawers popped into existence halfway along, facing each other from the left and right sides, complete with lit table lamps.

They exchanged a quick glance before running straight along the newly-made and largely invisible corridor. The carpet didn't budge so much as a millimetre below their feet, and in a few moments they reached an archway that led into a glass-lined space that could have been the longest conservatory Lewis had ever seen. It stretched for what seemed like three football fields in length, and vines climbed some of the floor-to-ceiling windows. Beyond the panes there was only snowfall, with no ground for the flakes to settle on. It could almost have been a tunnel through deep space, and Anne tore her gaze away from it when it started to make her feel dizzy.

They were panting and out of breath when they finally left it behind, plunging down yet more stairs that bizarrely started well before the rear wall of the soaring conservatory, dropping away in a juxtaposition of stone and wood in alternation. These steps were deep enough to be troublesome, and Lewis felt each footfall jarring his knees, but this was no time to slow their pace.

He dared not look behind and above, because the sound was terrifying. As if street after street of buildings were being torn up in a cyclone, crushed and shredded, and spat back out again. Worse, there was an inescapable sense of compression, and a growing pressure in his ears, which had started to pop every half minute or so.

It's being pulled back to wherever it came from, he thought. *The whole other house, however big it is.*

It was half guess and half instinct, but one thing was very clear: he didn't want either of them to still be within the walls of this version of the house when the process reached its conclusion.

Lewis heard Anne gasp beside him even as they jogged onwards and downwards, and he saw the cause of her reaction a moment later. His piano teacher when he was a child was standing to one side at the foot of the stairs, smiling and indicating the leftmost of the three corridors they could see fanning out from the bottom of the steps. They took her silent advice with gratitude but without hesitation, and the corridor quickly became a ramp downwards, becoming gradually steeper until gravity became their ally as they barrelled forward with whatever strength they had left.

All at once the surface levelled out, and at last they burst out into the main entrance hall, just as it had always been, pursued by a cacophony of sound from above. Anne came to a halt and looked up, and her mouth fell open in shock. Lewis couldn't help but follow her gaze.

It must have been miles high. A twisting, shuddering, writhing mass of half-remembered pieces of the house, all in a state of constant change, kaleidoscopic and sickening, and all against a barely glimpsed backdrop of the same light from before — and it was all coming steadily down towards them.

Lewis grabbed Anne's arm and dragged her across the atrium in seconds, his ears popped again, and as he released her to grab both doorhandles, he looked up once more.

It was all held in place for an instant, and then everything fell. All of it, rushing downwards, folding and breaking and compressing in on itself, materials shrieking under impossible stresses.

He tore the doors open, blinded immediately by the glare beyond, and reached sightlessly for Anne. His fingers found her, and he threw her and himself out into whatever lay beyond.

There was a sound larger and louder than any he had ever heard, but there was no sensation of an explosion or an implosion, and then suddenly there was the pain of a tumbling collision with something solid and rough and jagged.

The light was nowhere to be seen now, and Lewis found himself on his hands and knees, blinking, as he slowly realised he was outside in the gravel-covered turning circle.

The real one, he thought, feeling the truth of it in every part of him. Anne was there beside him, also getting to her feet, and they both turned around together.

Pale House stood silently watching them, weak light coming from the lamps in the perfectly normal, intact, and grand but sensibly sized entrance hall they could see through the open double doors. There was no wreckage. Every pane of glass was intact.

It was just a house, which had once been a home. To Lewis, for the first time, it looked small — and perhaps even lonely.

Anne startled when she felt something cold touch her neck, and it was only then that they both realised it was snowing. Flakes fell like ash from a heavy grey sky, night birds and animals made their sounds, and a light breeze blew through hundreds of pine trees, bringing their scent along with a crisp hint of frost.

Lewis and Anne exchanged a look, and he glanced at his watch. He was both stunned and not at all surprised at how much time had passed. As his eyes adjusted to the dark, he thought he could just barely detect the first distant wash of light from beyond the horizon.

It was not yet dawn, but for both of them the long night had ended.

Friday

Chapter 24

When the sun rose, it found Lewis and Anne dressed more appropriately for the weather, and once again outside. The snow had stopped, and steam from two mugs of coffee curled into the morning air.

Sleep seemed a futile pursuit, but Lewis was certain there was no more danger to be found in Pale House, so they had explored the entire place together, room by room. Including the small guest bedroom where Donald had ended his life, and the bare room that must surely have been meant as a nursery, and the music room, and the ballroom, and the attic, and every other corner of the entire sprawling mansion.

They had found nothing out of place, and nothing added. There was no knife, and there was no Agnew, nor were there any signs that either had ever been there. The snowfall had surely taken care of any marks the man had left when he arrived the previous evening. Lewis wasn't at all sorry to avoid any attempt at an explanation to outsiders. He doubted that Sergeant Howarth would even begin to understand.

The house was quiet, with no sense of anything beyond what could be seen, and its grounds were the same. Lewis and Anne had taken a walk around the immediate area once there was enough light in the sky, and they naturally found their feet taking them to the rose garden and the orchard. Lewis stood there for a long time, looking at the unremarkable and compact stretch of earth which they'd each seen excavated so recently, and which had in reality been untouched for many, many years. There was nothing to be done in that regard. Justice had been served, in a certain sense, and beyond that the matter was better off left alone.

The real conservatory still held many beautiful plants, and Lewis had brought a *myosotis* from there, in a deeper colour than the one that had been pressed into his mother's diary. He laid it at the foot of the marker tree, and he quietly said a few words that were no-one's business but his own. Anne came forward to join him when he had finished, and they both stood in a brief vigil of remembrance while dawn took hold.

Now they were sitting on a marble bench on the opposite side of the house, wrapped in warm coats, clutching their mugs and watching the forest and the world awaken around them.

"How do you think that he… that he got away with it?" Anne asked, and Lewis took a long, slow breath.

"I don't think he did, not ultimately, but I'm not sure what happened at the time," he replied. "I know that my mother covered it all up, and even this is the kind of thing you can make go away when you're an important family in a small place. I think she felt responsible — you can tell from her letter — and probably hushed it up out of some mix of shame and propriety and just devastated grief."

"I really feel for her," Anne said after a few moments, and Lewis nodded.

"I wonder if she was afraid of him too," he said. "That must have been part of it. But she turned the tables in the end."

There was silence for several minutes, and then Anne asked the question that was running through both their minds.

"It all really happened, didn't it?"

Lewis took a gulp of his coffee, and then set the mug down on the bench.

"Yes. It happened," he said simply. He lifted his arm with a little bit of difficulty, and pointed with his thumb towards the place on his shoulder where Anne had cleaned and bandaged the flesh wound he'd received from Agnew's knife when Donald had animated the corpse in a final attempt to kill Lewis. He thought for a few moments, then he began to speak again.

"I think that the man who came here — Agnew — was every bit as broken and damaged as Donald was. Maybe more so. I think it made him vulnerable to that influence. Donald found him the same way that lightning finds a conductor to earth. He was a puppet, but a willing one. I wouldn't be surprised at all if he'd killed people before."

Anne shivered, shaking her head even though she knew it was the truth. She would remember the man's face, with those other eyes looking out of them, shifting restlessly between colours, for the rest of her life.

"He was wrong, though; Donald, I mean," Lewis said. "I think he woke up when this all started, probably when my mother had come to the end of her life with a profound regret and a terrible secret, and he thought that this was all his own quest for some kind of revenge and justification. But it was never about that. Pale House was always in control."

"Because it wanted to tell a story," Anne said, and Lewis smiled at her. Of course she understood. She understood everything more quickly than he did, including the key realisation that some of the memories couldn't have come from Donald or from himself.

Lewis stood up now, needing to get some warmth back into his legs, and Anne set down her cup beside his and joined him. Together, they began to walk slowly around the paved area where the bench was positioned to catch the morning sun.

"I think that when a place lives with a tragedy that never has any kind of release, say because it's hidden and covered up, then there have to be consequences," Lewis said quietly. "Cause and effect. Like physics. I think there was a, a kind of… energy within the house. Something bad, made out of grief and guilt and loss, focused on and obsessed upon in private. It needed to be released, and when she died, there was nothing left to contain it. So Pale House woke up. I don't think it meant to bring Donald back, though. Maybe he just willed himself back from sheer spite and entitlement. Or maybe the house felt he was a necessary part of it all."

He thought the latter explanation was more likely, but he didn't discount the other possibility. One thing seemed certain: his mother had ultimately died of a broken heart. She had paid a last visit to the marker tree, perhaps even knowing that she had very little time left, and then barely managed to return to the house before she passed away.

Anne looked at the house, scanning the visible windows, and Lewis could see that she half-expected to see a face in one of them. A face of madness and evil, incandescent with rage, eyes coal black, and a face torn and broken but somehow still functioning. He put a hand on her shoulder, and he could feel the tension that was still in her small frame.

"It did what it needed to do," he said. "A house can't speak, but it can see — it can see all the things that take place within it. All the people's lives that pass inside its walls. Those memories were its vocabulary. And I think the fact that all of our memories are distorted things around little fragments of clarity, is probably why it took on the forms that it did. In a way, there are two houses: the one that's standing right there, and the one that's from every time all at once, knitted together by the narrative of what happened there. I guess that's the truer version of the place too."

Anne was still looking at the house, but more thoughtfully now. She walked over and laid her palm against the stonework, letting her skin drag across the rough surface.

"The true house still exists, though," she said, and again Lewis slowly nodded.

"What we saw at the end, I think, was it going back to wherever it came from," he said. "That's the poetic justice part. Donald hated nothing more than living there with my mother when I was still around. Or actually, I think that was the second-worst thing for him: the worst was having his own child, a baby, to endure too. And so the true Pale House is the most terrible place that could ever exist for him. Because it's made of all his worst memories, without end."

"He built his own hell," Anne said. "And now the other monster he brought in can live with him there forever."

It was mid-morning when Lewis and Anne stepped out of the main entrance doors, closed and locked them, and went once more down the handful of wide steps to the gravel of the turning circle. The sky had cleared, and while there would certainly be rain at some point, the day was brighter than it had begun.

"I feel like there's something we left behind," Anne said, "or something we haven't done."

Lewis glanced at her, pocketing the keys of the house as he adjusted the backpack on his shoulder. He shrugged.

"We left a hell of a lot behind, and I can think of plenty things we haven't done," he said.

She smiled. There was a lightness to him now, and if anything it reminded her of the boy he'd been when they were young. Back when everything was still possible.

"It's over now," Lewis said. "The past is in the past where it belongs."

He turned to look up at the house. It was a beautiful old building, grand and impractical, from a different age. A relic, looking always inward despite all the eyes of its windows now taking on the pale blue colour of the sky.

"It said what it had to say," he continued. "I think she can rest now, out here at least. And I also think a part of her will be over there too, making damned sure that he never forgets what he did to her."

"All morning I've been opening doors and expecting to find myself back there," Anne said, and Lewis put his arm around her.

"I don't think the true Pale House can be reached anymore," he replied. "I think it was a one-night-only performance. And I think I'd like to work hard on forgetting as much of it as I can. As for this place, there's nothing here beyond what we can see. It's just a house."

Anne nodded, then leaned her head against his shoulder, first double checking that it was the uninjured one. Lewis saw and understood, finding the gesture incredibly endearing.

"So what do we do now?" she asked, and this was a question that Lewis was ready for.

He turned to her, and she lifted her head to look at him. He reached out and gripped her fingers in his as he leaned down. Her hands were cold, but her lips were warm. When they parted again, he smiled at her.

"Now, we live," he said.

They left Pale House together, passing through the gateposts, and Lewis didn't look back.

Afterword

Dear Reader,

Thank you so much for reaching this page. I'm Matt Gemmell, the author of this book. This letter is for you.

I hope you've enjoyed reading Middleshade Road. I deeply appreciate the investment of time and trust you've made. Writing is a tough job; what makes it worthwhile is the idea that someone, somewhere, is reading your words.

If you enjoyed the book, I'd be very grateful if you left a brief review on the online store of your choice. Authors live and die by those reviews. A minute of your time would mean a great deal to me.

I'd also love to hear from you, and keep you informed about new books, behind-the-scenes articles on writing, bonus and deleted chapters, and more. Here's how we can stay in touch:

My newsletter: mattgemmell.com/news-subscribe
On Twitter: @mattgemmell
On Facebook: facebook.com/MattGemmellAuthor
My web site: mattgemmell.com

Thank you for reading.

Matt Gemmell
Edinburgh, Scotland
26th January, 2022

Acknowledgements

Some books are just stories — which is fine and proper — but some are more like confessions. It's wise not to confuse one with the other, or to try and force a square peg into a round hole. If you do, it'll fight you.

Each tale wants to be told in its own way, and resisting that process is an exercise in futility. The sensible thing is to go along for the ride. I think that's one of the lessons that Dair Lewis learned, isn't it?

Middleshade Road was the toughest book I've written so far. Not because of the genre, or the plot, or the emotionally challenging scenes that crop up here and there. It was difficult to write because the book had a different opinion than I did on what its own essence was. Its perspective was fixed and constant; a certainty, whereas mine had to undergo a journey to reach consensus. It took a lot longer than I wanted it to, but probably not much longer than necessary. Some stories are lies that tell the truth.

I'd like to thank my wife, Lauren Gemmell, for… just all of it. Her love and support. Her belief. Her understanding, and her willingness to keep going when understanding wasn't viable. For her own certainty, I suppose. This book exists because of me, but I exist because of her.

I'd also like to thank our dog, Whisky the labradoodle, who's my mascot, spirit animal, role model, firstborn son, and indefatigable biggest fan. The mirror of a dog's eyes always shows your best self, and we can only strive to live up to a fraction of their purity and faith. Thanks for your silent leadership, big pal.

There's a new addition since the last time I wrote one of these acknowledgements sections: my second-born son Calum, who's human rather than canine, but none the worse for it. As I write this, it's a *dreich* and drizzly Sunday morning, he's a year old, and he's just discovered one of the universal truths of the human experience: boxes are much more fun than the stuff they initially contain. I'd like to thank him for sleeping whenever he does, so that I can still do this thing. Without him, the book would certainly have been finished sooner, but I'd know a lot less about myself. I think it's a fair trade. This is a learning process for me, too.

This book is about memory, and how we can simultaneously live inside of it but also hide things there, which end up holding us back. Pale House is, of course, a physical representation of the junk-drawer of our minds, complete with poignant objects, tangled and knotted cables, treasures, and a lot of stuff that should probably be taken out, assessed, and thrown away. Opening the drawer often hurts us, but we can't stop reaching towards it. As our story's protagonist undertook his journey to find his own truth and perspective, I did too. My enduring thanks go to Sally Wright for her guidance along the way.

I'm grateful to everyone who helped ensure that my mistakes of typing, thinking, planning, and everything else were covered up before they could embarrass me further. You're a weird and wonderful breed. Special commendation goes to Lloyd Nebres, who read the whole thing before I had the chance to check my email again.

This book wouldn't exist without the kind, generous, wonderful people who support my work, and allow me to have this strange job. Writers write to be read, and thus you're the final piece of the puzzle — I provide the words, but the pictures are all yours. I appreciate the collaboration.

Most of all, dear reader, my thanks go to you.

If you enjoyed *Middleshade Road*, you'll love Matt Gemmell's ONCE UPON A TIME, an ongoing anthology series of ultra-short stories in genres including horror, science fiction, and more. Available as a paperback compendium and multiple ebook volumes, there are more than a hundred tales to intrigue and entertain.

Matt Gemmell is also the author of the explosive KESTREL techno-thrillers series. CHANGER is book one in the series, followed by TOLL, with further instalments on the way.

Each book stands alone, and you can read them in any order — though you may enjoy some additional (but non-essential) references if you've already read the earlier stories.

CHANGER

DESTINY CAN BE CHANGED

Jutland, Denmark: a billionaire industrialist seizes control of a top-secret project that the European Defence Agency calls Destiny, manipulating it for his own ends.

Edinburgh, Scotland: physicist Neil Aldridge's life is saved by an elite EU special forces team, codenamed KESTREL, drawing him into a race against time to prevent a disaster that will claim millions of lives.

As the chase leads to London, Amsterdam and beyond, Aldridge and his allies must battle a ruthless adversary: a trained killer with an unnatural ability, who seeks to hasten the cataclysm.

With time running out, Aldridge discovers that he and his enemy share an astonishing secret, which may be the key to salvation — or cause death on an unprecedented scale…

TOLL

THE PERFECT WEAPON LAY BURIED FOR SEVENTY YEARS. NOW ITS DEADLY POWER HAS BEEN UNLEASHED.

The Norwegian Sea: a group of eco-activists disappear from their vessel. Only their dental fillings remain.

Owl Mountains, Poland: a wealthy environmentalist resurrects a secret experiment forgotten since the close of the Second World War, determined to heal our ravaged planet.

When a dossier finds its way to the desk of Dr. Neil Aldridge, the elite EU special forces team codenamed KESTREL is drawn into a dangerous pursuit across Europe and beyond, to prevent a cull of Earth's greatest threat: humanity.

As the final countdown begins, Captain Jessica Greenwood faces the ultimate choice: fight to prevent the dark future ahead, or help make it happen…

Non-fiction by Matt Gemmell.

Raw Materials

An anthology of personal essays about nostalgia, fear, humanity, memories, and the author's journey through life. Notes for each essay are included.

Writing a Novel: Resolving Plot Issues

One of the most challenging stages of writing a novel is preparing for the second draft. What's wrong with the plot? What changes do you need to make, and where? These are daunting questions that all too often lead to stalling.

This book walks you through a technique for finding the issues with your first draft, working out how to fix them, and preparing a list of needed revisions.

Writing in Markdown

Markdown lets you write plain text in a way that's not only readable as-is, but can also easily be converted to other formats. It's intuitive, it follows very common conventions, and it's simple to learn and use.

This quick guide will get you started with Markdown in about twenty minutes.